I0583648

BLOOD CITY CHRONICLES Vol 1

VIOLENT SOULS

BYRON BARTLETT

Cover Design, Interior Design and Distribution by Bublish, Inc.

Book formatting by FormattedBooks.com

ISBN: 978-1-64704-108-3 (paperback)
ISBN: 978-1-64704-109-0 (eBook)

This book is dedicated to Ashley. I love you.

PROLOGUE

The blade from my neosiri is stuck in this guy's rib cage. Annoying. When I finally pull it free, he falls to his knees, spitting up blood—choking on it. I point the blade at his two kids in the corner. I can't tell their ages, but they have fresh skin and childish fat around their faces.

"Leave," I order.

At first they try to help their father up. I kick one in the ribs with my shoe. I said, *"leave."*

The blue haired girl I kicked spits at me and says, *"Cea tam wewe digna metodsceaft."*

That means a monster like me "deserves death" or "to die." Depends on the translation. It's one of those phrases where the meaning has been muddled over time.

This is a better cut—right in her stomach. She curls over at the stomach, blue hair covers her face. Unlike her father, the blade slides in and out easily. I repeat it, a little to the left. *Her* left, not mine. Her father is motionless and she's soon to join him. When I turn around, I see that the other kid has run outside.

On a desk in the corner of the workers' space is a carving of CEO Saevus. I walk over and inspect it. Real wood. I'm surprised they could afford this. The corporation foreclosing on this town keeps an inventory on everything an employee owns, they would know someone nicked it.

I walk back to the street and watch the workers run away while I wipe down my neosiri. I'd use my guns, but this contract specified blade weapons only.

In the backyard across the street, Drake is chasing a little girl around a tree. She's wearing blue pants with kittens on the legs and a yellow kitty T-shirt. She's screaming for her mommy and he's laughing and mocking her.

"Mummy!" he yells, looking up to the sky. "Where are you, Mummy?"

He could catch her, but Drake always enjoys the children, likes to draw it out.

A drop of rain hits my left arm, as a light rain begins to fall. I spot a red flash in the corner of my eye—a weather warning from my phone.

"Open," I say, and a projection of a poorly rendered storm cloud pops up on the screen. The animated cloud delivers a flash flood warning for this area. "Close."

I look back and Drake has the girl pinned against the tree. I can only see his back, and the child's legs kicking and thrashing about. She must be terribly afraid. I register the idea, but can't relate to the emotion. This is how it works. If your town goes insolvent, the corporation gets to foreclose. The workers knew the deal when they came out to the suburbs.

Foreclosures are great pay for *bongers* like me. (A *bonger* is a slang term for assassin used in our business.) A few hours of work can cover my rent for months. Unlike Drake and me, there are some bongers who can't stomach this type of work. Auntie Belle, the assassin who trained me, never takes these jobs. Not that she's sentimental, but Drake and I have certain advantages for some of the dirtier jobs. In my case, I had the surgery to remove my empathy. In Drake's case…well, he's just a *kichaa woda* who enjoys other people's pain.

The little girl's legs have stopped thrashing. They jerk a couple of times, then go limp. When Drake steps back, I can see he's pinned her against the tree with his *beadomece*—a longer, heavier version of the *neosiri* I use. He waves me over, like a proud child begging for Mom to come look at his drawing. I ignore him and walk deeper into the 'burb.

My shoes are clicking in rhythm on the concrete. The area is starting to clear out now. Behind me, I still hear screaming, but in front of me, it's quiet. The foreclosure has been going on for half an hour now, and most workers have either escaped or are dead.

To my right, in a white stucco house, I hear a baby shrieking. I keep walking. There's a hint of grilled *hund* in the air. *Hunds* actually graze the fields just west of the 'burb. The baby is still screaming…that sound where only half the scream comes out and the rest is so forced, it ends up muted. And for the first time in years, I feel a twinge.

I stop in my tracks. No one is going to help the child. It'll starve to death. Not really my fault, though. But still, there's that *twinge*.

I enter the house and follow the screaming. I pass a couple, slumped over each other, eyes wide open, mouths ajar…probably the parents. I open the door to reveal a bedroom painted light blue—and there, in a blue and green bassinet, is the source of the cries.

Ugh. If I choose to save it, I'll have to carry it all the way to safety. Looking down, I can't really bring myself to kill it, though. I want to believe this is a rational, humane choice by me, but that would be denying what's happening to my surgery.

I scoop the baby up, wrap it in a blanket with the picture of a *Leona* sewn in, and head out. I go through the backyards so none of the other bongers see me. I'm almost home free, when—

"Hey, Sa! Wha'cha got 'ere?" Drake cries out. He starts walking over to me, leaving the woman he was doing whatever to on the ground. His lime-green metallic shirt is splashed with blood.

"Nothing, just some stuff I'm nicking for myself."

Drake catches up. "Yeah, what's…*ahhhhhhh*." His yellow eyes go wide when he realizes what I have. "Can I see it?"

Drake's voice has gone up a notch.

"No," I say. "I'm taking it to a *kuokua locus*."

"Wait—wait! I didn't find any of these! Let me have it?"

I shake my head. Whatever this *rudder* is going to do with it, I don't want to know. And I'm not letting it happen.

He curls his lip and spits out, "Give it to me!"

"Fuck you."

He points his sword at me. "*Now*, gods damn it!"

His head is trembling with anger. Good. I hope it fucking explodes.

I smile at him as a taunt. As I start to walk away, he grabs me by the shoulder—a quick flourish of my right hand provokes my *brasu cnif* to pop out from its holster. I stick it through the arm that's grabbing me. Drake shrieks, maybe louder than the baby did, and falls back on his behind.

"You rudder! Fuck you, Sa!"

I walk away and leave him there to kick gor and cry.

As I go, I can't help but look down at it—and I feel that *twinge* again. While it's good for this baby, it could be very bad for me.

CHAPTER 1

My Home Life

I'm in the middle of a dream, standing at the bottom of a waterfall—the one from my childhood home on Riestovik. I can see my *hund* grazing on the lily pads. He's grunting and swatting at flies with his tail. When I wake up, I have to pee so badly it hurts to straighten my body. *Alright, I'll pee and then get going.*

Two more hours and I'm still tired. That's one of the side effects of the surgery: no matter how long you sleep, you're never fully rested. I start to get up, but the mattress makes a strong case for staying in bed.

Thirty minutes later, I'm still groggy while halfheartedly playing with myself under the covers. It's a weak attempt but enough to wake me all the way up. I used to have a man who would do that for me. *Groscek.* We lived together for four years. He's dead now. It was my fault.

My bedroom is spartan. No pictures, no posters, no hope chest. Just the bare essentials. I rub my eyes and walk barefoot to the closet. I don't have a lot of choices. Grey or dark blue tops. Matching pants. Most of the closet space has been taken up by my gun locker.

I have to brag—it is high-end, a real schway piece of art. The outside is a mix of chrome and bronze—*Brasu* bronze, which can only be mined on Riestovik. It's indestructible (for all intents and purposes). DNA saliva scan to open it. Ammo monitoring with auto-refill (I paid extra for that). Anti-theft weight system was standard, but I upgraded it to the osmium package, which adds 100 kilos when tripped. When you open the door, there's a gold plate with each job I've done marked by an X.

A green light flashes in the corner of my left eye.

"Answer."

A hologram appears in front of me. I have the low-end PIP system, so there's a lot of lines and flickering on my images. But honestly, these things fritz out so much, it's a waste. And that includes ones that cost ten times as much as mine. My mom called such items "mierrends," which translates to "expensive cheapness."

"Lovely, Sasha." Burgealdor Spencer greets me with a toothy grin. Spencer was elected Burgealdor a short while ago. I don't pay attention to politics so I don't remember when exactly. He's the leader of the business section of Chicago. It wasn't the best paying position in government, but it came with an immense amount of influence.

"Burgealdor Spencer. It's a pleasure to speak wi—"

"Are we ready for today?"

Gods, he interrupts me *constantly*. "Yes, I've taken all the ness—"

"Oh, that's just wonderful, my dear." He puts an extra kick in *wonder*.

"They seem to be gathering outside the guild hall right now." Spencer sighs through his nose. "You know, I won the election. I really shouldn't have to be bothered with frivolities like these."

"I couldn't agree more, Burgealdor." I do not agree, but he's paying the bill.

I can hear Spencer speaking to one of his assistants, "Francis…oh, Francis? Would you be so kind as to put the gold plates at the head of the table yes? You can use the silver for the diplomats, but the CEOs need to have the gold plates."

He comes back to me. "I'm in such a fright right now—the last thing I need is a bunch of deadbeats chanting and marching and trying to block my guests tonight. Now you're *sure* you'll be enough, yes? I can afford to pay another kill…assass…I'm sorry, but I don't have the foggiest idea what you prefer to be called."

I fake a chuckle. "Assassin is the term I use on my tax forms." That's true.

"Well, whatever you're called, you come highly recommended by General Williams. And if you can impress that lot, you must be fantastic."

I keep a disarming smile painted on my face. It seems to make my clients feel secure. "I'm professional and discrete. And most importantly, *ruthless*. That's the important part, considering what you're asking for."

"Yes, the General says you are distinct in your class. And you have no qualms about . . . dealing with a child? More machine than human, they say. Yes?"

I ignore the slight. "Burgealdor, I beg your pardon, but I need to get fixed up for today."

"Right, right. Well, I have so much to attend to...I must be going."

"And the payment—the second half will be transferred tonight at midnight?"

"Right, right."

I walk into the bathroom to get ready for the job. I brush and floss. I wash my face and arm pits. Gargle with an alcohol-free mouthwash and pick at a pimple on my neck until it bleeds. Cover the pimple with a *bindele* that soaks up the blood. I study my face in the mirror for any other flaws. My eyes have turned gray since the surgery, and I have black bags under them. Some crow's feet. But other than that, I look quite valuable and trustworthy.

As I walk down the hall, I hear the crackle of bacon. Jorge never gets up this early, which means he was up all night.

"Sash, 'sup? Got the bacon frying."

"Good morning."

I adore bacon cooked the old-fashioned way, in a pan. Groscek used to do that, and now, so does Jorge. Growing up, my mom red-eyed everything. It was efficient, quick, but left all the food bland with a metallic aftertaste.

"Here ya go: eggs and bacon and a slice of vercillion, fresh from Riestovik."

"By fresh, you mean picked, frozen, and shipped thousands of miles?"

"Don't be literal," Jorge complains. For some reason, he fills two more plates with food.

I fake a smile and nod.

I'd like to clarify, 'cause it's a misconception that annoys me to no end, that surgery doesn't mean I can't feel any *pleasure*. It just takes a lot of effort on my part, and is short-lived. The same way for grief, but why would I want to work at feeling *that*?

"Any good, Sash?"

"Yeah, it's the best you've made."

"Nah, come off it."

We're sitting on opposite sides of the kitchen table. There's yellow waridira in a slim glass vase in the middle. You can see the petals starting to wilt. The standing microfilter fan is oscillating back and forth between us. I bought it, after much consternation, with my last paycheck. You take that out, with groceries and rent, and there's hardly anything left over for fun. Or my approximation of fun.

There's a bit of stirring from Jorge's bedroom. I hover my finger over the button on my belt that releases the sidearm. It's rare, but interested parties can find out who you are if they know the right people. So once in a great while, you'll come across a widow or a son looking for revenge. Their attempt at killing is not legal. It's extrajudicial and we live on a planet of rules and order.

Jorge is busy with his eggs when I see a shadow cross the doorway. I pull the gun up and take aim at—

"What the hell are you doing?" Jorge asks.

I nod toward his bedroom and whisper, "Someone is breaking in. I told you to get the windows twimilted shut."

"That's *Alva*," he says, like I'm supposed to know who that is.

I shrug, the gun still aimed.

"She's the woman I told you about."

Told me about?

I lie. "Oh, yeah. *Alva*. She works in. . ."

"The finance department," Jorge finishes, brows raised. "Can you put the gun down now?"

"You sure? I can do it and we can backdate the paperwork to say you hired me."

Jorge chuckles. "Yeah, I'm sure."

From Jorge's bedroom emerges a woman about one foot shorter than him. Her head is shaved with a bald stripe down the middle. But my focus is drawn to her eyes—a lush, emerald color.

"So, hey, I'm Alva." She extends her hand out to me.

I stand up and reciprocate. "Jorge's roommate, Sasha."

"Yeah, Jorge told me. You work as an assassin, right?"

"He is really not supposed to advertise that."

Alva smiles. "I just thought it was cool. My dad was an assassin."

"Oh, yeah? Who was he?"

"Waldofo Adsworth."

I squint my eyes. I know that name for some—

Ohhhh, shit.

"Oh."

The whirring of the air purifier is the only sound for a minute.

Alva's smile fades. "It's okay. I've gone to a lot of therapy. I'm super over it now."

Desperate to change the subject, Jorge asks, "So this is the big day for you, eh?"

"Yeah," I say.

"I'd ask if you're nervous but . . ."

"I feel nervousness still. When it's in regard to me. But when you hear a mother talk about being nervous for a child, *that* I can't approximate."

"But your first political job—that puts you up there in the big time."

I finish off my toast. "Yeah, no more clipping cheating spouses in parking lots."

"I'm going to have to start looking for a new roommate with the money you'll be making."

Gods, I wish he was correct. I'm still in debt for the gun safe from five years ago. *'Praemia Sunt Juu'* (the rewards are at the top) was my profession's motto. And I was still struggling in the middle.

CHAPTER 2

PLANNING A PLANET

The Ruling Class of Riestovik, the Ealdorman, felt threatened.

Strikes had been coming in waves, disrupting the cozy life most ealdormen lived. Any good will or hope for compromise broke down when a fanatic bombed the Staracy Hotel, where a meeting between high-profile politicians was being held. Two politicians were killed, along with their families, who were staying in the penthouse when the building collapsed. Everywhere, the media projected the image of two-year-old Oconomowoc, his head severed, laying among the rubble. The eyes were wide open: gold, with long lashes. Those eyes, more than any strike or any bomb, spurred change.

A year later, a proposal for a new planet was voted on by the Big 3.

Abakalic was responsible for the new technology that could create a planet. The history books advertise the breakthrough as the brainchild of the Spiltrany twins. The twins were the picture of perfection in Abakalic society…over seven feet tall with deep hazel eyes and trim, muscular frames. They also fit the planet's beloved narrative of rising up from nothing to change the world.

In Abakalic, rebellions and strikes were of no concern to the Ruling Class. The underclass was held in check by a strong *bucco derosa arfast* (there isn't a direct translation, but it has to do with honor and work ethic). The poor believed the struggle to become rich was the true joy in living.

The Ruling Class reinforced this by glorifying the rich who built their wealth and vilifying those who inherited it. (Incidentally, to be a part of the Ruling Class, you had to be born into it.) They gave them the title nouveau riche. Nouveau riche were smarter than everyone else, more industrious, mentally stronger. Their perseverance was fetishized as a boon to all of Abakalic.

Bolstering the idea were projections and books exulting the narrative arch of the nouveau riche. The most common went as such: The hero begins in a single room cabin on the outskirts of the city, preferably deep in the Mauti or Akutshi forests. You get a sense of the *gor* beneath his or her fingernails and in his or her hair, the blood staining the rags worn. A most important part of the formula was the patient and persistent push to *improve one's self*. You must always be *improving one's self*. The sleep sacrificed to learn a new trade, the family neglected to work endless hours at a new business, the loneliness endured to achieve a most important thing: *ricea*, preferably untaxed.

Then the narrative would hit a bump during the rise—maybe a rival to battle, one who isn't quite as scrupulous as our hero—leading to the triumphant moment when our hero squashes his enemy. It would end with a shot of the hero dead in the business he created, or the *aleacraft de cwaltt* (artful death of honor).

Of course, all of the networks running these projections were owned by moguls who had passed down the networks for generations. But that was neither here nor there.

Abakalic was known for consistent weather. This might seem unbelievable, but the weather on day 200 ten years ago was the same as day 200 five years ago, and two years ago, and so on. It was a dream for agriculture. And the Abaks had thrived for centuries. The nutrient- and oxygen-rich *gor* put them in a constant position of strength when trading, thanks to surpluses in food and grains. Throughout history, while they maintained a good relationship with Riestovik, they bitterly fought with LaRocca.

This *fahmann* crystallized at the turn of the century during a crisis on LaRocca. LaRocca was in the middle of a famine unseen by the three planets. Abakalic held its prices steady. To the Abaks, they were performing a charity—their economic norms dictated people in a position of power should raise their prices. From the LaRoccan perspective, this broke their code of *ahneswork por welcem* (charity till poverty, give until you can give no more).

When the talks for a new planet began, the delegates from LaRocca were all for it. Despite being a planetary philosophy, their code, *ahneswork por welcem*, was an ideal many fell short of. It was mostly used by religious leaders to engender guilt into the populace. Biscops would joke that *ahneswork por welcem* was responsible for more churches than the gods themselves.

During the famine, a dark side to the wealthy emerged. Many blamed the farmers for overworking the land, for not believing enough in the gods, for exposing the belly of LaRocca to the other planets. The Fullfremens (perfect ones) tried to hog what little resources were available. They convinced themselves the survival of LaRocca depended on the survival of their children. This hoarding exacerbated the famine for decades, ironically weakening LaRocca and strengthening Abaklic.

The Fullfremens became the most popular among the poor. The poor began to lash out at each other. The wealthy fed the backstabbing. The media was filled with stories of *layabouts* and *slakful*, sucking up the charity of others and giving nothing back, like ticks fattening off the blood of a *hund*.

Wealthy Fullfremens organized and marched on the capital city of Berkwin. Day after day, week after week, the wealthy protesters disrupted daily life in Berkwin. Chaz, the leader of the party, gave rousing speeches praising the idea of Earth. The day before the vote, he gave the famous "cruelty of love" speech.

Here is a sample:

"…true to their nature. But should we also suffer? Have we earned the right to walk to a movie theatre without being hassled for feoh? When I sleep at night, I dream of a LaRocca free from the pestilence that is the poor. A dream where we no longer are blackmailed into guilt by the sight of sick and dirty children. A dream where our hospitals aren't choked by the malfeasance of creatures too lazy to pay for their healthcare. And my friends, Earth…is…this…dream!"

Many of the wealthy protesters broke down in tears at the beauty of it all. Their children bounced up and down chanting, "We want Earth!" Chaz celebrated on stage by chugging expensive barrel-aged *baerodast*, imported from Riestovik. He wrapped himself in a resplendent fur coat and waved to the crowd as he walked off stage.

CHAPTER 3

THE NEW KIDS

"**W**ell, you're just a wisp of a thing, aren't you?" the waitress says to Jonas Cello.

He pushes his stringy black hair away from his eyes and grins, nervous from the attention. "I, uh . . . I guess ma'am."

The waitress taps her watch. A menu projects in 3-D on the table with prices, cook times, and pictures. A couple of the pictures are black and white, indicating these items are out of stock. The pictures in green are the specials.

"All right, son—just swipe what you want. Keep the cooking times in mind if you're really hungry."

Jonas swipes three times on the omelet but nothing happens.

"Cheap Abakalic crap." The waitress jiggles her watch. The menu flickers and then steadies. "All right, try again."

Jonas is successful this time.

"And how about you, young lady?"

Jessi Cello looks at the menu with her lip curled. "I don't see quinoa."

"Quinoa?" the waitress replies as if she is shocked anyone would even ask.

Jessi sighs. She has short, platinum hair and is bigger than Jonas in both height and width. "No edamame pods?"

"Girl, this is a *bryce* shop, not Lucciano's Steak Hus."

Jessi cracks her knuckles and glares at the waitress. "I don't eat meat, and I don't eat anything *not* from Earth."

The waitress reiterates, "I understand, but you have to stick to the menu."

"Waitress, I think it's best you find something to meet my sister's diet," Jonas says under his breath, trying not to draw any attention.

"I have…a very specific diet." Jessi is burning a hole through the waitress with her eyes. "I can get sick easily."

"Ma'am, do you have an arugula salad?" Jonas asks.

"I don't—we have regular lettuce."

"From Earth or imported?"

"Look I have other customers," the waitress snaps. "Pick what's on the damn menu so I can get going."

Jessi emits a growl—deep and guttural—which causes the table to vibrate and the silverware to rattle.

Jonas keeps his voice calm. "It's important—what do you have that hasn't been imported, purely grown here on Earth?"

The waitress looks at the menu. "I don't know, probably the potatoes. Those are only native to Earth."

In one motion, Jessi grabs the waitress by the shirt, jerks down, and slams her head into the table. She slams it again. And again. The waitress lets out a scream which causes the whole shop to notice. The table starts to crack. And again. The napkins are getting stained with blood. And again. It's hard to tell if the crunching is from the table or the bones in the waitress's face. And again.

Jonas shakes his head as Jessi lets up. "Come on, now we gotta go somewhere else."

A cook from the back runs out, screaming "Julie! Julie! My god, what have you—"

Jonas sticks a *neosiri* through his throat. Then he uses his foot to push the cook off, freeing the blade. Blood gurgles from the wound. The cook collapses on top of the waitress.

Jonas looks around the restaurant. There's an elderly couple in a booth in the corner. They're trying to hide under the table. There are three kids wearing college T-shirts at a round table starting to flee. And one woman—who appears to be in her fifties, with sleeve brandings up her arms—calmly sipping her coffee at the counter.

Jessi chases down the college kids. She snaps the necks of the first two. The final one, she punches in the throat over and over until the flesh wears away and the spine is exposed. Jonas walks over to the elderly couple and dispatches with them quickly, *mercifully*, with his katana.

Jonas patiently glides over to the woman at the counter. She's polishing off some poached eggs with a side of *percic*. He stands behind her, holding his sword at his side. She betrays nothing. No shock, no fear, just an impermeable focus on her eggs.

Her voice was drowning in phlem and sounded like she gargled with whiskey and nails this morning, "Yeah, whaddaya want?"

Jonas studies the woman. "H-H-Hey, were you an assassin?"

"What's it ta ya?"

Jonas points at the brandings up her arm. "I'm looking for someone. . . someone who we can train under."

"Ya? You wanna be like me? Be a bongar like me?"

"Well, me and my sister—she's the one with the temper—we want to become Cysta Por Ruverno."

The lady wheezes out a laugh and reaches in her pocket. She pulls out a blue mask and covers her mouth with it. The mask comes alive and shoots down her throat. She coughs a few times, then takes a deep breath.

"Dream a little dream, mi boy," she says, looking him up and down. Her voice is crystal clear now. "You can't weigh more than eight stone."

"I'm really trying to show you a little courtesy, professionalism. If you would give me a name or address to work with, I can be on my way and you can get on with it."

"Professional courtesy?" she says with a high-pitched, mocking tone. "Boy, one thing you learn real fast is there's none of that in this life."

"I don't know if you watched what Terror Girl—that's my sister's avatar—is capable of."

"I saw; I seen it before."

"Hmmm, probably not like this."

"Like what? Why you actin' so damn weird? You . . . You're a real *geneat*."

Jonas opens his eyes wide. "That's not very nice ma'am. How would you like it—"

Before he can finish, the old lady takes her knife and sticks it in his throat. He smirks, flicking the blade with his index finger. He tries laughing, but the blade interrupts any sound coming out. The blood drips onto his white silk blouse, ruining it.

The old assassin blinks and the knife is gone, back on the table. Standing in front of her is Terror Girl, who has spittle dripping down her chin and is rocking back and forth while holding onto the counter. Jonas's blouse is clean, with no sign of the blood stain.

"How the fuck—"

"You know how."

Old lady squints her eyes, looking at Terror Girl. "No…no one does that anymore. No surgeon would even think of it."

"Wouldn't they?"

"No one would be stupid enough to get it."

"And yet, here we are."

The old assassin braces herself against the counter. "I only knew of rumors, tales of old heads who had it done." She reaches out to touch Terror Girl, who has recovered. "Why'd you do that? Do you know what happens?"

"I'm going to kill her now," Terror Girl says as she starts to come back.

"She's useful for information. We should take her," Jonas cautions.

"None of you taking me anywhere."

Seconds later, Terror Girl is dragging the unconscious, retired assassin through the door. Jonas follows before pausing to look at the bodies of the waitress and the cook.

Jonas dips his fingers in the neck wound of the cook, coating the tips in blood. With it, he draws a giant "K.K." on the floor before wiping his fingers off on the cook's apron and leaving the bryce shop.

CHAPTER 4

THE JOB

I want you to know I still have a concept of the value of life.

In the concrete sense. The value of life is *Yearly Output* minus *Salary* times *Number of Years Remaining* with a modifier, depending on how age will hurt production in said field.

There is a white-noise hum emanating from the protest crowd. People are packed together so tight you can't make out a sliver of concrete. This is one of the largest protests I've seen. (I reckon they have been growing in size and frequency the last decade.) It was an impressive showing. The people must be *really* mad at Burgealdor Spencer.

The *magistratus* (police) are in a line, shoulder to shoulder, behind the crowd. Their weapons, a mix of blades and guns, are drawn at this side. A few of them are dispersed throughout the crowd.

Many protestors have signs depicting the Burgealdor in all sorts of violent situations. In one, a mythical kipanga is clawing at his stomach and tearing out Spencer's intestines. As someone who has seen the insides of more than a few people, this was unnervingly accurate. I used to *love* The Kipanga Stories as a kid—they were prominent in this collection of stories about the first CEOs to tame the workforce of Earth. The Kipanga Stories featured lots of violence and sweeping acts of sacrifice and heroism. I used to get such a visceral thrill reading the violent parts over and over.

Two days ago, I scouted out a perch on top of the book-*dryre*, but the stage was placed a couple blocks further than anticipated. The new spot, on top of an aging *guistarn*, is covered in gravel. I'm already annoyed; I have a couple of pebbles in my right shoe. The stage is planks of wood nailed together and tied on top of some concrete blocks. It did not look altogether safe.

As part of my ritual, I take a bite out of a red *wuddupple*. This time of year, they tend to be bitter if they come from Earth, so I'd paid extra for ones out of Abakalic. I place the *wuddupple* to my left. I pull out my *Fealca* Vision Glasses—top of the line, cost a bundle. At least for the assassin I'd killed and took them from. Franco. . . Frank . . . Francis? Something like that. He had this really pretty blond hair, which was stained red when I domed him at short range. I felt a pang of guilt about that—it was *gorgeous* hair.

My favorite tale from The Kipanga Stories involved the CEO from Stubbs Eastern Concern, known as "The Gnashing of LaRocca." This was shortly after the farm wars, when a brutal landlord, Saevus, seized power. Saevus was a heavyset man with a booming voice. He was greasy and unkempt, smelled like rotting *hund*, and had a face that was scarred and disfigured from years of fighting. Saevus was only concerned with main-taining his position on top and thought the workers little more than *hnutu* on the blocks for slaughter. His mantra, "The Lengo del Vita es Tumikia Saevus," or "The goal of life is to serve/service Saevus," was carved into boards, which were nailed to people accused of treachery. Their bodies hung up across the land to intimidate the workers.

My mind wanders as I listen to the chanting of the crowd. My surgery, performed years ago, is starting to wear off. You see, the "humane traits," like feeling guilt or empathy, would start to come back, in most cases. And I know, on the old planets, the *askofus* would point to their texts and speak about my humanity growing back. My soul is repairing itself. But they can keep my soul, I just need the money and the surgery to get right.

My project, Kergan Satre, is scheduled to give a speech. She is the leader of this tribe. They call themselves, "Et On Weardo Tutti" or "The Ones Who See All." Very anti-corporation. These types usually grow up in the woods outside the capital of Chicago. The woods are filled with citizens obsessed with the idea that the corporations on Earth were fascists. Women like Kergan would come in the city only to kick a *hyrnet*'s nest. It was disruptive and harmful to people like me who participated in society.

When I talk about the old CEOs, they were different than today. They were people borne through the fire training on Riestovik. (Heck, they don't even do that training anymore—it was deemed too brutal for polite society almost a century ago.) Their bodies and minds had been pushed to extremes. They were capable of staying awake for days at a time. Their skin was impenetrable. It was said they took on traits of machines, with brazen focus on their tasks. So, when Karl Stubbs arrived on LaRocca with his *kipanga*, Kifuta, he was as if cut from Brasu bronze.

There's a man dressed head-to-toe in fur giving a speech right now. He's definitely from the forests; that style is only acceptable out there. I can't hear anything he's saying, but I'm sure he's complaining about how "this CEO did *this*," or "this corporation did *that*."

"Display time," I say out loud, triggering the PIP system. It's a couple hours until the Burgealdor's event. My project isn't visible yet.

Saevus and Karl almost destroyed LaRocca. In quite a literal sense. Saevus sacrificed tens of thousands of workers trying to slow and wear down Karl. But Karl could dispatch workers with a flick of his wrist. Like smashing a *fleoge*. At Saevus's *ufalme*, Karl was greeted by rows and rows of *iboras* (archers) with their arrows drawn and ready to shoot. Saevus charged the *ufalme*, only to stop when he saw the faces of the *iboras*. They were children—children of the *workers*—some hardly able to draw back their bow.

I'm spreading out my bites of *wuddupple* so it lasts. It's terrible being stuck in a perch and hungry. Thought she would go on sooner than this. This man is really droning on.

I wore a grey pullover, but the Andetnes star (the sun) is determined to make me sweat. Sometimes I wish I was on Abakalic. I take the pullover off. I'm wearing my usual gear—grey top, dark blue pants, soft-soled shoes. The air is thick. When you take a breath, it feels like work. It's the biggest negative of the city. You get far out enough towards the forest and it's like a different planet, air quality-wise.

Karl was stuck. Even a heart as hard as his had a line. And even his loyal *kipanga*, Kifuta, shied away. Slaughtering an army of children was more than their conscience could bear. He turned around and retreated. Far away, he dug a hole straight down for a mile to escape and pray. When CEO Karl wanted to consult with the Founders, he needed complete sensory deprivation.

The Founders were three sexless beings who created the three worlds. That's a different story, though.

There she is, my project. Short and wide, and like the previous speaker, covered in fur. Her hair is brown and down to her knees. I don't get that—why don't the forest people take better care of themselves? She's trailed by a child, built just like her with the same hair color. The child looks nervous and keeps petting a tiny green frog pinned to her sleeve. I watch the project kneel down and speak sternly to the child before walking to the podium. The kid is immediately engulfed by three large men who looked like bodyguards.

That's going to make this job more difficult. I can't even see the second project behind them.

Then, for a split second, I feel relaxed—more than I have been in a while. Usually, I'll get anxious, not having eyes on a target. Strange.

There's a bit of a commotion, and my project moves back into a crowd on the stage. She's yelling at two men off to the side. I can't quite get a view of her; she's moving around too much. I slow my breathing, which helps twofold: patience and accuracy. When I first started, I had an issue with holding my breath, which was causing me to tense up when I pulled the trigger. To train me, my aunt would stand next to me at the shooting range and kick me in the ribs if I held my breath. My aunt . . . Well, you'll meet her.

CEO Karl paid respect to the Founders by offering them ricea. Ricea is a mix of blood and gold. He pressed them—what could he do in this predicament? And this is when the Founders grant us the gift of the surgeon, CEO Karl being the first. The knowledge of how the brain works was poured into him by the Founders. Every impulse and every signal, he can trace from point to point. Behaviors, feelings, memories—the puzzle had been solved.

CEO Karl is able to close off certain receptors. In this case, the ones specific to empathy and sympathy. The next time he and Kifuta attacked Saevus's *ufalme*, the children stood no chance. Mercy to those who died quickly. Those that didn't were so mangled and injured, they wished they had.

Karl and Saevus fought head-to-head. The walls of the *ufalme* shook, cracked, then collapsed. Kifuta attacked Saevus' eyes, dislodging one before Saevus caught him and snapped his neck.

I keep peering through the glasses. I take my shot. It was clean, through the neck. The project collapsed like a dying *hund*. I'm looking for any signs of movement. The child is screaming and holding the project's hand. I can see her tears dripping off her chin and mixing with the project's blood. These glasses really *do* have fantastic clarity.

I can't tell, but it *looks* like the project is still breathing. Disappointing. I had a one-shot-kill streak of eleven before today. I could hold out and hope she bleeds to death, but this is a government contract and is too important. I put another slug in her chest and one in her head. I focus in on the girl. I have a clean shot for a second, but I don't shoot—and she's dragged away by the guards.

I start to clean up my perch. Hopefully, Jorge is making something with *hnutu* for dinner. Why didn't I shoot? He fries up the best *hnutu,* and I'm famished.

Now, I'm anxious. I just screwed up my big contract. *Gods!*

But the damage is done and Saevus has been worn down. CEO Karl had too much stamina .All that was left was to decide how Karl would end it. On that day, Surgeon Karl was born.

CEO Karl left his family to save LaRocca, but Surgeon Karl was the one who returned. At first, he faked it…feelings for his wife and eight kids. But after a few months, the mask of humanity started to slip. His responses were cold and mechanical, and he greeted most emotion with disdain. Why were the kids crying? Why did they complain? Why were his kids so weak?

So, he fixed them.

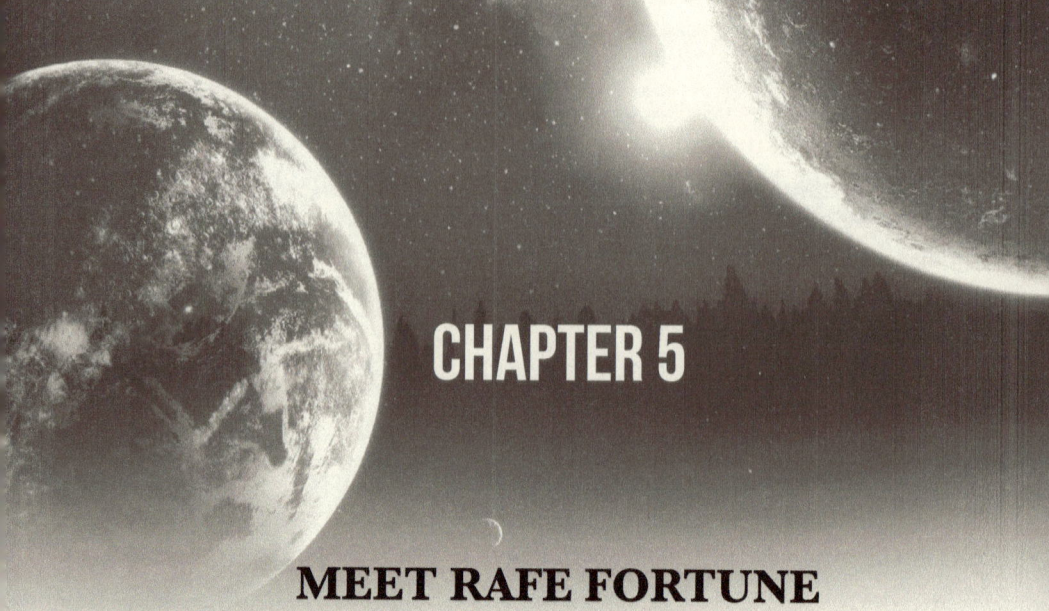

CHAPTER 5

MEET RAFE FORTUNE

Rafe Fortune can smell the metal in his own blood as he ties a *bindele* around his thigh. This was a weird mutation Rafe "suffered" from: his sense of smell being as strong as a black *mordu*. Rafe had never known his parents. Growing up, the kids often teased him, saying that *mordus* were his real parents.

Home is a giant ship off the western coast of Chicago. It has housed Rafe and thirty or so of his *weaoruds*, of all genders, for the past decade. (*Weaorud* is a slur that means, in polite terms, *hund* waste. They take it on as a badge, anyway.) Could house more—*used* to house more—but not many people can handle the lifestyle.

Micel Rudes burst into Rafe's quarters without knocking, living up to his last name. M, as Rafe liked to call him, was tall, awkwardly so, and had to duck to avoid hitting his head on the doorway. His face was covered by a red beard, and his hair was trimmed in a short box-like shape.

"Aye-aye, Rafey—you gonna be all right? I know my knife might'a bit you hard, but I held back as much as a could," Micel said with a giant belly laugh. He pulls out a bag of *pulveris*, about the size of a fist, pinches a bit of the powder, and snorted it up his nose. Micel's hair starts to glow white and his eyes cloud with black, then silver, then purple. This switching repeats for a minute while Micel tries to hold steady against the bronze desk in the corner. Micel pushes the bag towards Rafe.

Rafe ignores the offer and replies, "Of course, you silly rudder—I wake myself up with a bite like that."

Micel keeps staring at Rafe. Rafe grins. The grin fades. He bites his lip. Then he falls down on his bed. "Fine, it hurts."

Micel laughs till the point of coughing.

"You should take it easy with the *pulveris*." Rafe is staring at the wood ceiling of his room. The ship was composed of metals, but Rafe had used laser sculpting to give it the feel of the old Reistovic war ships. Of course, this ship was nowhere near flight-worthy and hadn't been for years.

"Just a pin after a good SNP." Micel was referring to a Sifa Njema Pug, which was a fight-style demonstration. "Sparring" is not quite the right word, as the level of violence depended on the combatants. Sometimes, it was nothing but rolling around, punching and kicking. Sometimes, it ended with someone getting a knife in them. It was a fight but an honorable fight. These were common back when ships like Rafe's ruled the skies.

Micel extends his hand. Rafe grabs him by the wrist and they both give it one good shake.

"Hey, you remember when you gave me this?" Micel pulls open his blue and orange vest to expose a scar running along his right ribcage.

"Yeah, a lifetime ago. You were smaller then." Rafe puts his hand out to exaggerate Micel's girth.

"And you were prettier, didn't spend so many nights alone."

Rafe sits up and curls the corner of his lip. He spits out the words, "What do you know about it?"

Micel backs off. "No, I didn't mean . . . Look, Rafe, I know more than anyone."

But Rafe's already broken into a smile.

"Ah, you *stu-weaorud*," Micel says with a chuckle.

Rafe takes the *bindel* off and reaches under the bed, grasping with his left hand. He finds a *formeltan* iron (used to heal cuts, close wounds). Rafe shakes it to warm it up. He points it at the knife wound in his thigh.

Micel, who is glowing again, says, "You really outta get the bleedin' to stop before you use one of those."

Rafe ignores him and turns it on. Immediately, his thigh muscle starts to mend, strands connecting quickly.

"How old is that thing?" Micel asks.

Rafe looks at M and grunts, "Older than the pubes on a CEO's sack."

Blood starts gurgling from the wound, then splashing, with some hitting his cheek.

Micel shakes his head in disappointment. "See, you need to stop the bleeding first."

Rafe uses his blanket—already with plenty of stains on it—to soak up some blood, then continues with the repair.

"This room is 'bout half the size of your old one."

"Yeah, I hadn't noticed, M."

Micel asks, "How long ago did Cadyn beat you for your Brimwisa quarters?"

Rafe shrugs. "Long enough; I'm used to this one."

"Rafe, Kergan Satre is here to see you," a woman with orange hair says from the doorway. "Says it's about a job."

Rafe and Micel look at each other with raised eyebrows.

"Have her meet me in the chumba room," Rafe replies.

Rafe limps into the room with Micel behind him. Kergan Satre is sitting on one of the steel chairs which surround the table. Her legs are crossed and she's chewing on a *wuddupple*. A bit of juice runs down her chin. She wipes it with her hand and then wipes her hand on her animal fur pants. The pants expose her from the knee down. She's wearing a top which is obviously from a different animal: darker and visibly more coarse.

Standing behind Kergan Satre is a young girl, maybe twelve. She bears a strong resemblance to Kergan.

Rafe opens the dialogue, "Look at this, Micel—Kergan Satre, in our humble abode."

"This place stinks," Kergan says while chewing.

"That's…the dead things," Rafe replies, with a shrug and a flourish of his left hand.

Kergan uses her fingernail to pick food out of her teeth. "You look like…the business end of a *hund*, Rafe. What the hell have you been doing with yourself?"

Rafe leans against a chair; the wound hurts when he sits. "Waitin' 'ere for your lovely presence."

Kergan laughs—a giant, *wuddupple*-spitting laugh. She hands her leftovers to the kid. "Throw this out."

Kergan sucks on her teeth before saying, "I need to hire you and your band of . . ." She looks at Micel, who returns her look with a giant grin exposing a mouth of broken teeth and bleeding gums. "Of whatever it is you call this."

"Well, you've come to the best on Earth, you know that."

Kergan taps the table twice, "Hmmm. Mostly I know I can trust you; you don't care about politics."

"Not in so much as I get to keep my *feoh* away from the government."

Kergan laughs. "You still think the government is the one taking your *feoh*, huh? You know, last year, the top five companies on Earth received 60 percent of tax revenues?"

Rafe looks at Micel. "I didn't know that. Did *you* know that?"

Micel exaggerates a confused face, "I didn't know that."

Rafe looks back at Kergan. "We didn't know that."

"Gods, you still think you're gonna fly this graveyard off to retirement, huh?"

Rafe doesn't respond.

"Maybe you still think you and Sash—"

"Alright! Get to the job," Rafe interjects.

Kergan nods. "I'm going to be assassinated."

"I'm sorry to hear that," Rafe deadpans right when Micel says, with complete sincerity, "Oh no! By who?"

Kergan rolls her eyes and ignores Micel.

"Do we know where or when?" asks Rafe.

"No."

"So this is more of an *existential* threat, huh?" Rafe says.

"That's a big word for a *weaorud*."

Micel crosses his arms. "Hey now, we didn't show up to your hut and call you names, you—"

"Ignore her, Micel," Rafe says. "Living in the forest tends to ruin one's manners. So what," he goes on, now looking back at Kergan, "we're just gonna follow you around?"

"Come here," she says to the kid. The child complies. "This is my daughter, Kergan Satre II. This is who I want you to protect."

"Hey, kid." Micel grins at the girl. The girl pulls back and looks away.

"Close your mouth before you scare her away, Micel," scolds Rafe.

"When I'm assassinated, it will trigger a deposit into your account. A large one. Your job from there is to keep her alive until she can take over my position as leader. A year or two, depending on when I die."

Rafe frowns. "A year or two? She'll barely be a teenager."

Kergan's eyes pop with a deep sea blue. "That's how old I was when I took over for my murdered mother."

Rafe and Micel shift uneasily. The girl is very still, held by her mother, but not in a maternal way. Rather the way someone would hold a hostage.

Rafe traces his left eyebrow with his middle finger. "I assume once she hits the age to take over, we get another giant deposit, right?"

"Yup."

Micel holds his hands far apart, "*How* 'giant'?"

Kergan straightens her face and looks Rafe dead in the eye. "I'll give you the number when we're alone, but it will be enough to buy a working ship. Or fix *this* one, if you prefer this Earth I deathtrap or whatever you call it."

"And if she dies?" Rafe looks off to the side when he says this.

"You won't let that happen. It'd be bad if you did. *Very* bad, for you and your men."

"Hey, you can't threaten—" Micel starts.

"Micel, take the girl on a tour of a vessel while me and Kergan go over the details."

Micel protests, but ultimately waves the girl on. She walks behind him, like a soldier marching in line.

When they leave, Rafe continues. "That really your kid?"

"I got the scars to prove it."

"And so you came to the best-looking Brimwisa you knew."

Kergan lowers her heard but keeps eye contact, "You used to believe in what I'm fighting for . . ."

Rafe scoffs and looks away.

"You're *vaguely* good at what you do."

Rafe snorts and squints his eyes. He rolls his tongue against the back of his teeth and retorts, "Kergan, I am *excellent* at what I do."

Kergan sucks on her teeth before continuing. "And the rumor is your rakishi ex has the contract."

Rafe grunts, a smile sliding across his face.

"See? I knew that little bit of news would get you interested. You are so damn predictable."

"I like to disappoint my ex, that's all."

"Why should your breakup be any different than your relationship?"

Rafe scrunches his face. "Gods, you still bite like a sword."

Kergan looks Rafe up and down, pursing her lips. "You got any *ceren* to indulge in?"

Rafe raises his eyebrows. "I can have one of my men bring it up to my room."

Kergan stands up. "My daughter safe with that giant of yours?"

"Without a doubt," Rafe says with a nod. "At this point, she's basically a fleshy sack of *feoh* to us now. We'll guard her with our lives."

"Alright then, let's see if your room is as filthy as I remember it."

CHAPTER 6

JORGE'S JOB

The headset Jorge is wearing begins to emit a low-frequency drone, alerting him to the fact that he had not entered anything into the spreadsheet for five minutes. The drone was referred to as a PTA (Productivity Tracking Assistant), but functionally was a tattletale—every minute the worker ignored it, the drone would get louder until it was piercing. If you took the headset off, the border around your desk would light up red.

Jorge goes back to work, but can't help leaning over the border wall to check if Nalah was in her *yrfebin* next to him. She's supposed to be coming back from a leave of absence today, after being gone for a week following her four-year-old daughter's funeral. She would have been out longer if she weren't out of WAPD (Work Absence Paid Days). As of right now, her border is lit up in a bright yellow to indicate she's late for work.

Jorge eyes the clock and squirms in his seat. Just a few minutes until lunch. He pecks away at the spreadsheet, then looks back at the clock. *No movement.* Pecks away again. Looks back at the clock. In his head, he groans. *No movement.* Jorge finds himself typing blindly now, just clock watching.

Finally his border lights up green and he's free to take off the headset and go to lunch. In a straight line, the workers on the third floor lumber toward the staircase. Their footsteps create a thumping rhythm down the stair case. The walls of the lunchroom are a dark grey. The tables line up in a single row and have plastic red stools attached to them. Everyone sits in the same spot day after day. Everyone shares the same meal, with consideration for allergies. Across from Jorge is an empty seat where Nalah usually sits.

Most workers keep their heads down, reading a book, or listening to music. Jorge looks around, trying to catch someone's eye. When he finally does, he can't remember his name. "Hey, um . . . Do you have any idea about Nalah? She was supposed to come back today."

The person shrugs, then starts talking to someone else. Jorge keeps looking for someone else to ask, and connects with Gerwid, a worker in the planning and development department.

Gerwid has forest green hair and matching eyes. She's wearing a black hooded shirt and black pants with brown boots. Her eyes are bugged out, but not because she's excited—that's just how they have always been.

"Hey have you heard anything about Nalah?"

Gerwid shakes her head, "Bits and pieces. And it's a damn shame how the company is…"

Out of nowhere, Nalah appears in the empty seat—her hair unkempt, long, down to her neck. The outfit she has on is a clash of colors: red, blue, orange, pink. Her dark brown eyes are sunken, with blue bags under them. Her lips are chapped and have bits of skin sticking up.

Jorge says, surprised. "Oh, hey, Nalah!"

Nalah nods her head to acknowledge him but doesn't say anything.

"Hey, um…I don't know what to say, but how are you feeling?" Jorge cringes, realizing how stupid the question is now that he's asked it.

Nalah, much to Jorge's relief, ignores him. They finish their lunch without incident. As the workers march back to their desks Gerwid whispers to Jorge, "*That* is what the company thinks of us." She nods towards Nalah who is walking ahead of them. "Imagine being forced to come back to work after watching your child…" Gerwid shakes her head instead of finishing the sentence.

Later that day, everyone is back at work. Nalah's border is red as she hasn't bothered to put the headset on or do any work at all. Jorge can see Wildorlic, from Notitia, walking down the aisle. Jorge uses his peripherals to eye Wildorlic, who passes him by and goes to Nalah's desk.

Wildorlic speaks in a slow measured tone, "Excuse me, Nalah. Can we see you in our office?"

Nalah stares ahead, blank.

"Nalah, I'm Wildorlic from Notitia. The department noticed, along with being extremely late, you haven't started any work so far today."

Nalah doesn't respond.

"Now, we understand you have gone through a traumatic event—"

"If you understand," Nala interjects, "then why'd I have to come in?"

"Well, that was addressed by the department when we called to check on you last week."

"You called and told me I was out of WAPD and was due back at work."

"Well, you were the one who burned through them earlier in the year."

Nalah's eyes spark and she flares her nostrils. "I *burned through them* taking care of my dying child!"

"And we were supportive of you then, as we are now. But we need you to hold up your end."

"Fucking sack me, then!"

Wildorlic takes a deep breath. "Nalah, you have the option to quit, whenever you'd like."

"Great! I quit."

Wildorlic's voice raises, "I am recording this and this will serve as your official resignation."

Nalah stands up and starts to leave, but Wildorlic blocks her. She tries to move around him, but he handcuffs her.

Jorge is just tapping the same key over and over, concentrating on what is going on in the Nalah's yrfebin. He realizes she's been handcuffed and starts looking around the office for someone to step in.

"You remember the loans the company gave you to cover the child's *baelbys*?"

Nalah snorts. "Yeah."

"Well, we need you to work off the loans in servitude."

"Why? I'll pay them back when I get a new job."

Wildorlic sighs through his nose. "We can't trust that'll happen. You will have to submit to servitude for a couple of months."

Nalah's eyes are wide open. "I can't do that! I have two kids still at home!"

"Well you should have gone with a pauper's funeral. Or you could have donated the body to the surgical school."

Nalah kicks her desk, "I'm not donating my *child* to a fucking school!"

"And that's why we are here." As Wildorlic says this, two members of his department show up and flank him. "If necessary, we can forcibly remove you."

Jorge stands up and clears his throat. He raises his hand and asks: "Hey, um . . . May I talk to her?"

Wildorlic looks Jorge up and down before nodding in agreement. Wildorlic backs off with his subordinates.

Jorge walks over to Nalah, who is breathing heavily and fighting back tears. He starts to put his hands on her shoulders but is greeted with a sharp, *"Don't!"*

"All right. Hey, I know it's almost impossible to ask this of you. I don't know the kind of pain you're in. But I know you have two kids at home also going through a tremendous amount of hurt. Two kids who need their mom."

Nalah breaks down and buries her head in Jorge's shoulder, whispering, "I couldn't afford to pay for my own daughter's funeral. Cause I'm a failure as a parent and as a worker."

"No…No you are not. You come here every day with love for your children in your heart and work your butt off."

Nalah starts to regain control.

Jorge whispers so Wildorlic can't hear, "We both know if you go into servitude, you'll never get out. They'll keep finding things to charge to you."

Nalah coughs and nods. "I know." She looks at Wildorlic. "I don't want to resign. I want to stay."

Wildorlic signals for his cronies to leave. "Nalah, that's reassuring to hear. Rash decisions make for sloppy mistakes, am I right?"

Nalah bites her lower lip and nods.

Wildorlic, "I'll leave you to get back to producing."

Over the next week, Jorge overhears Nalah breaking down a couple of times a day at her desk—but she always manages to work through it. He'd often bring her baked goods that he or Alva made—a treat for breakfast.

At the end of the week, as the workers are dismissed, Jorge hangs out on the sidewalk and waits for Nalah. He waits. Waits a little longer. The big star in the sky starts to go down. Finally, Nalah emerges. When she sees Jorge, she closes her eyes and hangs her head.

"What happened?" he asks, walking closer.

Nalah's voice is high-pitched and scratchy, "They released me from my contract. Said I was bringing down the mood in the office. That I needed to learn to keep my personal life at home."

Jorge looks back at the building, "Gods, I hate this place. I get why there's so many damn strikes and protests these days."

"Well, it's what I wanted, I guess." Nalah sucks on her top lip and says, "Maybe I'll become an assassin like your friend."

"That's not you, Nalah."

Nalah agrees with a nod. "Well, I gotta figure out *something*. Eventually. Thanks, Jorge. At least by voluntarily sacking me, I don't have to pay back the loan. I'd be in servitude if it wasn't for you."

Jorge goes in for a hug, but Nalah shakes him off and sticks out a hand. They shake and head off in opposite directions.

CHAPTER 7

THE KIDS AND THEIR TOY

"Toy?"

The old lady starts to come to, realizing she's on top of a bed. She's dizzy, but remembers what happened at the *bryce* shop.

"Toy?" a child-like voice asks again.

The old lady grunts and hacks. The bed squeaks as she sits up. She rumples the blue sheets with her fingers, trying to get her bearings.

"Are you awake, Toy?" Jonas asks in a sing-song fashion.

She tries to say something, but the words bubble out as spit.

"Oh dear, let me get that." Jonas uses a towel to dab at her mouth. "There, that's better."

As her eyes adjust to the light, she can see Jessi, or Terror Girl, leaning against the wall. She's staring at the old lady while picking at her cuticles, some of which have been picked so badly they're bleeding. When the blood starts to run, Terror Girl licks it up.

The room smells of antiseptic, but most of the lower-end motel rooms do, since they're cleaned by a service machine. Service machines were last manufactured about twenty years ago, before being pulled from the market. They would occasionally turn violent and murder a family pet. While the masses didn't care so much about the poisonous chemicals these bots used to clean their children's dressers, they *did* care about dead kitties and puppies. So, Slymart Global Concern pulled them from the market due to the public backlash.

This was the only time a product had been recalled in the last fifty years. Slymart was quickly bought up by Spumea Local Greening Co-Op and the name disappeared from the market. Since the recall, the only places you could still find these antiques were hotels and motels, since they were usually pet-free.

The walls are painted a putrid brown color, except for the parts that are cracked, exposing the white drywall. The ceiling has splatters of pink and yellow and a fan with one blade missing.

"Water?" she asks, barely above a whisper.

"Sis?"

Jessi starts tapping her foot and looks away. "This is *your* thing, Jonas. Not mine." She looks the old lady in the eyes, a brutal gaze that portents a violent end to this encounter. "I'd of disposed of her already."

Jonas clasps his hands together. "All right, I'll be right back. Please don't move, cause my sister will obviously kill you."

The old lady sits up. On a dresser in the corner are her keys and a couple of knives. The window behind it displays a fake sunset, so she can't tell what time it really is.

She looks to Jessi. "I'd ask you the time but you probably don't worry about that anymore, do you?"

Jessi just stares daggers back.

Jonas interrupts their staring contest, "I tried to clean this *canne* as much as possible, but. . ."

He hands her a glass of brown-colored water in a *canne* stained with . . . *gods know what.*

The old lady looks at it, then rolls her eyes up to look at Jonas. Finally, she pinches her nose and chugs the water as fast as possible, trying to avoid it lingering on her tongue. Some of it runs down her chin. After finishing the glass, she gasps for breath.

"More," she says, handing the glass back to Jonas.

Jonas returns with more water and the old lady repeats the ritual.

Jonas takes a seat on the bed. He uses his index finger to stroke a long grey hair hanging in front of the old lady's left eye. He pushes it behind her ear and puts his hand over hers. The old lady is repulsed and pulls back.

"Well, out with it. Let's get on with the questions so you can let me go, or kill me, or whatever."

Jonas paints on a grin, "I do appreciate your enthusiasm."

He stands up and walks over to his sister, holding out his hand. Jessi reaches into the desk drawer and pulls out a pad of paper and a pen, slapping it in Jonas's hand.

"Thanks much, sis." Jonas spins on his heels and heads back over to the bed. He pulls a chair up alongside it and, like a psychiatrist or a journalist, readies his pen over the paper as he asks his first question. "Name?"

"Antibelle Sojourn."

Jonas writes it down. "Pretty. Can I call you Belle?"

She shrugs.

"Belle, I admire how calm you seem to be through all this. Dare I ask, what surgery did you get?"

"They went in"—she points to the front of her forehead and taps a few times—"took out me anxiety. Me nerves."

Belle puts out her right hand. "Used to shake like a serpent's tail before I got sliced and diced."

Jonas makes some notes. "How long did it last?"

"I dunno. So far, so good."

"It didn't wear off?" Terror Girl spits out some cuticle as she asks.

"Nah, that's . . . whatchamacallit . . . Those special traits, right? Like guilt, empathy—stuff that affects the soul."

"What about mine?" Terror Girl asks. For the first time, there's a hint of innocence in her voice. Maybe even some hope.

But any hope washes away as Belle laughs. *Loudly.* Shaking the bed. Slapping her hand down on the mattress. As she wipes a tear from her eye. "You know what's gonna happen to you? The same thing that happened to Surgeon Karl's youngest child."

Terror Girl scoffs and looks down. She turns and punches the wall, leaving a hole the size of a human head. Then she leaves the room with a slam of the door.

"She starting to regret it?" Belle asks Jonas.

"Yeah, something like that." Jonas continues, "Who did your surgery?"

"Slyve Cohen. Skilled man."

Jonas eyes widen as he leans forward. "Do you still know where he lives?"

"Yeah, Corporate Byrignes of Chicago."

Jonas drops his shoulders and frowns. "So, he's dead."

"I was at his *baelblys*. Gave 'em a good speech. Talked a lot, drank a lot. It was a fun time. Danced with his widow. Best *baelblys* I've been to. And I been to my fair share, you know what I mean?"

Jonas follows up. "Do you know of any other Surgeons?"

"No."

"Come on, you're a *bonger* for a living; you have to know one."

"The one I knew is dead. Why don't you use the one that sliced and diced your sister?"

Jonas mumbles out, "Don't worry about it. Suffice to say, we can't."

"Well, that's tough shit, ain't it?"

"I'm trying to find one who can fix my sister before it's too late." Jonas says.

Belle laughs again. "It's *already* too late. Now it's just a matter of time till she's drooling on herself, locked in a room somewhere."

Jonas is silent.

"There'll be nothing left of her, ya know. That surgery—it'll eat away at her till she ain't got no idea where she is."

Jonas becomes a little colder in his voice, sharper. "Who else do you know works as an assassin?"

She shrugs. "I don't fuckin' know, lots of people."

"Lots of people?"

"Yeah, you want some names? Amikba, Taylor, Mcloud, Sasha, Blair, Trumbo, Oluwatson . . ."

Jonas starts out writing the names, but stops at *Sasha*, circling her name a couple of times. "You have any last names?"

"Yeah, I got lots of last names." Belle shrugs.

"Do you know the current Cysta Por Ruverno?"

Belle scratches between her legs and answers, "As much as any celebrity, I guess."

"Great—how did he get the title?"

Belle curls her upper lip. "Hard work and dedication. The same way anything is earned, isn't it?"

"Is there a number he hit? A specific contract he carried out? What was his percentage?"

Belle shakes her head. "No, kid, for god's sake. Look, the CEO who appoints the Cysta is named Malcolm Ritchie. The current Cysta is named Malcolm Ritchie, Jr. The one before him was Uwezo Ritchie. Do the damn math."

Jonas waves his hand back and forth, "Come off it."

"Look 'er up then."

"Cysta Por Ruverno is the most sought-after position in our line of work. You can't just give it to someone 'cause they have your blood."

"Okay, I guess you'd know."

Jonas asks, "Well, how long was he an assassin before he got the position?"

Belle coughs out a phlegm-filled laugh. "He was *never* an assassin. He worked in a warehouse till he got fired, allegedly for stealing. Then he operated one of his dad's *bahati* shops till he was investigated for stealing *feoh* or something. Then he disappeared for a while until he got this position. The journals profiled him a whole bunch. Made him look bad, too. I was actually hired by his dad to whack the writer who did the profile. Netty James, I think. Anyway, he bled a lot. Ruined the carpet of the store I stabbed him in."

Belle coughs and spits out some phlegm on the floor.

"Ugh, we have napkins for that."

"Nah, good with da floor," Belle says, words slurring together to form one.

"How did you get into the job?"

Belle flashes a crooked smile. "Used me fucking charm."

"I can call my sister in here to crack your skull, leave you alive, begging for death."

Belle's smile fades. "I's an orphan. Got adopted by a *bonger*—Crispus Herodis. He was from LaRocca originally."

"Well that was certainly a lucky turn of events."

Belle frowns as she explains, "He used me as a maid and beat me without mercy any time I didn't comply. One time he choked me till I passed out because I used a red-eye on his meat instead of frying it." Belle sniffles slightly. "I didn't ask for this surgery, he made me get it. Last forty years of my life, I've never felt nervous or anxious. You'd think it's a blessing."

"Why isn't it?"

Belle replies, "Everything has a tradeoff. I don't feel any adrenaline *ruunt* at all. Everything is just . . . *swetwyrde del miji*."

Jonas seems to ponder this for a couple seconds. "I'm sorry that happened—that you don't feel any excitement. But I'd be willing to bet you got your revenge though, right?"

Belle shrugs. "One day, when he was training, I was kneeling on two bricks as punishment for not falling asleep when he ordered me to. He had a heart attack. Watched him die right there. Before the surgery, I would'a enjoyed it. Now, not even a flutter of me heart. Crispus, that *mafuta ombe*, took away the one joy me had—his death."

"Is there any other assassin you can direct us to? Someone who can help more than you?"

Belle shrugs, "I don't know. If it'll get me out of here, sure. Taylor will work with new—"

"*Sasha*," Terror Girl's voice booms from outside the window.

Jonas smiles. "We would be interested in meeting with Sasha."

"Her? Gods, why?"

Jonas relinquishes the smile, "It's not your business why. That's who we want to work with."

"It's just . . . She ain't the mentoring type. *Bongers* who have their empathy removed make terrible trainers."

"The training aspect for us is more about how to maneuver in the world as assassins."

"I know, but she's a salted dog, that one. She'll turn on you. Her last boyfriend—"

Jessi kicks the door open and marches to the side of Belle's bed. "Listen old bag, we want her. Give us an address or something to get in touch with her."

"It look like I have a fucking address book on me?"

Jessi has her head tilted down and glares at Belle. "Can I kill her now?"

Belle dives for her weapons. There's a flash and a pause. She finds herself back on the bed, no closer to the knives. Jessi is slack-jawed and bracing herself on the bed with her hands, frozen.

"If ya loved her," Belle says to Jonas, "you'd stop her from doing that. It's going to melt'er brain."

"Leave your weapons and run." Jonas is reading over his notes. "I want to extend this as a moment of generosity on our part."

Belle gets up, straightens out her pants, and walks to the door. "Son, I don't run from anybody."

Jonas snorts. "I guess you wouldn't."

Belle stops at the door and looks at Jessi, who is still frozen.

"It's lasting longer," Jonas says.

Belle throws out the most banal piece of advice she can think of. "Yeah, well, life's tough."

"Her mind, too. She's becoming more and more obsessive about little things, like where her food is grown or what color her shirt is."

Belle replies, "It's why you're not supposed to get that. I ain't think no one knew how to do it anymore."

Jonas answers, "She didn't choose it. Kind of like you, it was forced on her."

Belle sighs. "Who forced her?"

Jonas is too busy helping Jessi lay down.

Belle starts to say something, decides against it, and closes the door as she leaves.

CHAPTER 7

THE MEETING

Riestovik's leaders, CEO Prezbigly and CEO Podsteop, arrived in Abakalic a day before the meetings were to begin. They were the most cynical about the idea of jettisoning citizens from each planet who were deemed "unenthusiastic".

The definition of "unenthusiastic" was left intentionally broad. Maybe you were a political rabble-rouser. Maybe you were no longer usefully productive due to age or mental capacity. Maybe you were an orphan who would be a burden on planet resources. One thing that was clear was moving to the new planet would be more a demand than a suggestion.

Prezbigly was bald, with her company logo tattooed on each side of her head. You could see the bones in her arms and cheeks as she practiced the ancient Riestovikian art of *sumba ymbren*. This was an extreme form of fasting, left over from the old days when a CEO would refuse food until he or she passed out. During the time the person was unconscious, it was said it was the ideal time to come up with the best ideas. Prezbigly's skin was almost translucent, as CEOs saw very little of the outside, preferring to live in their offices.

Podsteop was strikingly tall. He had to lean down to avoid hitting his forehead on most doorways. He had black eyes, which occasionally sparked red, especially if he was excited. His platinum hair ran down to his buttocks, but he was currently concealing it in a gold *dupat* he recently received as a gift from Prezbigly.

His company tattoos were imprinted on the back of his hands. The scars up his spine were from brandings he submitted to whenever the company failed to meet profit objectives—*margin* profits, not cumulative. Podsteop's company, Podsteop Community and Manufacturing Concern, had the distinction of being the most fined company on Riestovik. This was actually an honor, as it was a sign of *fremueac euc feo andet*—meaning the company put profits above people.

LaRocca sent Episcopius Mauricio and Papal Marcado to the meetings. Mauricio had taken/won control of the state church and therefore became default leader of LaRocca. In his younger days, he was a picture of LaRoccan beauty. Today, though, years of seven-course feasts and gorging on expensive *ceren* had taken its toll. His eyes bulged out, and his cheeks were plump to a comedic level. He was wheeled around in a wheelchair—not because he couldn't walk, but because it was beneath him (no pun intended).

Marcado was his lover. One of them, at least. A beautiful lad half of Mauricio's age, Marcado was something of a prize to the esteemed Episcopius. Marcado's position was, well . . . *ceremonial* would be a kind way to put it. It had been created by Mauricio out of thin air. Basically, Marcado accompanied the honorable Episcopius to dinners and *surrexerunt luderes*.

Finally, Abakalic, the host planet, was represented by General Guvata and President Ajabice. Guvata was part of the a Nouveau Riche after working her way up the military chain. Ajabice was the fifteenth in his family's line to be Abaklic's President.

Guvata had lines on her face, baggy eyes, and calloused hands. She wore the uniform well. It was as if the gods themselves sewed it for her—wine colored pants with a matching shirt. The hat was slung low on the left side (a style she adopted when she became General) and displayed her awards made of *brasu* bonze.

This partnership was tenuous. The press held an almost fanatical love for Guvata. This, in turn, had won her the hearts of the public. Ajabice was not quite as popular. Frankly, Ajabice enjoyed almost zero support from the media and was being propped up as president by Guvata. Guvata didn't want the responsibility of political office, but desired the power. Ajabice was desperate and weak. For Guvata's ends, he was, in a word *fremian*.

Night one featured the Spiltrany twins explaining the proposal in depth. They were thorough and answered all questions confidently. CEO Podsteop pushed hard, but the twins withstood even the most cynical of questions. Later that night, the CEOs admitted to each other that the twins were more than impressive, but they had to maintain the charade to position Riestovik as the major beneficiary of Earth.

This meeting also featured Marcado falling asleep after an hour and snoring loudly, much to the embarrassment of Mauricio. Papal Marcado was sent back to their room. Mauricio made a formal apology to the twins at the end of the meeting. This consisted of him genuflecting on one knee and kissing the back of their hands. *Misericordiae autem in contumeliam*, as it was called on LaRocca. The gesture impressed Guvata and Ajabice and did much to calm tensions for the time being.

CHAPTER 8

I GO TO A CONCERT

’m getting call after call from Burgealdor Spencer or his assistant or somebody. It's definitely a government number, as the screen goes yellow when the caller reaches out. I don't want to talk about this right now. There's a bunch of messages, too, but I've deleted all those without listening.

Jorge looks around, "Man, was it a left or a right from here?"

We are at the corner of Dust Street and 35th. A wind pops up intermittently, but it's a calm night otherwise. Opposite us is a two-story Reistovikian restaurant called Cancetung Bridd. I dined on the bottom floor there once with Groscek. The top floor is supposedly stunning, filled with artwork, live music, room to dance. The bottom floor, well, not so much. Also, I heard the menu is different, with the top floor serving premium cuts of *hund* and *cicen* wings. On the bottom floor, everything is red-eyed with a ton of salt to give it flavor.

"We went down the street, where the coffee place is," Alva says. She's holding hands with Jorge, their fingers interlocked. Their arms swing in synchronicity when they walk. They aren't wearing matching shirts, but the colors complement each other.

"Oh, yeah, I wanted to try that place. We have time before the show," Jorge says.

Alva seems excited and they both look at me. I shrug. I'm not much of a coffee person. Tastes like burnt water to me. At least on Earth, the prices are cheap. I guess the CEOs found it keeps people alert and productive.

Hence, it was made accessible to even the poorest of Earthers. I've always found it makes my hands shaky—obviously a detriment in my field.

Alva treats us all. I thank her and start to choke down my flavored water. The sidewalk is busy tonight. I keep bumping into people. I pet my side piece beneath my jacket. Crowds like this make me nervous. I'm vulnerable to a *blodwracu*—the son of someone I shot, or the brother of someone I stabbed. When we head down an alley, I breathe easier. It's quieter. I can hear someone coming.

Jorge stops in front of a wall. He puts his hand out to touch it and his hand goes right through, disappearing.

"Yes! We found it again," Alva says as we start to walk through the illusory wall. "This place is just . . . so *werdylic*, right?"

"I don't know, Alva. We just entered," I reply. Gods, I'm *trying* to be nice, I forgot. So I add on, "But yes, so far it seems *werdylic*."

A quick note: We are at a subterra club. That's why it's cloaked on the outside. It's an attempt to hide it from the *magistratus*. And why do we have to go to a hidden club to see a concert? Because all of Earth's musicians, the licensed ones at least, belong to Liccetan Recording and Hundry Partnership (LRHP). Before I was born, LRHP maneuvered a politician—a woman—into a place of great power. She then created the licensing system which is monopolized by LRHP.

It's created a much more efficient music scene for Earth. The music is approved by LRHP, and the quality is guaranteed. And when you think about it, if the musician is licensed, it's going to be high-quality. I don't always like the music, but I know it's all good music.

There are a few people on the fringes of society who scoff at the idea of needing a license. Which is ridiculous. I mean, *I* need a license to operate. If you want to have a bonding ceremony, you need one. If you want to have offspring, you need one from your employer.

But yeah, they throw these shows outside of the legal market. It attracts young people mostly, some kids from the forest. And I'll be honest, none of them seem to want to do harm. I believe they just love the music, even if they risk servitude.

Alva has a giant smile. She runs her fingers over the bald stripe on her head. "This is the first time he's playing a subterra gig, so this should be pretty good."

This evening's entertainment will be provided by Jata and the Nyundo. They are a formally licensed group. Jata was born on Abakalic. She's nearly six feet tall with red and yellow curly hair hanging down over her face. No one in the public has ever gotten a clear view of her face—a marketing ploy to keep her mysterious.

Jata has butted heads one too many times with the CEO of LRHP and had her license suspended. Something about "pay discrepancies," or whatever. I think if you're spending your time playing music, you should count yourself lucky and shut up. Besides, when she was part of LRHP, her music was very enjoyable and . . . placid.

Jorge and I walk up to the bar together. As I'm paying for drinks, he surprises me with, "We're thinking of having a baby."

I can't imagine why one would do that. So I ask, "Why?"

Jorge laughs. "I don't know. Alva wants to create the family she lost when her dad died. I just . . . I love her and I've always pictured myself as a dad with three kids running circles around me. I think it'll be fun to watch them learn and grow."

I chuckle.

"What? You don't see it?"

"No, quite the opposite. It's perfect for you."

I get an uneasy feeling and turn to look in the corner of the room. There's nothing but a draest box filled with empty cans. I say to Jorge, "You know, it's weird, but I feel like there's this couple watching me...a guy and girl—young. See 'em out of the corner of my eye, but when I turn, there's nothing.

"I'd say your paranoid but considering your line of work." Jorge hands me a ceren, "I'll keep an eye out and let you know if I see anything."

I could tell from the intro of the first song that Jata had not continued in the corporate mold. And as the speed and volume of her new music assaulted me, I catch a brief glimpse of the girl: tiny, brown-haired, petting her frog. But her hands—they had blood on them. I close my eyes, breathe slowly through my nose, and relax my shoulders. When I open my eyes, she's gone.

The music is still here, though.

After a bit, the band takes a break. The three of us line up against the wall, Alva in between us. There's some idle *frofro* about the band, and then Jorge heads off to the bathroom.

"So I heard you're going for Cysta Por Ruverno?"

I drink my mead and say, "Yeah, that's the plan."

Alva asks, "When do you find out? Is there, like, a test you take?"

"Well, it's an appointed position. So you work hard, put in your time, don't get killed, and they promote you to CPR."

"Seems like kind of a long shot though, right?" Alva's voice cracks a bit on the word "right."

"How do you mean?"

"There are lots of assassins, but only one Cysta. And didn't I read something about how the current one never even killed anybody?"

I shake my head. "That's outsider news garbage. If you read the *Pura Iuncturam Venutre*, it presents a concise and verified list of projects he worked on."

"I don't read company news. Is that how you refer to the people you kill? Projects? That seems ugly."

There's some silence. Then I realize I know nothing about Alva. "You know, I know nothing about you, Alva."

"What did you want to know?"

"How old were you when your father died?"

"Seven."

"Do you know who did it?"

"No."

"Did you try to find out?"

"My mom did, and still does, when she . . ."

"When she what?"

"When she can keep her wits about her."

I want to get to it, no more foreplay. "Do you hate me because of what I do?"

"*No*," she snaps. She rubs her head and continues, "What do you know about my dad?"

"In regard to what?"

"I want to know him—as an assassin."

"Waldofo was well-respected, efficient, calculating. I studied some of his techniques as far as scouting locations and preparing for the job."

Alva looks down at her feet. "How did he die?"

I sigh. "You realize because of my surgery, I don't mince my words. I don't have a kind way to say it."

There's a beat while she ponders this. Then replies, "I don't hate you."

"Awe, well, I don't hate you either."

Alva is back to looking at me. "Is Jorge safe living with you?"

Hmmm…She asked if Jorge is safe, not if *she* is safe. "Jorge is aware of what he signed up for. And the odds…"

"So he's not?"

Man, she is a *docga de paenitebit*. I respect it though, so I'll be honest. "No. Compared to living with an accountant or a program designer—no, he is not."

Alva picks some lint off her sleeve. "I don't want to see him get hurt."

"I'll point out that he was well aware of my chosen profession before he moved in."

"And he wanted to flirt with excitement—I get it. We talked about it."

"I'm very good at what I do."

"So was my dad."

Damn.

Alva finishes her drink. "What does he do for you?"

"He doesn't judge me."

"There's more, though," she says, officially prying. "What else? You don't really need him to pay your rent."

"Maybe I'm cheap."

Jorge returns with an armful of drinks. "All right, I got two for every-one! Put 'em up."

We hold our metal cups high in the air.

Jorge deepens his voice for the toast, *"Fac amici vivendo sunt experiendae."*

I nod. "To the gods and CEOs."

Alva nods, "To the people."

We slam the first drink, then the second.

"All right, we need more 'cause I'm out with my two favorite people, and this is a celebration. Hey, Sasha, you think you could tell the story about the pond again?" Jorge is rubbing his hands together.

I have a lot of pond stories; I liked to lure projects there. Open space, clear sight lines. Honestly, I did so many there, I mix them up. So I say, "If you get me some good *ceren*, I can and will."

Again, I see the couple out of the corner of my eye, sitting up from by the instruments. But when I squint, nothing.

"Hey, are you Sasha?"

The voice is on the higher end of the register—timid, shaky even. I turn around and see a group of four looking at me. I put my hand on my gun. "No, you're mistaken."

A black-haired boy asks, "You're not Sasha, the assassin?"

"No. Go away."

A girl with the same color hair, done up in a bun says, "We have *feoh*—lots."

I push a welcoming grin across my face and reply, "How can I help you kids?"

CHAPTER 9

AN ATTENTION-GRABBER

"I think she's still moving." Jessi points at a body. The kids are in the front room of a three story mansion. The body Jessi is pointing at is of a woman in her forties with a pool of blood around her abdomen. It's soaked through her light blue dress, highlighting the fibers. Her camel-colored shoes are a few feet away, resting where she kicked them off in the struggle.

Jonas studies her. "I think that's just a muscle spasm."

Her leg twitches and Jonas points at it. "See? Just a spasm."

"Don't be lazy—*check*."

Jonas groans. He's lounging in an antique LaRoccan chair, designed during Episcopius Donatello's reign. It was called the Bloodless Reign, as for the first time in LaRoccan history, there were no major wars. He achieved this through ruthless politicking and murdering rivals, but those deeds wouldn't come to light until well after a forty-foot statue of Donatello was erected. Jonas's hands are rubbing blood all over the arms of that chair.

"Come on, I had to run the kid down," Jonas argues. He points at a small boy, maybe seven lying face down next to the chair.

"Jonas, how are we going to be assassins if you don't finish the job?"

"Okay, I'm the older one—*I* should be nagging *you*."

Jonas drags his neosir at his side and lumbers over to the body. He uses his *hund*-tanned boot to kick the body over. It kind of lulls on its side. Jonas makes eyes at his sister as if to say, *see?*

Jessi makes a slashing motion across her neck. "Just slit the throat or something to be sure."

Jonas looks at his sister and then bends down, rolling his eyes. It's enough to give the woman on the floor the jump on him. She manages to thumb his left eye and send him sprawling. She tries to get up while pressing her hand against the wound across her stomach. As she struggles to get her footing, she see the body of the seven-year-old boy and screams, the piercing sound echoing through the room.

Jessi stomps over. She twirls a metal mallet above her head and slams it right into the woman's skull. It cracks a hole in her head about the size of a peach. She falls like someone flipped a switch and turned her off. Blood runs out onto the LaRoccan carpet, also from the Donatello period.

Jonas is holding his hand over his eyes. "She really got me. Gods! It hurts."

Jessi inspects her mallet for bits of hair, "That's your fault for being careless."

"Not now, Jessi—I'm in real pain here."

"Let's have a look."

Jessi studies Jonas's eye. Flares of red are shooting towards the pupil. She has him look up, then down, then side to side.

"It's not great, but the most you can do is cover it. I don't think we have a *formeltan* iron that's safe for eyes."

"I wouldn't trust it, even if they said it were. Too many bad stories in the forest of people burning their eyes out of their sockets."

Still, go to the bathroom and wash it out." Jessi demands.

Jonas stretches and gets up. "All right, can you do the letter thing—with the blood?"

"Jonas, I don't *care* about that. That's your thing."

Jonas walks down the hallway, yelling, "It's our calling card, Sister. Do it opposite the mirror, it'll look cool."

Jessi dips her fingers in the woman's blood and starts painting the letters "TG" and "KK" on the wall, as Jonas requested.

Jonas comes back, a towel covering his eye. "Besides, how else is Sasha going to know it was us?"

"Can we go? I'm dying for some cold *barafu maziwa*. I saw a place a couple of blocks down that serves it."

"All right, but I'm hoping this meal doesn't end with us having to flee."

"I'm hoping this time you don't kidnap anyone."

Jonas puts his two fingers over his heart and taps twice.

Jessi and Jonas step outside and are briefly blinded by the Andetnes star. A young girl in a blue and white jumper pedals a unicycle down the sidewalk. An older lady chases after her, telling her to "slow down" and "be safe!" A man wearing short pants and a grey blouse, which hangs untucked, walks by, reading the news off projections from his watch. He does take a second to nod at Jonas and Jessi. They nod back.

"I thought the industrial clouds above the city were supposed to block out the Andetnes," Jonas states.

Jessi shrugs and they walk shoulder to shoulder down the street. The walkway is pristine—not surprising in this part of town. On the left side is a row of silk ficus trees. They require daily care by city workers or the silk will fry and die under the Andetnes heat. Kid Kill and Terror Girl marvel at the size of the houses they are passing. These homes seem to be unending palaces to them, one bigger than the next. Some of them even had *lacus* for swimming.

Jonas speaks in a soft, dreamy voice. "It's a shame we can't just kill the owners and live in one."

"Well, we just have to kill enough. I heard the Cysta Por Ruverno gets a giant building that is built on an island in the middle of Estmere, Chicago."

Jonas asks, "But isn't he worried about flooding if the Estmere rises?"

Jessi shrugs.

"Do you have to take a boat every day to get to land?"

Jessi thinks for a second and replies, "I guess."

"I don't know how to boat."

"You can probably hire someone to do it for you when you're making Cysta money," Jessi speculates.

They leave the residential area and are immediately hit up by an *esne*. He is short, with a broken metal stick under his left arm for support. A brown-haired *geboeric* is sitting next to the *esne*, panting in the heat. The rumors are *esnes* kidnap *geboerics* from the rich to make their situations look more sympathetic when they were busking for *feoh*. There hasn't been a provable case, but conventional wisdom and the media suggest it's true.

Jessi squats down and looks at the *geboeric*, his hair matted at the rear end. She cracks her knuckles and balls up her hand. Slowly she reaches out with a closed fist. The *geboeric* sniffs a bit. Jessi opens her hand. The *geboeric* sniffs again. When the tail starts wagging, Jessi grins and rubs him on the head, right between the ears.

"What's your name?" Jessi asks him.

The *esne* answers, "He's Kyle, and I'm Henry. I'm sponsored by the Clean Energy Consortiums and Food Stuffs."

Jonas' face contorts into a confused look, "What? They sponsor you?"

Henry nods, "Yeah, starting this year, any *esne* on the streets busking has to have an official sponsorship. Supposedly for our safety."

Henry sniffles and pulls out a tissue. After wiping his nose, he explains, "Yeah, you have to be sponsored now or you can end up in servitude."

Jessi and Jonas look at each other.

"It's not so bad, but they charge us weekly if you want to keep your spot."

Jessi playfully roughhouses with the Kyle. "What? Come on."

Henry shakes his head. "Yeah, they just passed that last year. Guy over on 24th Street? They took his *geboeric* from him."

Jonas is looking east, in the direction of 24th Street. "What did they do with him?"

"What do you think? They have no use for one." Henry rubs his forehead.

Jessi looks up from Kyle, "Gods, some people are monsters."

Kyle rolls over, inviting Jessi to rub his belly. She happily fulfills her end of the unspoken contract.

Jonas pulls out some *feoh*, fanning out the bills, and places them in a yellow *pazia*.

Henry reaches in his back pocket and reveals a white glass orb. Jonas shakes him off.

"You don't have to do that, Henry."

Henry waves Jonas in close. "Sir, I'd feel a *byrpen* if I didn't. Please."

Jonas nods for him to continue.

Henry squints one eye at the orb and lines it up on his palm. He starts to spin it faster and faster until tiny holographic figures appear inside. They resemble Jonas and Jessi. They are on a boat on the Estmere and appear to be fishing. Jessi pulls back her rod and flings it forward, but it catches Jonas's hat and takes it into the water. Jonas grabs his head, then starts looking around for the hat. He taps Jessi on the shoulder, and she shrugs. Then she reacts as if a fish is on the line. Jessi starts to reel it in as Jonas prepares a net. But it revealed all she has on the hook is the hat. Jonas rips it off the hook and puts it on his head. There's a wiggling under the hat. Jonas takes it off, reaches in and pulls out a fish. Jessi grabs the fish by the tail, holds it up and smiles with pride. Jonas frowns and slaps the fish out of her hand, causing it to fall safely in the ocean. They both sit down in the boat, looking opposite ways. Jessi reaches back with her rod and the story starts again.

Jonas forces a chuckle, "Very funny."

Henry puts the orb away, "I know it's of the older sort."

"Ah. It's neo-classic," Jonas suggests.

The two wish the *esne* well and continue their jaunt into the heart of the city.

Jonas remarks to Jessi, "Do you ever wonder about our nature?"

Jessi rolls her eyes. "No. And I don't really care to."

Jonas shrugs. "Eh, it's probably not that important anyway."

CHAPTER 10

A NEW JOB

I do love the smell of the *wapenus*. The dust from sharpening the long-swords hangs in the air and fills your nostrils with every breath. Probably unhealthy, but it's a welcoming smell to me. The way my reflection is caught by the *brasu* bronze weapons makes me look more valuable than any mirror I've come across. And the best part of it all is, everyone keeps quiet and to themselves.

The one I'm at is called KNBY (Kucheza Na Bunduki Yangu), which is my favorite in Chicago. As with most Abakalic stores, you have to take off your shoes, but KNBY makes up for it with a thick and soft carpet. It's like walking on pillows. And the *beomador*, Belladonna, is the kind of young Abakalician who greets customers with fresh-made ginger spice tea and a sweet-cookie, baked that morning. I've tried other *wapenus* around the city, but even if they were cheaper, the experience is better here. And KNBY's arms are *always* first rate.

Right now, I'm sipping my tea as Belladonna talks about a tiny *frosc* she found and took in. She shows me a picture—it's no bigger than the palm of my hand, with blue dots on its back. It looks slimy to me, but Belladonna assures me *froscs* are quite the opposite.

We finish our tea, and after she convinces me to eat one too many sweet-cookies, we get down to business. I settle a previous debt of mine, then take on a new one to pay for more ammo. Belladonna tries to upsell me. I stick with my tried and true brand. It comes in this reflective blue box, its trademark. After scanning my tag, she tries to introduce me to some new arms, specifically, a new set of knives made of Abakalic steel. They are well out of my price range, but I feign interest anyway.

Following the trip to KNBY, I walk down the street to a *wico tabernam* and order a cold sandwich and a *wuddupple*. I sit down at a table and start in on the sandwich. It's not great; the *flaesc* is too salty. But at a place like this, you're paying for calories, not quality.

I'm sitting here, choking down my meal, when a bald, wiry man stumbles in. He looks like a mess, with a ripped long-sleeve shirt and a hood pulled over his head. *Oh shit, I know what he's going to do.*

He walks up to the counter, pulls out a pistol and points it at the worker. Hm . . . *Someone* is going to lose their tag if this guy gets caught with their gun. I worry I might get caught up in a police investigation for witnessing this. The worker is completely compliant and gives up the money without incident. Then the robber turns to me. I push my sleeves up and expose my branding.

This should end it. Most criminals would recognize I'm an assassin and steer far away. He looks at it and says, "So the *fuck* what? Gimme the box of ammo." His hand is shaking so much I doubt he would hit me.

I scratch my nose. Then I perch my right elbow on the table and rest my chin in my palm. "You *have* to be smarter than this. You could just leave and be fine."

"*FUCK. YOU.* Give me the damn bo—"

He doesn't even know where the first shot comes from, but since he isn't watching my other hand, he wouldn't. He drops down, grabbing his knee, screaming. His gun falls to his side—useless at this point. The robber is breathing in quick, short bursts—almost panting. Tears form in his eyes, wasted on me.

The barrel of my gun hovers over his head, waiting for my finger to give the order. Then the light in his magenta eyes will die. I wonder if his family will mourn him. Or if he *has* a family to mourn him. Why am I wondering about that? What makes him so desperate he would resort to robbery? And a *wico tabernam* at that, before the afternoon rush? That's not worth much.

"You ever do this before?" I ask. He doesn't respond—just kicks his healthy leg against the table. So I get down and put the gun in front of his left eye. That grabs his attention. "Have you ever robbed a store before?"

All he can force out is a whimper.

"I'm not gonna waste the bullet." I say out loud. I pick up his gun and hand it to the shop attendant; it's of no use to me now, since it was used in a crime against a business. The door slides open with a wave of my hand, and I step back onto the sidewalk.

When the door closes behind me, I hear the pop of the gun. I look back and see the attendant spitting and cursing at the robber, who I'm going to assume is dead. And even though he put a gun in the attendant's face, and even though it's the attendant's lawful right to purge the robber, I still feel a twinge.

I let out a sigh—deep, from the gut. The twinge goes away.

I'm on my way to the residential area for that job the kids paid me (*excellently*, I might add) for. At the crossroads between business and residential, I come across an *esne* and a *geboeric*. I don't make eye contact. He's probably going to use an orb or a child's holograph to show me a short story, try to guilt me into giving him *feoh*. Old rudder.

I haven't mentioned this yet, but I'm dressed as a *byrpling*. I have had an almost perfect record with this outfit. Since people are so excited to get packages, they'll open the door without even asking for ID. I got this years ago when I killed…well…a *brypling*. It was a revenge job for a scorned lover. I didn't ask or care about the details. When I was following him around, I noticed the advantage the uniform could give me. So instead of my usual method, I waited until he went to the bathroom and wrapped a thin piece of rope around his neck. He got urine all over the pants as I was working, so I had the uniform cleaned by professionals. I still keep that length of rope in the pocket as good luck.

I check the time. I'm right on target. The project should be dressed, lounging on the couch watching TV. The husband is off at work and the kid is at school. I'll pop over, ring the doorbell, she answers/opens the door. *Zip zap. Job done.*

But when I arrive at the house, there's a commotion. *Magistratus* going in and out like ants. I stay on the sidewalk, suddenly feeling like a rudder in my uniform. I get the attention of one of the MAGs. His eyes are puffy and red, like he's been crying.

"Hey, what is going on here?"

The MAG motions for me to leave, "Please, move along. We are doing some work."

"But I have a package for Carolin Alderine. And *that's* her house."

MAG waves me away again. "Go on with that package. This is a crime scene."

What happened?

"Hey, I'm just trying to get this delivered to Carolin Alderine. Is she home?"

"Look, Carolin Alderine is part of the crime scene. Leave the package and go."

I put my hand over my mouth; I need him to confirm the project is over. "Oh my—is she dead?"

"Her and the boy. What kind of assassin would kill a boy, though? *Sick*, they are!"

Oh, man, I hope he doesn't notice my branding.

The MAG sniffles. "They even painted letters on the wall with their blood. What kind of person does that?"

"Wow, thanks."

As I'm walking away, I can hear him call out, "Wait, what about the package?" But I ignore him. I'm lost in thought. I could have sworn Brubaker Consortium Company has a story about a diner where the killers used blood to paint letters on a wall. I call up the news sites and search for the story. Headlines flash in front of my eyes. It happened outside of Chicago, so the coverage was small, but I get a hit.

My reading gets interrupted by the clients. One of the girls is on the video-phone.

"So?"

"Project is complete."

"Fantastic. We will send the rest of the *feoh* to your account. And our dad wasn't there?"

"Nope. A kid was though."

"Wait—what?"

"A kid was there. They got done, too."

She shakes her head. "What do you mean? You killed the kid?"

"In a manner of speaking."

"What the—" She looks to her side. "Aye, she killed Geri."

Off-screen, I hear, "The fuck for?"

She looks back to me. "The fuck you kill him for?"

Ugh, gods, *this* is why you try to only kill the person you were hired to kill.

"Look, honestly, they were dead when I got there."

"What? So who killed them?"

"I don't know. Is this going to affect my payment?"

Another person—a guy who was off-screen—pops up and splits the picture in half. Their calls are separated by a wavy line down the middle of my view. He's on the left, she's on the right.

"If you didn't kill her, why would we pay you?"

She puts both hands palms up, "I can't believe you killed Geri!"

The guy follows up with, "Yeah, what the fuck is that? He's a kid."

"I'm sorry, but I'm not sure why you care—you paid to have me *kill your mom*."

He adds, "Nonbiological."

She looks disgusted and won't make eye contact with me. "And that was for money—it was a business transaction. Killing the kid is crazy, it's *woda de faereld*."

He flares his nostrils and says, "It's just *wrong*."

"Look, I'm not the one who killed the kid. In fact, I didn't kill either." This client was starting to annoy me. "I'm keeping the first payment for my time. And I consider our transaction complete."

She starts to yell at me, "Hey I want my money—"

I wave my fingers and the projection goes away. They try calling back. "Phone, block number. Go silent for the next hour."

I don't know who did my job for me, but they cost me a lot of *feoh*.

CHAPTER 11

THE FOREST PEOPLE
ARE PEOPLE, TOO

Rafe Fortune uses a sword to slice a path through the grassy plain. At this time of year, the straw is a rich green and especially tough to cut. The grass comes up to his forehead and leaves a sticky green residue when cut. The residue is dulling the blade, making the mission even more of a chore. This plain was the last parcel of land before reaching the forest.

Rafe is flanked by Micel and Cadyn.

"I'm not made for this," Micel shouts, "I should'a stayed by the ship and drank spicy *ceren* all day." After wiping his brow, Micel takes a swig from a water bottle. The shirt Micel wore used to be a bright white color, but time and sweat had stained it yellow and brown.. The bottom of his belly hung over his belt and was covered in curly brown hair.

Rafe hums out a response, "But, that's what you did yesterday."

Micel agrees, "And I had fun yesterday—the parts I remember. I mean, we're protecting 'er, they could'a dropped 'er off."

Rafe replies, "I thought it was too much of a risk having her go through the city to get to us."

Cadyn spits from the side of her mouth. "We take too much of a risk, coming out here."

Rafe, "Did you think you signed up for a holiday cruise?"

"There's no point in getting paid if you're just going to get killed by some *leona*."

Rafe smiles. "You hear that Micel? Cadyn's scared of a little fluffy *leona*."

Micel is too engaged in wiping off sweat to acknowledge the comment.

Cadyn hushes her tone and uses her best sales pitch voice: "Look, we already got half, which is a great amount. Let's just ditch out. There's plenty of easier jobs we can take."

Rafe snuffs out any hope Cadyn had, "*Kwa heshima tunayoishi.*"

Cadyn slaps her neck, killing a bug. "Fuck that Abakalic 'survive by honor' garbage. I'm gonna get *cruento* disease from these damn bugs."

Rafe is still hacking away at the tall grass. "Cadyn, I love you, but shut up until we meet up with the girl."

Micel uses his height to peer ahead. "I see 'em in the distance, edge of the forest." There's a beat before they half whisper, "*wow.*"

Cadyn looks at Micel, "Wow, what?"

"There's a lot of 'em."

"Ugh, as if one of them's not bad enough. Bunch of *victos*," Cadyn spits out.

Cadyn is as tall as Rafe but distinctly lankier. She carries scars all over her arms and hands, and when she walks, it's with a slight limp on her left side. Up and down her body, wounds and scars tell the tales of old battles and scrums. Her eyes are a deep blue and so is her hair. She dresses in a swirl of orange and fuchsia colors, topped off by an ever-present pendant. Cadyn once explained that the pendant is a replica of Riestovik.

Once the trio reaches the edge of the forest, Rafe and Cadyn realize what Micel meant by "*wow.*" There are about thirty people waiting for them, lined up in two rows. As the trio approaches, a man in his late sixties steps forward.

Rafe says to the man, "This is a larger group than is needed, I think."

The man offers his hand. Rafe grabs him by the wrist and they shake. "Gilead. Gilead Lakes."

"I'm Rafe—that's Cadyn and that's Micel. You have the package?"

Gilead appears taken aback. "Is that how you refer to her—as a *package?*"

"Ah, industry term, 'sall."

"She's back in our *apulder*. Things are very difficult for her now."

"Yeah, moving is a big deal."

Gilead squints, "I was referring to her seeing her mother assassinated."

"Also…a big…dea— *Micel*, you wanna jump in here?"

Micel shakes his head and shrugs his shoulders.

Gilead turns to look at Micel, "Micel? Are you Juan Micel Colon?"

"Yup," Micel answers curiously.

Gilead smiles for the first time. He walks over and they shake hands.

Gilead whispers something to Micel and then walks back in front of Rafe. Rafe gives Micel an eye but Micel ever so slightly shakes his head *no*.

"Rafe," Gilead begins, pacing back and forth with his hands behind his back. "We have decided keeping young Kergan here with us is for the best. So you and your friends have made a trip for nothing. We do apologize for taking you away from drinking and brawling."

The group of forest people laugh.

The trio look at each other with brows raised.

Rafe slowly responds, "I'm not sure what you mean"

Still pacing, Gilead continues: "Kergan The First was wrong to hire outsiders. It's a plan we never agreed to."

"You don't think she did what's best for her daughter?" Rafe asks.

Gilead stops in front of Rafe and gets nose-to-nose with him. He's close enough that his spittle hits Rafe in the eye as he says, "See? You don't know the *first thing*. Kergan didn't raise a daughter, she cultivated a replacement. Something to continue her battles, finish her war."

Rafe, not one for backing down, replies, "And she entrusted *me* with that replacement. Now if you could show us where she is."

Gilead pulls out a knife and puts it at Rafe's throat. "You're not getting her. And that is final."

Rafe already had his hand on his belt. Gilead didn't notice. Rafe pushes a button and a tiny arrow shoots out, piercing Gilead in the stomach. He stumbles back, waves his arms, and the battle commences.

Rafe and Cadyn are swarmed, but people avoid Micel. Probably because of his size. Until one young man, about fifteen-years-old, walks up to him with a metal mace at his side. The mace has seen better days; it's mostly rust at this point. He swings it around his head to gain steam and runs at Micel. Micel catches the head of the mace with one hand, yanks it out of the kid's custody, and tosses it to the side.

"Run away—*now*," Micel says to the kid. And before he can finish the word "*now*," the kid is nothing but a trail of dust.

Rafe briefly notices Micel is not being attacked but has no time to address the situation.

Cadyn appears to be holding her own, using everything at her disposal. She has her kintana in one hand and a blade shooter—similar to the one on Rafe's belt—in the other.

Rafe's having a time of it. A woman tackles him to the ground and starts biting his arm. Rafe uses a blade hidden in his wristband to slice her cheek and get her to retreat. A man of medium build, with red paint on his face, charges Rafe immediately after, aiming a spear at his chest. *An amateur move,* Rafe thinks to himself. *It could never pierce his chest place, let alone his armor.*

Rafe lets the tip of the spear break trying to pierce the armor. Then he pulls the wooden handle from the attacker and conks him on the side of the head.

Cadyn and Rafe are back-to-back now, fighting off attackers, repelling them with great success.

Micel bellows, "That's *enough*, Gilead!"

Gilead, still on the ground, whistles and waves his left hand in a circle. The forest people back off and start helping the injured with *formeltan* irons.

Cadyn is panting. "Where the hell are ya going, *iboras?*"

Micel puts his right hand up. "Relax, Cadyn—it was a test."

Gilead confirms this, as he's being attended to. "Juan Micel Colon is right."

"Fuck that." Cadyn starts to go after a young woman who is tending to her wounds. The woman falls back and scoots away in submission. Micel grabs Cadyn by the shoulder. Cadyn, without looking, turns and punches him with the butt of her sword. Micel snorts and shoves Cadyn to the ground with little effort.

Rafe says to the pair, "All right, all right—*relax*." Then he turns his attention to Gilead, "I'm gonna have to take offense to that little ambush there."

"If you can't defend yourself against us, then you don't deserve to take care of Kergan Satre II." Gilead retorts.

Gilead stands, clicking his tongue in a steady rhythm as the militia group starts to line up again. Gilead, looking at Rafe, holds up an open hand. The militia stands tall. He closes his fist and the militia turns on their heels and marches into the forest. "Well, let's go get your package."

Gilead leads on with the trio in tow.

Once they get into the heart of the forest, a clear path opens up. To the left and right, the calls of various birds and critters vibrate the bushes. This time of year, the *amethystine* bushes are flowering and giving off a light blue glow around the pedals. The glow attracts bugs, which are then trapped by the sap of the bush. Birds come and eat these bugs, taking bits of flower—which contains the seeds—with them. And this is how the *amethystine* bushes have come to all but dominate the forest floor.

Micel points to a gold and green creature slithering on the side of the path. "That's a *pura migale*. We used to raise them for their eggs."

Rafe smirks, "I always forget you grew up out here."

A beat passes before Rafe asks, "Do you miss it?"

Micel snorts. Without looking at Rafe, he replies, "You can go back home, but you can't *get back* home."

To be honest, Rafe didn't really get what Micel was driving at, but the reply was so melodic, he let it be.

CHAPTER 12

AUNTIE BELLE COMES AROUND

I don't believe it.

Aunt Antibelle Sojourn is marching up the sidewalk to my *bolttimber*. I figured she was dead.

I'm sitting at my window, drinking a bittersweet *ceren* while my projector plays an old movie I watched as a kid. I tried to masturbate a bit ago, but couldn't get there. Then I had a nagging desire to see "Candy Island and Fantoozlebum." It has this part where the Fantoozlebum finally stands up to the lazy Unioberlum. See, the Fantoozlebum was initially lured in by the Unioberlum's promises of more candy and more free time to eat the candy if Fanto joined his team. However, our hero, Fanto, sees through the lazy Unioberlum's lies and gets back to picking candy from the Candy Island trees. In the end, the Unioberlum comes crawling, begging to eat, but Fanto kicks him away and Unio dies as he lived: a useless *esne*.

Belle stops at the front door and without looking up, yells, "Well, let me in, ya *victos*!"

"You're as pleasant as you ever were, Auntie."

"I'll snipe you from here if you don't open the door."

I press my thumb against the top of my watch and announce, "Door unlock—15 seconds."

I look at the projection; Fanto just came across the magical *hund* that carries her to the other side of Lemon Mountain. Ugh, Belle has the *worst* timing.

We're both in the worker space. (Some call it the residential space, but on Riestovik we called it a worker space, which makes more sense. You're defined by your job, not simply where you live.) I'm sitting on a yellow-striped chair, which used to conform to my body type before Jorge spilled *ceren* down the back and shorted it out. Now, it's permanently stuck in his favorite position.

Belle stretches out on the *fearh*-skin *kitanda* with her arm draped across her eyes. Looking at the lines on her face and the yellowing of her finger-nails reminds me how long it's been since we saw each other. Also, that she never took particularly good care of herself.

"You look old now."

"That's fuckin' rude, Sasha."

"It's the only thing I know about you."

"Well, I was just tortured by your fan club so, ya hafta forgive me for not wearing my best face."

"Do you want something to drink?"

Belle nods *yes*, as she slips her arm down to the side. "Man, that surgery of yours . . . You wanna ask how I'm doing?"

I thought that's what I *was* doing, though in a roundabout way. Besides, the fan club thing has piqued my interest. "What was this about a fan club?"

"Yeah, a couple of real rudders. Brother-sister team, looking for you. Said they want to train under you."

"How did—"

"The *drink*, Sasha. Can you get me a damn drink?"

"Yes, hang on."

When I come back from the kitchen, I hand her a glass of water. Belle takes a sip.

"Ugh, what *is* this? Water? I said a *drink*. *Ceren* or stronger. Take this back."

I return with something strong. She downs it in one gulp.

"That was . . . not cheap," I say.

With a belch, Belle replies, "Yeah, tasted damn good."

Belle massages the back of her neck with both hands and lets out a groan. "I miss the days when I was your trainer—when I had you to massage my neck."

"I do not."

Belle rolls her head around and belches again. She takes a *voluptatem stilla* out and squeezes some of the gel on her finger—rubbing it into her left eye, squeezing it shut. Belle lets out a pleasurable groan and smiles. She holds the finger-sized bottle out to me as an offer. I shake my head. *Stillas* put me on edge. I think that's why Belle got addicted to them—they let her feel a bit of nervousness/anxiety again. I guess she missed those feelings, for some reason.

Her left eye is now a milky-white color. She uses a dirty tissue to dab at the eye's corner as some of the gel runs down.

"They kept my damn weapons. My *cnif*, my silver cutler, my red and bronze *oeorfsear*—even the one you gave me to accept you as a student, the Riestovikian brass neosiri. I really liked that one. It's why I took your sorry butt on."

"Thanks." I mean it. This was Belle's version of a compliment.

"You were nothing back then. A fragile doll. I thought long and hard about how that first night would end for you."

When you submitted for training, you had to first find an assassin who might take you on. Present him or her with a weapon. Then promise your life in servitude to the person. Once you did that, legally you were bound to that person. If the assassin didn't find you worthy, he could dispose of you as he saw fit. Seriously. A lot of kids didn't make it through that first night. Either the gift was *undeore*, which was common, since most kids wanting to train were poor and on the fringe (think about the kind of people this work attracts). Or the kid didn't show enough deference the first night. Or, the assassin just enjoyed killing. Some of us do. I find killing part of the job. I like the art in the preparation and the strategy. But the actual kill has always felt like filing paperwork. You have to do it to get paid. But some, like Belle's teacher, liked the essence of the job, the taking of someone's future.

"No, you didn't—you loved me at first sight." I smile.

She sort of grunts and looks away.

"The kids screwed up a job for me. Went in and killed not just the project, but ancillaries around it."

"Sash, you were a fuckup in the beginning."

"Why are you soft on two kids who tortured you?"

Belle had her head all the way back, resting on the couch. She's staring at the ceiling and occasionally dabbing at her eye. "They had a real *ingenii* (natural ability) for the art. Not like you."

"I get the job done and move on."

"I respected their commitment."

I pause to think, then reply, "Is this your way of suggesting I take them on?"

"Actually, I wanted to *warn* you, more than anything—about Terror Girl."

"Terror Girl?"

"That's what she goes by, I dunno. The other one's Kid Kill. Today is all about getting attention, everyone wants to be Cysta. You still chasin' that *genip*? Tryin'a catch smoke with ya hands?"

"It's not a *genip*; it's a real goal I am working towards. With focus and planning and—"

She yawns loudly, drowning me out.

I cross my arms and look at the window. "All right, what is the warning?"

"Terror Girl has the *planus wakati* surgery."

Honestly, I don't even remember what *planus wakati* surgery is. I've heard it before, but—

"Gods, you haven't a clue?" I shrug, and she says, "It's the *time* thing."

"Huh?"

"Where time goes all *fylleseóc*."

I shrug again. I don't know what she is talking—

Oh.

"You mean the surgery Karl did to his kid?"

"Yeah," she says as she rubs more gel in her eye, "the time loop shit."

"I didn't think anyone even knew how to do that anymore."

She's too busy with her *voluptatem stilla*.

I think for a second, then ask, "Doesn't it make you go *fylleseóc*?"

"I've never knew anyone who had it, but yeah, s'what they say." Belle arches her neck up. Her tone takes on an almost whisper. "This one, she's halfway there already."

"And the other one—what was his name?"

"Kid Kill. He's more the leader. More studied and patient than Terror Girl."

"You sound like a parent bragging about a child."

"I need more drink."

I'm not too sure that's true, but old habits die hard so I serve my former sponsor without questioning her. I was lucky. Belle still has most of her emotions firing, even after the slice and dice. She treated me as well as she could, considering her background. When we got to the end of my training, I searched for a *donum magnam*, as was custom. I wanted to kill her trainer, Crispus, but he was already dead. I ended up getting her a new weapon safe.

As I hand her the drink, she says, "I'm gonna get wasted and stay here on the couch."

"I have a roommate."

"Yeah, what's with that? Ya 'ave your empathy cut out, but ya still want to empathize with people?"

I lock my fingers behind my head and stretch. "You said it before—these surgeries aren't always what they're cracked up to be."

"What's that about?"

I shake my head. "I think mine is wearing off. I keep seeing the face of this girl..."

"You kill her?"

"No, that's just it—I *couldn't*. And now I see flashes of her, with her mother's blood on her hands."

Belle gets serious. She clears her throat, then speaks in sharp jabs, "Ya hafta get that surgery done again."

"I've been thinking—"

"Don't think. You hafta get it done. You hear me?"

I'm puzzled and look at her with my brows furrowed.

"Look, empathy, guilt, sympathy—all of these emotions grow back. And as they do, you'll start thinking about everything ya done in the past, everyone ya killed. You'll dwell on 'em more and more. When was the last time ya felt it? Can ya even remember?"

Belle has this tone that cuts, makes me feel like a little *bearn*. And now, it's more effective than usual. I leak out an answer with my eyes cast to the side, "No."

"It'd be devastating, child. You lived as a vicious *bonger*. Can't change that now. It's too late to go back."

All I can manage is a shrug.

"Sasha, the longer you wait, the more you'll start to feel. And for rudders like us, feelings are as dangerous as a sword."

CHAPTER 13

THE APPLICATION

"Jorge, come in here." The voice comes from *dihtere*'s office, soft but confident.

Jorge stretches as he gets out of the chair. He pulls his arms behind his head and then cracks his knuckles before heading in to see the *dihtere*. As he leaves, his cubicle's border turns grey, indicating he's in a meeting.

The office is barely large enough to fit Jorge. It consists of a desk, on which rests his department's *dihtere*. Developed by the Miles Corporation and Water Concern, this model, the Dihterematic version 2.1 was, according to the marketing materials, "A dream come true for ruling and controlling a department." It consisted of a black box, the CPU, and a speaker about the size of a plate. Newer versions put the setup inside an animatronic humanoid figure. This older model, though, was just a speaker on a box. The speaker didn't even have a protective case anymore and was littered with dust.

"You can have a seat."

When the *dihtere* talks, there's a lighting strip which blinks along with the syllables. Or there should be—the lights on this one burnt out years ago.

Jorge looks around and says, "Um, there aren't any cha—"

"Great. I hope you're comfortable."

Jorge just shrugs.

"Jorge, I see you have been with the company for six years." The speaker is so loud it distorts the sound. Jorge looks for a volume button on the sides of the box but can't find anything.

"And you have been given a raise each year," the *dihtere* continues.

"That's right."

"Unfortunately, you have not been promoted in that time. And are still a level A-*siphoda* employee."

"I'm happy with what I'm doing. Honestly, I haven't looked to move anywhere."

There's a beat before it responds. "That is good to hear." Another five seconds go by before it continues. "We are going to need you to take a pay cut, as we cannot justify your salary at your level."

"What?"

The box shoots out a hologram projection which shows a graph. The projection is fuzzy, with wavy lines running through it. The graph lists salaries for Jorge's position in the company, in the area, and on the planet. Next to all of that is a bar representing Jorge's salary—it's slightly taller than the other bars.

"As you can see here, Jorge, you are making about five percent more that the upper twenty percent in your position."

Jorge squints his eyes, taking in the chart. "I mean, is that accurate?"

"This updates constantly. Our database compares employee salaries in this manner every minute throughout the day. When someone hits this threshold"—as the speaker explains, a line appears at the top of the graph and slightly cuts Jorge's bar off at the top—"we have to recalibrate their salary."

"I don't get it—last time I was in here, you praised my numbers and said I was a top performer."

"And we will continue to expect that output. However, we do have to realign your salary based on the market. You do believe in the market, don't you, Jorge?"

Jorge fidgets, but concedes, "Yes."

"And so you know, the market is correct. And if you are breaking the market, it's kind of like you are stealing from us."

"I don't see—"

"Now we know you wouldn't want to steal from us," the speaker interrupts. "You're a good guy. And we want you around for years to come. Just at a salary which reflects market values."

"Right, but when you hired me you were paying me below market value."

"Well, we are sorry but that comes down to what you negotiated. It has very little to do with us."

Jorge hangs his jaw open and then says, "I can't tell if I'm more angry or confused right now."

"Wonderful. We here at MK Ultra Pet Supply Depot Incorporated do have a heart. So instead of cutting your salary all at once, we will diminish it by five percent a month for the next three months. That should bring—"

Jorge walks out before the sentence finishes. He walks past his desk and over to Fran. Fran started out with Jorge, and they bonded over a love of old-time pictures. Fran stands at a black desk with two computers on it. She's manipulating graphs with her fingers, working on shipping goals and forecasts.

"Fran."

"Hey, J-dog, you old *ursa*, what's the good word?"

"They just called me into the *dihtere's* office and cut my salary." Fran doesn't respond. "And worse, they, like, *blamed* me for it. Like it was my fault I was—"

Fran runs her right hand through her silver hair. "Offending the values of the market?"

"Right."

"Yeah, that's an old line. I'm sorry, J."

Fran is wearing a tan skirt and matching V-necked top. She wears two necklaces: one with a gravity-suspended gem on it; the other with a small picture of her kid.

"I mean, I should quit, right? This is bullshit."

"And go where? What company isn't dogmatic about the market? You're going to lose your seniority for the same salary."

Jorge scratches his temple. "Those rudders!"

Fran nods. "I know."

"This is why people—you know I'm going to say it—this is why there are protests almost *every damn day* in this *andred*."

Fran turns around, scrunching up her face and shaking her head. She whispers, "Go back to your desk and pray no one in Notitia is listening."

Back at his seat, Wildorlic, from Notitia, is already waiting for Jorge. "Jorge, we need to chat, would you follow me into the Notitia Office?"

Jorge follows, dragging his feet and going as slow as possible. Wildorlic opens the door and holds it for Jorge. When Jorge enters, he's greeted by two other members of the Notitia department. The lighting in the room is a harsh white. The light, when it reflects off the metal table, is blinding to Jorge. All the members of the Notitia wear dark glasses.

Jorge sits down. In front of him is an application he filled out the day before.

Wildorlic stands in the corner like a guard. The two other members are dressed in similar light blue gowns. Their hair is parted, one on the left side and one on the right. Their hands are folded neatly in front of them, and they sit up straight as a pole.

The person on the left taps the desk with his index finger three times. "Jorge, we are here to discuss your application for *kuzaliwa kwa mtoto*."

With the salary cut, he had forgotten about it. Alva and he had discussed it for a while now. Both had reached the age window to apply and since it can take multiple applications to get approved, they wanted to start trying.

The person on the right tilts his head slightly. "Can we hear from you on why you want to have children?"

Jorge sits up straight and puts on his deep, professional voice. "I don't know that we have a specific reason. I've always imagined having kids."

Left replies with a serpent-like hiss in his throat. "And you know one of the highest responsibilities you can have is molding a young resource into a valuable asset?"

Jorge grins. "Yes, I do." It was not believable.

Left and Right look at each other.

Right continues. "And you would be responsible if the worst happened. If the resource was not useful."

Jorge keeps grinning. "Of course."

Left taps his lips three times with his index finger before explaining. "It is very important that this privilege is given to those who take the responsibility seriously—not just to the child, but to the company that approves it—and that your family respects our values."

Wildorlic walks over to Right, whispers something, then walks back.

Jorge eyes him the whole time, worried that maybe what he said to Fran will be used against him. Then he thinks about what a disappointment that would be to Alva. The thought makes his stomach cramp.

Right places both hands, palms up, on the table. "If we gave you this, what would you give us?"

Luckily, Jorge was prepared for this inevitability. Everything is a negotiation in Chicago. "I'd be willing to put in eight hours of unpaid work a week for the next six months." He hoped to end up at a year.

They both shake their head *No* before Left explains. "That's generous, but we just need you to help out Wildorlic when he needs it."

"So if I work with Wildorlic, Alva and I are approved?"

Right nods. "Right."

Jorge is so excited he finds himself fumbling his words. "I accept. Yes, ab…absolutely."

Wildorlic walks over and puts his hand on Jorge's shoulder. He flashes a crooked grin. "I can't wait to work with you."

CHAPTER 14

TIME TO FEAST

Rafe, Micel, and Cadyn are sitting in a small *byre*. There's barely room for them and a round table.

"Is this another test? Locking us in a *byre* with no water, so we die of exhaustion?" Cadyen complains, hunching over the table and fanning her face with her hands.

Micel tried to explain. "They're used to this, they prolly haven't thought—"

"Fuck dat," Cadyn interrupts. "Show some damn respect for visitors. Or did you people not learn manners out here?"

Rafe puts his left hand up. "Aye, *relax*, Cadyn. We're all hot. They're bringing us mead."

Micel runs his tongue along his upper lip. "You're gonna love it. Fresh-brewed mead with *hordei ventilat*. Crisper and cleaner than either of you *weaoruds* have ever tasted."

Rafe runs his index finger up the surface of the wall behind them. "What are these walls made of? It's wood but . . . incredibly smooth. And I don't recognize the texture."

Micel strokes his chin, "Yeah, I was looking, too. I can't tell—maybe an ash."

"I think it's *lodrung*—they can cut down trees but we can't," Cadyn complains.

Micel's tone turns frustrated, "Chicago was destroying their way of life."

Cadyn rolls her eyes, "*Blah-blah-blah*, we weren't destroying nuttin'. Look at how much forest 'ere is."

Micel sounds exacerbated, "Cause they rebuilt it."

"Okay, great. They can build it *again*." Cadyn slams her fist on the table to accentuate the word "again."

They're briefly interrupted by an older man bringing them drinks.

When he leaves, Cadyn looks at the cup and grumbles, "They even use wooden cups."

Micel lets out a satisfying groan after downing the drink. "Cadyn, you are gonna be *abrugdon* when you see what they use for fire."

Kergan Satre II is led into the *byre* by Gilead Lakes. Kergan betrays no emotion. She has a stoic look, too mature and confident for her age.

"Hello, Kergan, I'm Rafe. I'm much obliged to meet you."

Cadyn flares her nostrils at the display.

Micel stands up and offers his hand, palm up. "Hey, if you remember, I'm Micel. I'm sorry about what happened to your mum."

Kergan places her hand, palm down, over Micel's, "Thank you. She will be missed by the community. And I do remember you, Micel. You snuck me some *ligaturas de scelerisque* from the kitchen. It was very sweet of you."

Micel blushes. "Eh, they was spoiled. But we'll see if we can do something 'bout that when you're with us this time."

Kergan speaks with a slight lisp. The pitch is deeper than one would expect for a young girl. Her purple eyes curve downward at the corners. She has a sprinkling of freckles on her cheeks and nose. She wears her brown hair in a sloppy bun on the back of her head. Kergan has a build almost identical to her mother—short and wide. On her left sleeve is the same tiny green frog she wore when her mother was assassinated by Sasha. There's a spot of red in the middle of the frog's back.

She turns to Cadyn. "And you are?"

"Your bodyguard. And that's all you need to know." Cadyn turns to Rafe. "Can we get going now that we got the package?"

Rafe cringes. "Aye! Don't be a rudder. Kergan is going to be with us for a few years." Rafe looks at her. "As far as we are concerned, you're a *weaorud* just like us."

Gilead, standing aside, spreads his arms wide. "We would like you three, with Kergan, to be guests at dinner tonight as Summo Honore's."

Micel tilts his head down in respect. "Wow, Gilead, that is a great . . ."

Cadyn has her arms crossed. "What's for dinner?"

Gilead appears to be startled by Cadyn's spouting out of the question. He flinches before answering. "It would be a traditional feast of *fúgol* and *foor*. The *foor* has been cooking for twelve hours and will *conflandum in ore tuo*."

Cadyn smiles and uncrosses her arms. "Well, that ain't too bad."

Rafe mumbles in Cadyn's direction. "I'm glad you approve." Then, to Gilead, he adds, "It'll be an honor, Gilead. Thank you."

As everyone leaves the *byre*, Gilead puts his hand up to stop Rafe. "Now that we're alone, there's something you need to know about Kergan II. You know the story of Surgeon Karl?"

"Nah, I'm not really the studying type."

Gilead leans in and hushes his voice, "Suffice to say, he was the first surgeon. And as the story goes, he experimented on his kids. Different ways to manipulate the mind."

"Sure."

"So he stumbled upon a way to influence how someone sees time."

"Yeah, the crazy-making thing. I've heard of it."

Gilead wipes some sweat from his brow. "People, humans, um . . . how do you say . . ."

"*Amittunt marmorum*," Rafe finishes.

Gilead leans back and squints. "I thought you didn't study."

"It's a phrase my mom used when me and my brothers were running around the neighborhood breaking things, making her life difficult," Rafe ends with a chuckle.

"Heh, I'm sure. Well, Kergan II, she has this . . . I don't know if *gift* is the right word, but she is a *puer temporis*."

Rafe shrugs.

"A child of time. She bends time at will."

Rafe scratches the stubble on his face. "Who gave her the surgery?"

Gilead dabs at his brow with the bottom of his shirt. "No one. She came from the ashes like this."

"She is slowly losing her mind, then?"

Gilead coughs into his fist and says, "That's just it. She's not. She shows no ill effect from it. Which makes her—"

"—invaluable."

CHAPTER 15

THEY FINALLY MEET

Tonight, I'm stalking a man and his mistress.. The window I'm peeking through is dusty, but clear enough to keep track of their movements. I'm on the rooftop just across the street waiting for them to exit. The aggrieved spouse who hired me was insistent I kill *just* the mistress. He wanted to deal with the man, Bernadino, himself.

The mistress ordered the fresh-cut *hund*. Not bad for a last meal. At the Nombe Ghali, where they were dining, it was quite an expensive dinner.

Off and on, I'm watching a *morgen pleghus* about an *esne* who works his way up to CEO. It came out last year; I'm just catching up. Most companies make it required viewing for their employees.

The first few years of Earth were smooth. The *unenthused*, sent by each planet, had a familiar bond. They were rejects. To the surprise of the *magistrates* who overlooked the transition, the new earthlings came together without violence or animosity. The *magistrates* theorized this was a short-term pact, which would dissolve as the natural drive to acquire resources ramped up.

I'm still watching the *andoleofen*. The couple is really *deliciae temporis*. The wind kicks up, and I can hear it billowing between the buildings. I watch as some *draest* blows around in the gutter. I don't know why people can't just throw the wrappers away. It's really irritating. The companies work hard to keep up a beautiful *andred*; it really shows disrespect. No one ever hires me for that—to kill people who litter. I'd do the job for half my rate.

The *fyllejnod* seems to float, suspended high in the sky tonight, illuminating the exposed parts of Chicago. I like doing jobs at night and watching the movement of the shadows as time elapses. The gradual movement feels comforting and reminds me of times with my mom, eating late-night snacks and her telling me stories of her home world.

Hm…now they're hanging out in the doorway. Maybe waiting for the wind to die down? Bernadino drove, so they're not waiting for a taxi. He parked just a block down; I can see the car from here. The car was my second option. First, I hope to get a good shot when they step out of the doorway. A lot of couples will kiss as they leave. I can get a clean shot then. Or when he stops to open the car door.

As I peer through the scope, the wind blows so hard it cuts my eyes and pushes the gun ever so slightly. Ugh, I may have to get down to the street and do this with my side piece. And this is such a good spot. What a waste. I call up the fire escape platform and ride it down ten stories to street level. I stash the *reafian* and hit the button on my belt to expel my pistol.

I'm leaning against the wall of a building, just in front of their car. When they exit, I'll casually walk up to them. When they pass, I'll put one in her head. Depending on how he reacts, I'll try and empty the chamber in the project's torso.

When they exit Nombe Ghali, they stop to kiss. The project starts to walk towards the car. I start to walk towards them. We are an arm's length away when the sound of screeching tires startles us both. Lights blind me and instinctively I back off to a safe spot. The project has no such instincts.

The mistress goes under the car. Bernadino ends up flipping over and comes to rest on the roof. I'm darting my eyes around the scene, trying to get my bearings. Both car doors open at the same time. Out comes a boy and a girl. The boy is a wisp of a thing, the girl is a tank. She grabs the project under the car by the ankle and drags her out. She raises her right hand into the air. For a second, light from the *Fyllejnod* reflects off the four metal claws attached to the hand. The girl sinks them deep into my project's stomach, pulls them out, and jams them in again at a different angle. Smart—she's trying to hit a major organ to ensure a kill. Though I would just…

Then she cuts the project's throat. *That's* what I would have done.

The boy pulls Bernadino from the roof. Bernadino's head lulls back and forth, but he's alive. Blood is slipping from the corner of his mouth.

The boy points at him with his sword and looks at me. I shake my head and the boy releases Bernadino, who collapses on the sidewalk.

They both line up in front of me. Now that the surgery is wearing off, I can sense the boy has a spark of excitement in his eyes. The girl...I can't feel her out.

"I really hope you are Sasha, the assassin," the boy states.

"That's me. Sasha...the assassin."

The boy claps his hands together. "Fantastic! I'm Jonas, better known as Kid Kill."

There's a pause. Jonas coughs, triggering his sister.

"I'm Jessi." Jonas elbows her. "Ugh...Also known as Terror Girl."

CHAPTER 16

ALVA AND JORGE

Jorge is sitting at the dinner table, alone for the moment. He set the table and put fresh *wudorose* in the middle. On Alva's plate is the approval for a child, freshly stamped with his company's logo.

Jorge made Alva's favorite: *egeswin*, pan-fried and drowned in lemon. The sides are legumes with slivered almonds and a salad.

He hears the eye scan whirring outside the door. It stops, and a warning beeps three times.

"Come *on*," Alva yells. The scan activates again, followed by those dreaded beeps. "Fuck you!"

Jorge yells through the door, "Did you try the print scan?"

"Come open the door, Jorge!"

"Wait—try the print scan. Sasha said it was having issues; I wanna see if I fixed it."

There's a beat of silence. Then Alva tries the door handle, to no avail.

"Damn it. Come get the door, Jorge!"

Jorge gets up and halfheartedly jogs over to let her in. When he opens the door, Alva pounces on him. She kisses his lips furiously and pushes him over and down onto the *fearh-skin kitanda*. When he's pinned down, she reaches into her back pocket and pulls out a silver vial.

"Here it is—our little *fasciculo gaudium*."

Jorge is all smiles. Alva is all smiles. He kisses her back, then gently takes the vial and looks at it.

Jorge is studying it when he asks, "So you...You put it in there?" He points at her vagina.

Alva is appalled. "Do I put the serum into my *vag*? Is that what you're asking?"

Jorge forces a chuckle. "Of course not."

This pause is an awkward pause.

Jorge asks nervously, "It doesn't go into my..."

Alva kisses his forehead. "Gods, Jorge, *no*." She takes the vial back. The light from the *Fyllejnod* hitting the silver creates a rainbow effect on it. "I just inject it into my thigh. One third, in the morning, over the next three days. And my systems are powered up."

Jorge claps with a silly smile. "Yay! Baby-making time!"

"There is a one-in-a million chance the serum can cause liver failure. But I must carry the baby, so I guess I should have to take the risk of death, too."

Jorge starts to say. "If I could . . ."

"Shut the fuck up right now."

Jorge looks down. "Right." He nods to the side, over at the dinner table. "How d'you wanna celebrate your work approving you? Dinner or playtime first?"

Alva is still on top of him. "Ain't approve me."

Jorge raises his eyes.

"They were acting like the business end of a *hund* about it. Turned me down last week, didn't I tell you?"

"No."

Alva is pawing at Jorge chest. "Yeah, so I got this off a *ceaster-wyrt*."

"A *ceas*—Alva, they're not even sponsored by a company. That's completely off the margins."

Alva sighs. Her stance on top of Jorge is more adversarial, with her arms crossed. "You just gonna sit around and wait for some data program at your company to tell you what to do? That's not you. Never been me."

Jorge rubs his right eyelid with his index finger. "I get that Alva, but this is *having a kid*. It's not like in our grandparents' day. If they didn't get their kid sponsored, they couldn't attend University. But you still got to raise them. I mean, have you seen the 'Pro-Active Training' programs they put the kid in if they find out? They're no good, Alva."

"That's why we have to be careful."

"Careful? What doctor is going to deliver it without a sponsorship? Gods, I can't think of a doctor we can use that isn't associated with a corporation."

Alva pets the side of his face. "Jorge, I understand if you don't want to go through with this without a sponsor. And if so, we'll work through it. But I have to be honest—"

"I mean, lots of people get rejected the first time, Alva. And my approval is good for up to five years."

Alva sighs. "Jorge, I have to tell you something."

"I'm sorry, I won't risk it—not when there are other chances."

"There are no other chances, Jorge."

Jorge crinkles his nose. There a ringing on his phone; it's Sasha. "*Ignore.* Tell her I'll call her back."

Alva gets off him and cracks her knuckles. She folds her fingers together and turns her back to Jorge before saying, "Not gettin' approved. I already, a few years ago, tried to have a kid with no sponsor."

Jorge says nothing. Alva's still not facing him.

"The serum I used was all fucked. The…I didn't come to term. It only lasted a couple months."

Jorge retorts, "*That* I needed to know."

Alva chews her bottom lip, "Yeah."

"Cause if we're going to do this, it would'a been better I didn't get approved either."

"What?"

"Well, now there's a record of me asking with—"

"You're still in?"

"Oh yeah, most definitely. You're as *bari* as any girl I've met. If I can't have kids with you, then fuck it, I won't have kids."

Alva turns around, smiling. "Thank you."

"How do we know this serum will work?"

"My cousin, the *boucher* painter, used the same guy. He deals to a lot of the underground artists who aren't signed to a corporation. Walnut used him. Fischer, the *morgen pleghus* writer, used him. The model, Feodiora Puchelli, used him."

"Walnut is hilarious."

Alva clicks her tongue. "Okay, my *gagel.*"

"They are."

"I guess? I don't really think the whole bit where they mock the people of the forest is funny."

Jorge shrugs. "I guess it's—I mean, that part isn't funny."

"It's half the act."

Jorge frowns and shakes his head. "I can't defend it, but their early work—about CEO Pariunt, especially—was *funny*."

"Focus here, Jorge."

He smiles. It's a wide grin. He can't hide it or fight it. He simply says, "We're gonna have a kid."

CHAPTER 17

FIXING HIS KIDS

CEO (now Surgeon) Karl was sitting in a metal desk chair, watching his youngest child. They were in a basement Karl had fashioned himself. It wasn't cozy, but it was utilitarian, and it provided the needed space, tools, and privacy for his experiments. His *aethebald* was slumped in a corner, covered up by sheets and blankets. Her eyes were open, the pupils dilated. Her jaw was slung open and her muscles were limp, exaggerating her shoulder bone's prominence. A fly landed on her lip, crawled into her mouth, then flew away.

Next to her, perched in the same fashion, was Ainsley. Ainsley's brain was exposed, and the top of her skull was in her lap.

Luckily for Karlton, Jr., his was the first successful surgery his father performed. Well, more or less. Junior was just regaining his motor skills and walking back and forth in the basement. Early tests were promising, though. Surgeon Karl had removed his fear. He exposed Junior to various creatures which used to terrify him, but now only drew a bemused curiosity.

Upstairs was Layton. He had survived a surgery to remove his sense of anger. Karl hoped this would create a person as determined as he was, without giving in to frustration. A rigid focus on tasks. Layton was the only one of his kids to enjoy his new "gift."

On the table was Thatcher. Surgeon Karl decided to give Thatcher what he thought was the greatest gift of all—he messed with Thatcher's sense of time. Karl didn't know what effect this would have, but he hoped it would open up a sense of mortality before unknown. Thatcher, he theorized, would see existence and the world outside of what anyone else experienced. He would, in effect, see it the same way the gods did. If it worked, Karl was going to try the surgery on himself.

Thatcher began to stir. His cheeks were flushed red and puffy—normal for a child his age. He blinked a few times in rapid succession. Then he rubbed his forehead in a circular motion and tried to regain his bearings.

"Father, my head hurts something fierce."

But Karl, exhumed of any sort of sympathy, didn't care. He asked, "How do things *look*, Thatcher?"

Thatcher squinted his eyes and looked around. "How do you mean, Father? They look normal."

"Do things feel any different? Are you experiencing anything new?"

Thatcher hung his head. "I don't know Father. My head hurts real bad, though."

"Do you have any sense of what is going to happen next? Is everything still happening in a linear fashion for you?"

"I'm not sure what you mean, Father."

Karl lifted Thatcher's chin up, "Are you seeing everything in the order you normally do?"

Thatcher starts to get nervous. Ever since his dad had come back from the war, he was not the same man. His temper was quick and he had a cold look in his eyes. Thatcher missed the father who rubbed his back while he tried to sleep. This new Surgeon? He was no father. That much, Thacher knew, even at his young age.

Thatcher stared hard and concentrated, trying to detect something new. Nothing stood out. With a timid shake in his voice, he croaked, "I don't see anything, Father."

"Go get some water, then come back," Karl grunted.

With the groan of a man fifty years older, Thatcher got off the table and walked to the corner. He didn't think to look under the sheets where he'd discover his father's failed experiments. He chose a steel cup, washed it out, and then filled it with water.

Walking back to the table, Thatcher collapsed and the cup of water fell to the ground. Karl gradually got up and walked over. Standing over his son, he said, "Are you okay?"

Thatcher looked up and made eye contact with Karl. Next thing Karl knew, he was back in his seat. He looked around, confused. The cup was back in Thatcher's hand, filled with water. Thatcher, however, was worse for wear. His left eyelid kept twitching and a stream of blood flushed from his nose.

Karl ran over this time, grabbing Thatcher by the arms. "Son, what happened? What . . . How did you do that?"

Thatcher went limp and let the cup fall to the ground.

CHAPTER 18

KERGAN MEETS THE CLAN

Kergan II is standing in the Chumba room, surrounded by members of Rafe's clan. Her eyes dart around as she reads the body language of the crowd. Their mood is not helping her adjust to the new surroundings. She wishes she was back in the forest already.

Cadyn is leaning against a wall, burning a hole through Kergan with a stare. Micel is next to Rafe, explaining the situation to the rest of the crew.

Kergan leans over to Micel. "How many of these *weaoruds* are drunk?"

Micel shrugs. "I dunno, all of them?"

Kergan wonders out loud, "It's pretty early in the day to start drinking, isn't it?"

"What makes ya think they stopped?"

Kergan, under her breath, says, "*Deorcynn…*"

Micel nudges her. "Hey, these 'ere are the best money can buy."

Kergan's eyes go wide. "Seriously?"

Micel nods in affirmation. Then shrugs. Then shakes his head side to side. "Fine, *no*. But we *are* very good. A few people we've protected have even *survived*."

Kergan hangs her jaw open before saying, "Wait, what?"

Rafe stops for a second and looks at Kergan. "Kergan, did you want to introduce yourself to the crew?"

Kergan looks the crowd over. Half of them are swaying back and forth, probably inebriated. The others a busy picking their noses or digging in their ears. With an annoyed grunt, she answers. "No."

Rafe turns his palms up. "Um…All right, then. Back to work, or drinking, or whatever it is you were doing. Micel, take Kergan to her *allor*."

There's a hum as the *weaoruds* start to file out past Kergan. Most give her the once-over, which Kergan reacts to by looking at the floor. A couple walk over and introduce themselves. Kergan acknowledges them with a halfhearted wave but doesn't say anything.

As Micel leads her out, they're stopped by Cadyn. She holds out her arm and says, "I'll take this."

Micel reach his arm out to block Cadyn. "S'all right. I—"

"Said *I'll* take 'er." Cadyn snorts and squints her left eye.

Micel's voice lowers to a growl, "What's your deal?"

Cadyn retorts, "Maybe I'm just in a hospitable mood."

Micel is still affecting that growl. "*Clifrin* that."

Cadyn grabs Kergan by the arm. "Let's go."

And just like that, Cadyn is dragging Kergan down the hall to her *allor*. She looks over her shoulder a couple of times and pushes anyone standing in the hall out of the way. With the coast clear, she tosses Kergan into a *greot* room, knocking over a mop and some brooms, all still in their original packaging.

Kergan grabs the unopened mop. "Did you know you can *actually* use this to clean?" Then she looks at Cadyn. "They're not just decorations."

Cadyn grunts out a response, "Shut up. That's rule number one. Keep your mouth *shut*."

Kergan stands up tall. "I'm going to be a leader of my tribe and—"

Cadyn punches Kergan in the gut, *hard*. "You broke rule number one."

Kergan doubles over, catching her breath.

"I know you think I'm a real *rudder* right now, but I'm going to be the one who teaches you to survive."

Kergan, still breathing heavily, shoots her a scowl.

"Number two, and this includes Rafe—I'm the *only* person you can trust here."

Kergan furrows her eyebrows. "Are you…"

Cadyn puts up her fist, points at it, then at Kergan's stomach. Kergan cuts herself off and bites her top lip.

"I put extra locks on your door. They're damn useless if ya don't lock them, right?"

Kergan nods.

"Finally, as much as you can, avoid bein' alone with anyone who ain't me—again, this includes Rafe."

Kergan starts to talk, thinks about it, and decides to just nod.

"You can ask me *one* question."

"If you all need me alive to collect, why wouldn't I be safe?"

"A Burgealdor has plenty of *feoh*. And they want you dead. Everyone has a price."

"What's your price?"

"I said you get *one* question." With that, Cadyn leads her out of the *greot* room by her arm.

Kergan squints at Cadyn. "You remind me of my mom."

Cadyn grunts. When they get to Kergan's *allor*, Cadyn tosses her in. Kergan looks around the room, searching for anything welcoming. No such luck.

"Remember, use the locks. No one enters alone. I'll get you in the morning."

"But it's too early—"

Before she can finish, Cadyn slams the door shut. Kergan walks over to the bed. It's soiled and damp. She takes the blanket off, lays it on the floor, sits down, and begins to sob. She cries until she falls asleep.

Later that night, she wakes up with a start, a powerful pain in her gut. Kergan rolls on her side, holding her stomach, kicking and cursing. She looks up to see Cayden standing over her with a cold frown on her face.

"The locks are useless if you don't use them, correct?"

Kergan is coughing.

"Correct?"

Kergan squeaks, *"Yes."*

"Next time I'll break something—something you need. *Unanielewa?*"

Kergan can only spit out her response, *"Naelewa."*

"Hm…You speak Abakalician?"

Kergan sniffles, rubbing her stomach. "My mom made me learn the three planetary languages. To help me unite people."

Cadyn spits on the floor, then wipes some spittle from her lip. "Why ain't you on the bed?"

Kergan furrows her brow. "Seriously?"

Cadyn inspects it. "All right, hang on."

Cadyn leaves. A minute later, she returns with a new mattress in tow and an angry and bleeding Rapunzel yelling at her.

"That's my gods damn mattress, Cadyn! You filthy rudder!" says Rapunzel.

Cadyn switches the mattresses and shoves Rapunzel and her new mattress through the door, locking it behind them.

Rapunzel kicks and screams, tries to open the door but fails, and eventually leaves, defeated.

"See? Lockin' the door works," Cadyn says.

"Thanks," Kergan says as she crawls into bed.

Cadyn starts to get undressed, "I'm gonna stay in here with you tonight."

"You said to never be alone with anyone."

"Well, I didn't mean me."

Kergan stares at Cadyn. Cadyn stares back.

Cadyn nods. "Good job."

******

Cadyn leaves and closes the door behind her. She listens for a second. When she hears the locks click, she retires to her own bed.

As she heads down the hall, Micel is standing in his doorway. Cadyn stops. They hold eye contact for a couple of seconds.

Micel asks, "She settled in then?"

Cadyn snorts, then rubs a drip of snot away with the back of her sleeve. "You remember your first night here?"

"Not really," Micel replies while mimicking drinking from a bottle. "I remember I tried to be friendly with you, but you stabbed me in the thigh."

"Thought you were coming onto me. Wanted to make myself clear."

Micel laughs and shakes his head, "Cadyn, when has that been an issue for you?"

Cadyn stalks away, giving her response with a single finger.

She uses a key and a fingerprint scanner to open the locks to her room. She looks around before slipping into her hiding hole. The locks engage with a series of clicks and snaps. Cadyn exhales audibly. She takes off her kitana and hangs it on the wall, pulls a knife from her wrist band and puts it on a metal desk, pulls another knife from her left boot, and then reaches to her back and retrieves another cnif that was held by tape. Cadyn pats herself down while counting the knives on the desk, then pulls down her pants, revealing a thigh holster with another large, serrated blade.

Cadyn walks over to her bed and looks under it. "How's it goin', Eorl?" She clicks her tongue on the roof of her mouth and taps the ground. As she backs away from the bed, she's followed by Eorl, a twelve-foot *hama*.

Eorl is mostly black, but sports a series of gold diamonds running down her back. She wriggles side to side; her tongue flickers, helping guide her. Eorl spirals up Cadyn's leg and ends up wrapped around her arm; she hangs on with the help of two tiny legs located near the back of her body, by the tail. These legs are the last vestiges of *hamas* of the past, which scurried rather than crawled.

Cadyn opens the desk drawer and pulls out a handful of dead *bitels*. Eorl greedily licks them up, swallowing each one whole.

"I'm sorry I was gone so long, but we had to go to the forest."

Eorl stares at Cadyn as she talks.

"I always wonder if you know what I'm saying, Eorl."

Cadyn rubs the hama's head with a circular motion. Eorl rests her head in response. Cadyn walks over by the closet. She picks up and inspects a faux wood guitar, looking down the neck to see if there's any warping. Then she takes out and inspects a flute.

Cadyn's room is spotless. The bed is neatly made with a huggable, fluffy duvet on top. Next to the bed, there's a metal stand with family photos on top. Against the wall hangs a series of flags from all four planets. Her pride is a light blue LaRoccan flag which dates back over two hundred years.

Before getting into bed, Cadyn leans over to smell trimming from a *pintreowl* she keeps on the bedside table. She hums a lullaby she learned as a child and sinks into her pillow. For the first time today, Cadyn is relaxed.

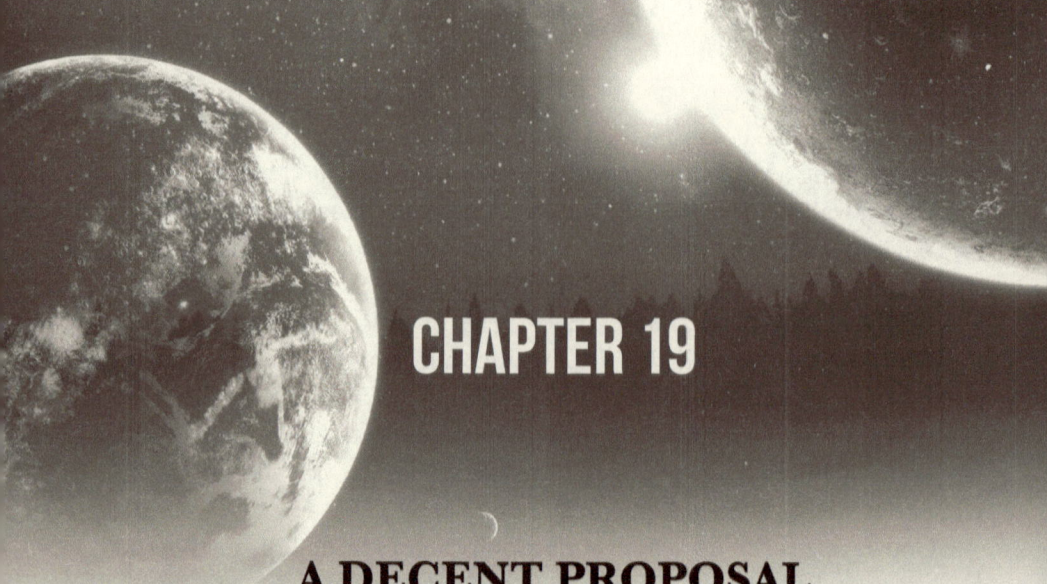

CHAPTER 19

A DECENT PROPOSAL

I'm sitting in a *winhus* on the outskirts of Chicago called Avem Ebrius. The tables are all made of metal, but painted to resemble wood. Same for the chairs. It's smells heartily of mead and whiskey.

The chairs across from me are occupied by Kid Kill and Terror Girl. We've been sitting in awkward silence for the last five minutes, waiting for a *ceren*.

A waitress with yellow hair and matching eyes brings over *bucs* (jugs) of home-brewed *ceren*. The pants she's wearing are covered with tears and stretches in the fabric. I don't get it. You're supposed to be representing a business. Why would you dress—

Kid Kill looks around. "So, is this a place you hang out at a lot?"

I shake my head and mumble, "*gods*, save me."

He squirms a bit. "So, do you have any other jobs tonight?"

His sister is looking around and tearing a napkin into tiny pieces. Every time we make eye contact, she rolls her gaze to the left.

"Or maybe tomorrow?"

The waitress is waiting for someone to pay her. I point at the kids. Kid Kill gets the hint, fishes around in his pocket, and pays. "How long have you been an assassin?"

Now *this* is just a power play. The longer I ignore his questions, the more desperate he'll get. It's really too easy. I take a sip and shrug my shoulders.

Kid Kill shifts a bit, then fires off again, "Is it fu— I mean, do you like it?"

Now I can reply, because I have something sarcastic to answer with; it'll put him more on the defensive. "Yeah, every day is a holiday. It's fuckin' Bata Kamili out there."

Kid Kill explains, "Our family doesn't celebrate that. We're Riestovikian."

Time to let them know I'm smarter than them. "You break into my communication server to figure out where my jobs were going to be?"

Kid Kill smiles. "Yeah, that was my work, I'm pretty gift—"

"Shut up."

He does.

Terror Girl curls her upper lip. "Maybe you wanna *thank us* for handling your work for you?"

"Maybe I would if you didn't kill everything in sight. The kid you killed at that house? He wasn't part of the job."

Terror Girl shrugs.

Probably due to the surgery wearing off, I'm excessively bothered by her indifference. I notice my jaw tense up. I'm staring at her, and she's glaring right back, the little—

"That's why we're here," Kid Kill interrupts. "To *train* under you. Try and avoid mistakes like that."

"You need to be trained not to kill kids?"

"I thought we were being thorough," he practically whimpers.

I've already made my decision, but I entertain them a bit longer. "Well, where's the offering?"

"Oh, yeah—*here.*" Kid Kill pulls out a bag and hands it over to me. I open it to find a blade made from *minerual yttrium*. I can tell from the dark gold coloring of the blade. It's caused by the heating, a chemical reaction when they forge it. The handle is adorned with blue and red jewels. I will say, this wasn't cheap.

I put it back in the bag and draw the string closed. "And what about her? Where's her offering?"

"Oh," Kid starts. "We—we just had enough to pay for that one."

"That's fine, it doesn't matter."

Kid's eyes light up. "So you're going to take us on?"

"Oh, quite the opposite, child." *Ew,* the look on his face when I say this. I have a twinge of guilt. "Look, I'm not the best person to train you. Thanks for the drink."

I pound the last bit of *ceren* and start to get up. Terror Girl grabs my hand. It's like a vise. I'm not sure if I can pull away, so I don't struggle and stay relaxed. I can't show weakness.

"You fucking owe us!" Terror Girl spits out.

I shake my head. "Typical of you kids—*everyone* owes you."

Kid Kill pulls on his sister's shirt. "Jessi, let's go."

Terror Girl turns her head to the side and squints at me. I exhale hard through my nose, never breaking our gaze. She stands up, knocking her chair over. She's released the hold on my hand but now has her hand on the handle of her mallet. I slip my hand down to the button on my belt in case I need to release my side piece.

"Outside," I say.

Terror Girl licks her lips and responds, "You'll die just as fast in here."

"If you destroy the property of a business, there will be hell to pay from the corporation that owns this place."

Kid Kill is standing; I didn't notice. To his sister, he says, "*Outside.* Let's go."

As we're leaving the Avem Ebrius, I slow down so Terror Girl is right on my heels. We get outside and I spin around with the handle of my gun and nail her in the temple. She's dazed and I'm able to grab her as hostage with my gun pointed at Kid Kill. Her hair is getting in my mouth as I give Kid orders, "Put the sword down, kick it away, and lie on the ground. I will kill your sister. And it won't mean much to me. So please."

He hesitates. His eyes dart back and forth between me and his sister.

"We can still leave here with everyone alive," I say. Most importantly, *me.*

I hardly notice it, but Terror Girl has turned her head to the side so her cheek is pressed against mine. Like the crack of a whip, she extends a blade from her wrist and jams it through her cheek into mine. Instinctively, I pull back and shove her to the ground.

Now I'm nursing a wound and they both have blades drawn on me. But I still have a gun. Though I'm gonna get into a bunch of bureaucratic crap, maybe have my tag pulled . . .

You know what, this wasn't explained. I have guns. Own 'em, use 'em, love 'em. Wonderful for the job. I had to go through two years of school, take on massive debt, and give four years to the service of a corporation. (I was randomly "interned" to East West Compass and Butchery Concern in the corporate espionage division. I oversaw suppressing unionization by employees. I was very good at it.)

Then, and only then, are you given a tag implant that allows you to buy guns and ammo. It's made of *aurum de abu*, which is a pliable metal found exclusively on Abakalic. Though it has a LaRoccan name origin. Go figure. Mine was inserted in my hip. So whenever I go to a *wapenus*, the tag is scanned and that gun or ammo is forever attached to me. If it's stolen and someone else uses it, I'm just as guilty as the person who stole it. That is an unfair law. But it does make you paranoid about losing anything, and I suppose prevents psychos from getting them. Unless they're really determined and patient.

The reason this applies now is, whenever I use a bullet, I must submit a form to some big shot in the CSD: Cum Sicario Disputabo. This is to ensure it was used in appropriation of a legal job I was hired for. Basically, I can't just kill some *weaorund* who rips me off, or shoves me in a line. If you lose your tag, you do not get it back.

The advantage I have right now is they might not know this . . .

"You can't use that gun on us, this isn't official work."

Of course. "Well, I would lose the tag, but you both would be dead and I'd be alive." I run my tongue along the wound in my cheek. It didn't quite go all the way through, but I need to get it closed soon before I end up with a scar.

Terror Girl is just letting the blood run down her neck and stain her yellow shirt. I can see she's focusing on me to ignore the pain. Impressive.

Kid Kill is grinding his teeth. "Just fucking train us! You owe us!"

I spit in his direction while moving the gun's aim back and forth. When I focus back on Terror Girl, I see the blood-stained frog pinned to her sleeve. I try to blink it away, but the frog persists. For the first time in years, my shooting hand starts to tremble. I need to go before they—

"Shit, her hand is *trembling*," Terror Girl notices. She smiles. "S'amatta? Too much *ceren*? Scared to be outnumbered?"

I slide the gun back into the holder. Kid Kill charges me. I pull out the offering they gave me and catch his *neosiri* as he slashes down. I push him off but Terror Girl's shoulder slams into me with the force of an *elpend*. I land flat back, roll to the side, and pop up. is twirling her mallet above her head. She charges and swings. I duck but can feel the mallet brush my hair. Kid Kill takes a jab with his *beadomece*, but he's unbalanced and fails to do anything but tear my blouse. *Thank god*, that was aimed at my stomach. Terror Girl comes back with the hammer—her arms are sinewy, like the ropes they use to dock ships—and it finds my shoulder. *That* was unpleasant, and possibly dislocating.

"Why are you fighting me? Just go find someone else to train you!" They both stop. Then Kid Kill grunts out, "Calude Beatty."

I remember her. I shot her in the temple. I think her employer hired me for that job. I'd have to think about it, though. "Yeah, what? She's your mom or aunt or something?"

"Wow, you really—" Terror Girl starts, then shakes her head and stops.

Kid Kill tightens his grip on the *neosiri*, "She was an aunt who raised us after our mother passed."

"Is this a revenge plot?"

"Not purely," Kid Kill responds.

"All right, so what is this?"

"Since our mom died, and our surrogate mom died, I wanted you to make up for it."

I don't get it. "Why would you want *me*, of all people, to be your new mom?"

"It's not *mom* mom." Kid Kill starts, his hair hanging in front of his eyes. I admit that I have a very motherly urge to tell him to get it cut. "It's more like, I dunno—*matrina lanista.*"

I look at Terror Girl. "And what about you?"

"I hate you, but I'm loyal to my brother." Terror Girl stretches her arms straight out. I never noticed before, but her face is young, no wrinkles or scratches. "If you accept us, I'll honor his wishes."

"And what happens if he changes his mind?"

Kid Kill holds out his hand with his fingers spread. He takes a blade to his pinky. His hand is shaking. Terror Girl looks at him. "Gods, Jonas, *don't.*"

He's looking at me. "I'll perform the *spiritualibus*. If you don't believe me, I'll cut my pinky off and offer it to you."

Ew, no. "What would I do with your pinky? Also, no one does that anymore."

Kid Kill frowns. "I read about it, though; it's a form of penance from LaRocca."

"Yeah, I didn't even remember the word for it. But, no, you don't . . . Actually, it would be interesting to see if you'd go through with it."

Kid Kill is darting his eyes between his hand and me. Ha, little *cicen*. I stare at him, focusing intently at his eyes, selling the moment. His hand is now rattling like a baby toy.

"All right, that's enough, I have no use for your appendages."

Kid sighs, and Terror Girl jabs him with her elbow, shaking her head.

I slide my index finger along the *beadomece* before sheathing it. "All right, well, see you both tomorrow."

"Is that it?" Kid says. "No, like, *ceremony*?"

I start walking away.

"Do we meet at your place?"

I keep going.

He shouts after me, "What about my sister? Does she still need an offering?"

I'm deeply regretting this proposition.

CHAPTER 20

MAKING BABIES

"And if you look to your left, you can see Episcopius Naomi IV give her victory speech after the Talmudic Wars. The Talmudic Wars lasted five years. Fifteen percent of the LaRoccan population was wiped out and a great number of those were civilians who starved to death."

The chariot keeps rolling along the track and the hologram tour guide points out the next attraction. Inside the chariot, or, more accurately, on the bottom, are Jorge and Alva. They are engaged in carnal acts not suitable for the history museum they're currently touring.

"Next, we have the visage of Episcopius Naomi V, daughter of Naomi IV. She would go on to start the second Talmudic Wars when a section of text in the good book sparked an argument of interpretation. This time, ten percent of the remaining population would die."

With their legs intertwined, Jorge and Alva are panting and sweating. Alva rubs the sore from where she took the serum. Three red dots had sprung up in the area, but this was a good sign.

The hologram, STACY—an acronym for a series of boring engineering terms—wears a smile. Her clothes change to match the era she's discussing. Her voice is cheerful, like a preschool teacher. It is as though she's a PR person for the planet. "And now we enter the era in LaRoccan history known as 'Pax Di Epoch' or 'God's Peace.' The wars had ended, and for the first time in LaRoccan history, the planet was united. It lasted for a decade and saw over twenty-five percent of the population killed through famine and disease."

Alva grabs her pants and fishes through the pockets. She pulls out two bottles, both containing brown liquid. These were *pombe tenebris* bottles, an imported cousin of whiskey. These were supposed to…*spur lovers into action,* would be the polite way of phrasing it.

Jorge takes one from her hand, "Hey, horny juice! Where'd you get that?"

"Off some *esne* selling them by the trains."

The bottle Jorge is holding is about the size of his thumb. "This stuff doesn't work, you know."

"Why not?" Alva says with a playful shove. "Down it and we'll see."

They both compete to see who can finish the bottle first, and both end up spitting out more than they drink when they break out into laughter.

Alva, using his shirt to wipe off a bit of dribble, says, "Awe, we wasted it. *Quae fortuna.*"

They're quiet for a minute and watch STACY.

Jorge reaches over and grabs Alva's hand. "This is kinda creepy."

"I dunno, the light coming off her is pleasant. Not too bright, but you can see what you're doing."

"It feels disrespectful." Jorge explains.

"To a hologram?"

"Well, it *is* modeled after a real person."

"Is it? I thought they generated a bunch of attributes and built these at random."

"No, I think these are actual people."

Alva shakes her foot back and forth through STACY.

STACY waves her hand, gesturing to the next exhibit. "And now, we approach the birth of the planet Earth."

Jorge starts slipping on his pants. "All right, this thing is almost done."

Alva rolls on top of him. "I thought we'd ride it again. Annnnnd I'd ride *you* again."

"Let's go over to the CEO tour. We can sneak off into one of the rooms in the castle."

"Yes! I like it!" Alva rolls off and starts to get dressed.

They're still buttoning up as the ride comes to a halt. Standing on the platform is the teenager who operates the ride, wearing a knowing, bemused look on his face. Next to him is a family of four waiting to ride. The parents are glaring holes through the couple. Jorge averts his gaze to the ground and Alva follows suit. They jump out of the chariot and shuffle off to their next destination.

They're standing on the moving sidewalk on their way to the CEO castle. While holding hands, Jorge observes, "That family was nice, right? Not the part where they hated us, but they looked good together. Kinda sweet."

Alva rises up on the tip of her toes. "God, such a sap. I love you."

They're kissing when the sidewalk jolts to a stop. Looking ahead, they can see a large man running full speed at them. In his left hand is a knife and across his shirt is a spray of red, like fruit juice. He has a green beard and matching hair. hould read His neck is as thick and as stump and his shoulders are square like boxes.

When Jorge realizes the man isn't slowing down, he hugs Alva and turns his back to the runner. But the man with the knife ignores them and keeps running. A few seconds later, two kids, maybe in their late teens, are giving chase and screaming obscenities.

"What *was* that?" Alva asks.

They start to walk to the end of the sidewalk. At the end, there's a circle of people. Some are whispering, some have their hands covering their mouths.

Jorge starts to push his way through the crowd, but Alva pulls him back.

"Morbid," Alva tugs on Jorge to leave.

"I want to see if the person is *sanu.*"

Alva is still pulling on his arm. "It seems like you want to gawk at someone who just got stabbed."

Jorge stops, and shakes his head. "Yeah, you're right."

As they walk away, Jorge cranes his neck to try and see. Alva grabs him by the chin and turns his head back around. He gives her a wry smile and a shrug. She responds by pinching his nipple.

"Did that excite you?"

"Huh?"

Alva replies, "The guy with the knife, that excite you?"

"Yeah," he replies simply.

"Think that's kinda fucked up?"

"Sasha does it for a living; it's a job."

Alva purrs in disapproval, "Right, but I'm asking about *you.* I think it's warped you *hoja ya minue* by blood and death."

"I dunno, I've always had a fascination with the morbid. It's something most people have."

"Most people don't live with—and I like 'er, but still—a *killer*."

Jorge inhales through his nose sharply. "No, I guess not."

A MAG approaches them. Both tense up, figuring the teenager or the family complained.

"I'm sorry, but we need you to exit immediately." He holds up a scanner about the size of his index finger. "I can scan your card, so you'll get one free admission for another day."

Relieved, they thank the MAG and leave through the nearest exit.

Alva pushes away from Jorge. Not in a mean way, but to let him know what she is about to say is serious. "Can't live with Sasha when we have a kid."

Jorge runs his tongue along his top row of teeth. The star above is blinding him and he uses his hand to block it. "I know, we talked about it. I know I have to leave Sasha."

Alva looks at him. Jorge reacts with a shrug.

Alva taps her watch. "Sooner rather than later, Jorge."

"So what, you mean tomorrow?"

"Tell 'er, at least. Get this thing moving."

"*Mi tibi kwako.*"

"So do I," she says right before leaning in to peck Jorge on the cheek.

CHAPTER 21

IT TAKES MORE THAN THAT

Kergan Satre III is standing in a banquet room at the front of the ship. The room is humid, damp. The air is thick and smells like a fish dinner that was left out for three days. She's bouncing a blue ball against the wall. There's a clang as it hits the wall, then a thump when it bounces off the floor. She keeps catching it in her left hand, then throwing with her right.

Clang…thud…catch.

The sound echoes, as the banquet hall is empty except for a crudely drawn ring in the middle. This is where they held the Sifa Njema Pug. Hence the smell.

Clang…thud…catch.

Rafe Fortune appears in the doorway, with Micel trailing. Rafe uses his shirt to cover his nose. Micel has a bit of the glow wearing off. Micel starts to take out more *pulvaris* ,but Rafe nudges him and, using just his eyes, tells him to stop. Micel puts it away.

Rafe runs his fingers through his hair. "Hey, Kergan. I was told you've been down here for a while."

Clang…thud…catch.

"Yeah, cause I'm fucking bored. I've been on this gods forsaken ship going on three weeks now. And either people avoid me like I have *cwild*, or they're too interested, like a *kushanga crustula*."

Clang…thud…catch.

Kergan is wearing a loose-fitting brown leather skirt and green sweater that covers her neck. So far, the wardrobe provided consisted of that outfit and a red piece more akin to a burlap sack than a dress.

"Rafe." There's a beat as she notices Rafe covering his nose. "Why are you covering your nose? You live in this stench."

"I'll thank you to know I have an extremely refined olfactory sense. One that is super sensitive."

Micel chuckles and says, "Yeah, kids used to tease him, saying his parents were *mordus*."

Rafe squints at them. "Thank you, Micel."

"So, like, how far can you smell?" Kergan asks.

"Depends on the strength. This room I can smell even when I leave the ship."

"Speaking of which, did you even think about the logistics of this? How to keep me from losing my damn mind?"

Micel explains to her. "Kergan, we know, we are working on things for you."

Rafe speaks in a slow, deliberate pace. "It's, uh—just one of those things. We are putting together some stuff for you."

Kergan scrunches her face. "How about we go get some food that isn't red eyed? Some food that doesn't have freezer burns all over it. I'm sorry, but most of it tastes like *draest*."

Micel shrugs. "Hey, the burns are what gives it flavor."

Clang...thud...catch.

"I'm very grateful to be here. Micel, you've been fun to talk to and play with. Cadyn, while a tiny bit . . . *brutal* . . . certainly has her heart in preparing and training me. And Rafe, you've made me feel like this ship is a *cantwaraburg*, completely safe."

Clang...thud...catch.

I'm very sorry," Rafe begins, "but the reality is our job is to protect you—not entertain you."

"Well, if I die from boredom, you won't get paid, will you?"

Rafe smirks and looks at the ground, "That's not likely to happen, now is it?"

"Let me put this another way. I'm getting *koroga impotente*, like a caged *leona*."

Clang...thud...catch.

Kergan snorts, then continues. "I'm going to try and escape. And you can probably stop me a few times. But eventually I'll get out. And instead of having one of you, or Cadyn with me, I'll be on my own."

Rafe and Micel look at each other.

"I wanna see the *andred*—I wanna investigate it, experience it. I've spent my life in the forest. The only experience I have with Chicago is holding my mother as she bled to death."

Clang…thud…catch.

"Is that what you want for me?"

Rafe sighs and looks off to the side. He kicks a piece of broken glass and sucks on his teeth. "We'll work something out. Give us a couple days. Come up with two places you want to visit; we'll scout them and see if they are safe."

Kergan tosses the ball at Rafe, but he misses it and it bounces down the hall.

Kergan puts her hand over her stomach. "I missed it once when Cadyn threw it at me and had to do sit-ups till I vomited."

Micel shakes their head. "I'll talk to her about—"

"No, I like being pushed. It's important for me to survive. And for you to get paid."

Micel explains, "Yeah, but his ex-girlfriend won't come 'ere."

Kergan looks at Rafe. Rafe is glaring at Micel.

"First off, I don't blame her. Secondly, what does your *cwyne* have to do with anything?" Kergan asks.

Rafe makes direct eye contact with Kergan. "We suspect she was the one hired to . . . you and your mother…"

"And she's your ex-girlfriend?"

"Right."

"So why don't you find her and kill her?"

"Then they'd just hire someone else," Rafe explains. "At least this way, we keep a step ahead. All my people know what she looks like. And finally, it's extrajudicial to kill her."

"But she's an assassin."

"Legally hired by a *burgealdor*."

Micel tilts his head slightly. "Her killing you? *Legal*. Us killing her? *Illegal*."

"No wonder my mom hated this system so much. Why didn't this assassin just shoot me with my mom? I was right there."

Rafe and Micel look at each other and shrug. Micel responds, "No idea. Took too long reloading, maybe?"

Kergan starts to pace back and forth. "Maybe she couldn't kill a kid."

They both laugh at her. Rafe explains, "Heavens Kerg—that was her specialty. She had her empathy removed, which, I guess, kept her conscience at bay." Rafe taps Micel on the shoulder. "I've got maintenance stuff to attend to, but I'll leave Micel here and he can get a list of places you want to visit. All right? We'll go from there."

The minute Rafe leaves, Micel takes out his jazz bag and snorts some *pulveris*. While glowing, they look at Kergan. "I better not catch you doing this. It's grown-up stuff, ya know?"

Kergan raises her eyebrows, but shrugs in response.

Micel stuffs the bag back into a pocket. "A'ight then, let's get chompin'. What places do you want to visit?"

"I've always heard about the Rali Navali in the business district. . Is it true it has the original train cars, from when they first built it?"

Micel squints and shrugs, "Eh, sorta. They use bits of the original cars, then fill in the missing pieces with new stuff. Also, I think Canton-Erie investors bought it and plastered its name all over."

"That's . . . a waste. It was real historical, wasn't it?"

"Well, the other option was it would be torn down 'cause it wasn't making enough profit. So. . . ."

Kergan continues to pace. "Okay, well…Scratch that one. Um, what about Aldhem Castle? That was the site of the first *biggencere* (worker) revolt, right?"

"Um, so that one was turned into a theme park for the Child Dodgers cartoon."

Kergan stops and looks at Micel. "Oh, come on."

"Well, the original site was thought to spark too much rebellion in—ya know—the common worker."

Kergan releases an exaggerated sigh, "Fine, sports. Take me to a *huntung* ."

Micel shakes his head *no*. "I can tell you right now, that is going to be too crowded to protect you."

"Gods, Micel! Well, can *you* think of anything?"

Micel shrugs. "We could go for ice cream?"

"Fine, let's do that. And somewhere I can shop for clothes. I feel like . . . like . . . like a *knob* in these things."

Micel, "Yeah, I can see dat. We'll take you somewhere."

"Where?"

"Kergan, does it look like any of us go shopping often? I'll ask around and find some places to choose from."

Kergan sighs. "Sorry, like I said, *koroga impotente.*"

"I get it—give us a couple days to scout, all right?"

Kergan's eyes start to well up. She starts to talk, but the words disappear into a cough. Then comes a second attempt. "I—miss—home."

Micel's arms were thicker than Kergan's neck, but it still brought her great comfort when they wrapped around her shoulders and pulled her in for a bear hug. Kergan doesn't hug back at first, but slowly relents and gently wraps her arms around Micel.

Micel pats her back. "I get it, Kergan. I do. Remember, I'm from the forest too. Way down on the south edge."

It's all right; I'll be all right." She starts to pull away.

"Don't be embarrassed."

"I'm supposed to be a leader. I can't let people see me like this." Kergan closes her eyes, squeezing them tight. She paces her breathing, slowing the rhythm down. There's a hum in the air around them.

Micel begins to say, "You don't have to—" But is interrupted when he stumbles. "Sorry, my head got light."

Kergan opens her eyes. The whites are sparking blue, first rapidly, then retreating until they're gone.

Micel rubs his temples. "Um, so as I was saying, give us a couple days to scout, all right?"

"All right. Thanks, Micel."

CHAPTER 22

THE KIDS SCREW ME

I'm standing in front of my *bolttimber*, waiting for Burgealdor Spencer and his cabal to visit. The wind is stirring leaves around on the ground, except for the ones stuck in the sewer grate. It's chilly, but not uncomfortable. If you're in the shade, you probably need a jacket, though.

My neighborhood smells of fresh-baked sweet *cecels*…sweet *cecels* drenched in berries and cream. Across the street is an Abakalician bakery which specializes in *cecels*. The man in the back who makes them is quite the opposite of sweet, though. Kali is . . . old. I can't say how old. He looks like he's lived all the years. His skin is dry and cracked. His beard is always unkempt and knotted, and it runs down to his stomach. His eyes are bereft of any color, and he has a lingering whooping cough that shakes the display case in front.

In spite of—or maybe *because* of—all this, he makes the best damn *cecels* you'll ever have. I'd stake my reputation on it. I purchased some to present to the Burgealdor for our meeting. The damn kids ate all of them. Normally, I'd have come up with some tedious or painful punishment for them, but heck, they're just kids and they didn't know any better. (Maybe Belle is right. Maybe I need to get sliced and diced to fix me.)

I'm still shocked he wanted to meet here. Usually, government officials avoid the residential areas at all costs. They prefer the heart of the city, living and interacting with their own. Jorge was disappointed he would be at work when Spencer visited. I don't think he has ever met a Burgealdor. I suggested he call off work, but I forget they have a company *lareow* who visits you. Ostensibly, it's to make sure you are okay and have the proper devices to heal. But, that explanation is a joke. It's really to make sure you aren't faking. Workers who fake being sick are subject to servitude and can even lose the right to retirement funds.

I'm startled as two cars pull up to the *bolttimber* with a screech. Out pops four, maybe five, bodyguards. Without warning, they take me to the ground. Two search my pockets, one holds me down, the others keep guns pointed at me.

Facedown on the sidewalk, I manage to see Burgealdor Spencer exit his car. He's dressed in a red and blue robe with a shimmery *faet* trim. His red hair is frozen in place, with the ends reaching the edge of his shoulders.

I'm able to mumble from my position, "It's a pleasure to see you, Burgealdor."

He waves his left hand. "Let her up, now. Let her up. I trust her as much as the word of the gods." He signals for a guard to come close and whispers, "Did you find anything?" The guard indicates no by shaking his head.

Spencer waves his hand again. "Please, let my friend up!"

They release me, but do not help me up. Fine etiquette.

Spencer is rubbing his ample stomach as he glides over to me. He extends his hand with the palm down. Ugh, if I was Cysta Por Ruverno, he'd be deferential to me. I lightly take his hand and kiss the top, with my eyes down at the ground.

Spencer looks the *bolttimber* over. "Sasha, would you be so kind as to invite me into your…" He actually clears his throat before saying, "home?"

Maybe the surgery wearing off is making it easier to swallow my pride. "It would be an honor, good sir."

I just got shivers down my spine.

Last night, I gave the kids a chore so they would be out for the visit. I didn't trust them in this environment, and I had a simple job I didn't want to do on the other side of Chicago.

I lead Burgealdor Spencer into the apartment. His bodyguards start rummaging through every nook and cranny.

"Sir, is that necessary?" I ask. But he's not paying attention. "Did you want to sit?"

"Hm? Oh no, that's quite all right. This will be—" He scrunches up his nose. "What is that smell?"

"Um, just people living?"

He takes out a *faet* handkerchief and covers his mouth and nose. "Oh, gods, yes. I remember my grandmother's lake *bur* had this smell. This and *ceren*." Spencer, speaking through the handkerchief, adds, "We need to discuss the matter of the child, yes?"

This is unavoidable. Even as I've dodged calls and pigeon messages (a letter sent via phone for the last month). I hadn't finished the job and it has been a lingering sore for everyone involved.

"You were hired because of your reputation, yes? A reputation that's taken quite the hit." He glides over to me, close enough that his stomach rubs my arm. "And you've left a threat out there, a threat against me and the profit margins of Chicago."

I turn my head to the side so I don't have to look him in the eye.

He whispers, "Some might worry it was intentional—that you're no longer supporting the proper side. What with your connection to that *weaorud*—what's his name?" he snaps his fingers at his assistant.

"Rafe Fortune."

Now I make eye contact with him. "What does he...*shit*."

"Yes. Shit."

They don't have to say it. This is exactly the kind of job Rafe would take. He gets to be a hero without committing to one side or the other. He can justify it by saying he is only protecting a child. Plus, he probably found out I was involved. To him, that's a bonus.

"So we need to keep up appearances, yes? We want—"

I start to wonder where his guards went. They disappeared towards the bedrooms in the back. I crane my neck to check they aren't fucking with my gun safe. I can see through a crack in the door...rapid movement and commotion. Two guards who were in Jorge's room dash into mine. The door closes behind them.

"—when we review the margins at the end of our year—"

Man, he's still going. My bedroom door opens slowly. Kid Kill slips through like an oiled-up *hama*. He has blood all over him and his *beadomece*. That is not going to help my case here with Spencer.

I try to shake him off. Kid Kill looks at me, asking a question with his eyebrows. I just widen my eyes and shake my head. I...I...I have *no idea* what you do here. It briefly crosses my mind to kill the Burgealdor. A couple of people have gotten away with it. Though they were able to get off the planet. The rest were flayed alive by *habari* procurement specialists. (Which is just a corporate way of saying *torturer*.)

"Burgealdor Spencer, please meet my trainee Ki—*Jonas*."

Jonas bows his head. "Ah, a Burgealdor—it's an honor, sir."

"What a well-behaved boy, yes?"

"Jonas, what happened to our guests, back in the bedroom?"

"Oh, man," Jonas starts. "Are they with him?"

I force a grin. "Yes, they're his guards."

Jonas licks his lips, turns around and runs back to the bedroom. "Hey Jessi, are they still alive?"

"Not all of them."

The Burgealdor looks at me and I shrug. "They're very eager to learn."

Jonas leans over the threshold, "Ok, leave the ones that are alive. Come on out, you can meet a real Burgealdor."

"Eh, fuck that."

Jonas looks back at us, chuckling. "All right, well don't kill anyone else, okay?"

There's a pause.

"I mean, this one is alive, but is bleeding out pretty fast so…" Jessi explains.

Burgealdor Spencer turns to me. "You understand there are going to be massive fines for this, right? The murdering of an elected official's *fehrwerd*. And since they're your charges, it'll fall on you." He turns to his assistant. "Please send Sasha a fine for a couple of murdered *fehrwerd*."

Half a minute later, my phone is flashing red. I open up the fine. *Gods, that's more than I'm getting paid for the job.*

"Gods, that's more than I'm getting paid for the job."

Burgealdor scratches his stomach. "So it is. Well, that seems a bit unfair since you didn't actually do the killing, yes? So how about this. How about you capture Kergan Satre II alive, yes? We have interests in her."

I ask, "Like what?" Because if this is some sexual *draest*, I'm—

Spencer drums his fingers on his belly and says, "There's rumors about her, and I want to see if they are true, yes?"

"What are…"

Spencer's assistant speaks in a measured tone, which indicates more threat than warning. "It is disrespectful to question the Burgealdor."

Jonas walks back over. His eyes are wide, and he's speaking too fast. "So, yes, a couple of them are dead—but I think the bleeding stopped for the one guy, so he'll live."

Jessi yells out from the room, "He's dead, too."

Spencer explains. "One more thing, Sasha. While I want the kid alive, I do expect you to kill anyone harboring her. No matter your…previous relationship to them."

"Burgealdor Spencer, he has a ship of people. I'd have to kill all of them."

Spencer shrugs and starts to leave.

The living guards limp their way out of my apartment. And they get blood everywhere. Jorge is gonna be pissed.

CHAPTER 23

AUNTIE BELLE'S HOUSE

Belle sets the kettle in the red-eye. It's an older model, analog. She stands back when she turns it on—the older models had a tendency to spray the beam when they started up. Getting hit by a stray redeye was painful and scarring. There was rust on the bottom which flaked off every time the door closed. The legs on it cracked and broke years ago, so she had it set on a pile of metal sheets, enough to keep it from scorching the floor. It takes a second. There's a bright yellow glow which shines through, since the door isn't flush.

Side note: they were called "redeyes" as a slang term. Funco Concern Inc. used *esnes* as the testers. They ended up blind, the light burning their retinas, leaving them a dark red color. On a positive note, the *esnes* were given five Funco Polyblend Coats as a settlement. Unfortunately, there were six of them. But, as the arbitrator said when the *esnes* complained, "Them's the breaks."

Belle retrieves the kettle and pours the piping hot *capulusno* into a plain black mug. She then opens the *andeleof* and grabs a carton of *beost*. She screws the light blue cap off and takes a sniff. It's a bit past its date, but the taste of the *capulusno* will cover it up. Well, that and the whiskey she adds. Belle adds a generous amount of whiskey.

She limps over to her comfy and well-worn *kitanda*. It has a perfect groove that wraps around her butt like a bird's nest around its eggs.

"Project, Game Channel," she orders, and the silver box in the front of the worker's room starts whirring. Light flickers from the top, then steadies. A green-colored word appears above it: *Loading.* There's a green light on the silver box which blinks rapidly to indicate the CPU is still working and not stuck.

Belle is sipping her *capulusno*, careful not to burn her tongue. An arm's length away from her is a blue humidifier, about three feet tall. Belle developed BHD (Burt-Hogg-Dube) four years ago. It was part of what drove her into retirement. The disease is manageable, thanks to medicine she mixes into the humidifier. When it was at full power, and properly mixed, the mist from it was light pink and in the air for an hour, waiting to be sucked in. Now it is spitting out a yellowish-brown mist, meaning it needs a refill of medicine.

Belle groans as she gets up and walks to a silver *armari*, which holds five bottles of whiskey and one bottle of medicine. She pulls out the white bottle. It's very light. She opens it and looks inside. There's nothing but a couple of drops.

Belle makes her way to the *kuoga locus* . She flips on a light and out of the corner of her eye, sees a furry visitor scurry into a hole in the wall.

"Don't run off, Valence."

The visitor sticks its twitching nose out of the hole. When it recognizes the scent, it comes back out. Valence is no longer than one's pinky, and almost as thin. Her left eye is missing and as is half her tail.

"Look at ya, a scared little *bonger,* ain't cha?"

Valence stands up on her hind legs. Belle rummages through the pocket of her black slacks and pulls out a thimbleful of crumbs. She lays them out in front of Valence, but Valence isn't impressed.

"All right, you, that's the best we can do. When my pension check clears, I'll pick us up some nice bread."

Valence seems to understand and starts to feast on the crumbs.

Belle shakes a couple of bottles, but they are both empty. She puts them back on the counter.

Walking back into the worker's room, she announces, "Phone. Call Louis."

It trills. Trills. Tri…

"Yeah, mom?"

Speaking fast, Belle explains, "I'm out of medicine, Louis. You were supposed—"

She's interrupted by the sound of kids yelling in the background.

Belle's phone projection is full of glitches. The colors are wrong and the image flickers.

Louis turns and asks, "Hey, keep it down, I'm on the phone."

A young girl's voice pipes up. "Who are you talking to?" Belle cranes her neck to try and see, but can't make her out.

Louis answers, "No one."

The words stab Belle and leave her staggered, but she shakes it off. "Louis, I'm out of medicine, I needed ya to send me more."

Louis sighs. "Mom, we talked about this. I can't do that anymore. The company tracks every bit of medicine that comes through."

She coughs, hacks, wheezes. "I know, but there ain't nothing you can do? At all?"

"You're going to have to buy your own, like everyone else."

"You know, the benefit of having spent all of my money sending my son to medical trade school was supposed to be *free medicine*."

"Always looking out for yourself, huh?"

Belle frowns and furrows her brown. "Come off it. You know I didn't… look, it's very expensive, you know that."

Louis diverts his hazel eyes to the side.

"Louis, without it, I'll wither away to nothing—this disease will eat my lungs."

"Yeah, mom, I know what it does. But we have kids in school, bills, clothes. I can't risk my job just because you—"

There's a beat. Louis pretends to be distracted.

Belle demands, "Because what?"

Louis doesn't look his mom in the eye when he responds. "You were the one who chose to do *pulveris*."

Now Belle is the one looking away.

"Frankly, it's selfish of you to even ask."

Belle meekly replies, "I know. I won't live without it, though, and I can't afford it every two weeks."

Louis clears his throat, then says, "If you were normal, you'd say you feel scared. But you can't feel that, can you?"

Belle, speaking softly without eye contact, replies, "I'm aware of my situation. That's enough."

"I gotta go, mom."

"Louis. Wait." Louis doesn't respond, but he doesn't hang up either. "I don't know why I can't talk to the kids at least, over the phone."

"Hm. Yeah, you do."

Belle tilts her head and adds a crack to her voice. It's half affected, half genuine. "Wouldn't hurt 'em. Raised you just fine, didn't I?"

"Mom, I don't think you'd hurt them. Freost doesn't feel comfortable with the kids being around an assassin. Her family is vehemently against it. They didn't trust me for years. She…we don't want our kids exposed to it."

"Louis, I don't even work anymore."

"Yeah, I know, I heard that over and over growing up. I have to—"

"I need my medicine, Louis. The coughing is worse."

"I have to g—"

"One last time. Please."

Louis takes a deep breath, then spits out in a rush, "*I'msorrymomIhavetogo*," and closes his screen.

Belle pours what's left of the bottle into the humidifier and sits back down. The projector is rebooting. Once it gets going, Belle watches "The Life Changing Challenge." She doesn't like it, but doesn't hate it.

It's going for two minutes before the projector shuts down again. Belle glares at the machine, as if she can intimidate it into working. Up projects the words, "Service Needed: Say 'AAA Projection' into your phone to get service scheduled." Then these words scroll up from the projector, "If you are ready to take the next step in entertainment, please say 'I'm a champion' into your phone and we will send you a new Burgealdor Model projection system. Bundle it with a new phone and save a ton. It's the sign of a smart worker, and we will let your company know of your bright decision."

Belle walks over to her table and sits down with her *capulusno*. It's cooled off considerably. She sits and taps the side of the cup with a chipped nail on her index finger. She looks at her reflection in the metal dish washer. The washer broke two years ago, but Belle never bothered to get it fixed. She never had company, so she never had enough dishes to need it.

"Old ya look, lady." She says to her reflection. Belle pulls on different parts of her face, trying to get wrinkles and crow's feet to disappear. Looks were never her calling card, by any means, but she had her suitors in her day. She studies her thinning white hair. Belle looks down at her hands, notices her knuckles, gaunt and prominent. The veins from the back of her hand protruding, blue, tracing all the way up to her shoulder. Her eyes used to spark the darkest of blues, were now sullen and grey. And her posture…

"What 'ave you let yourself become, old lady?"

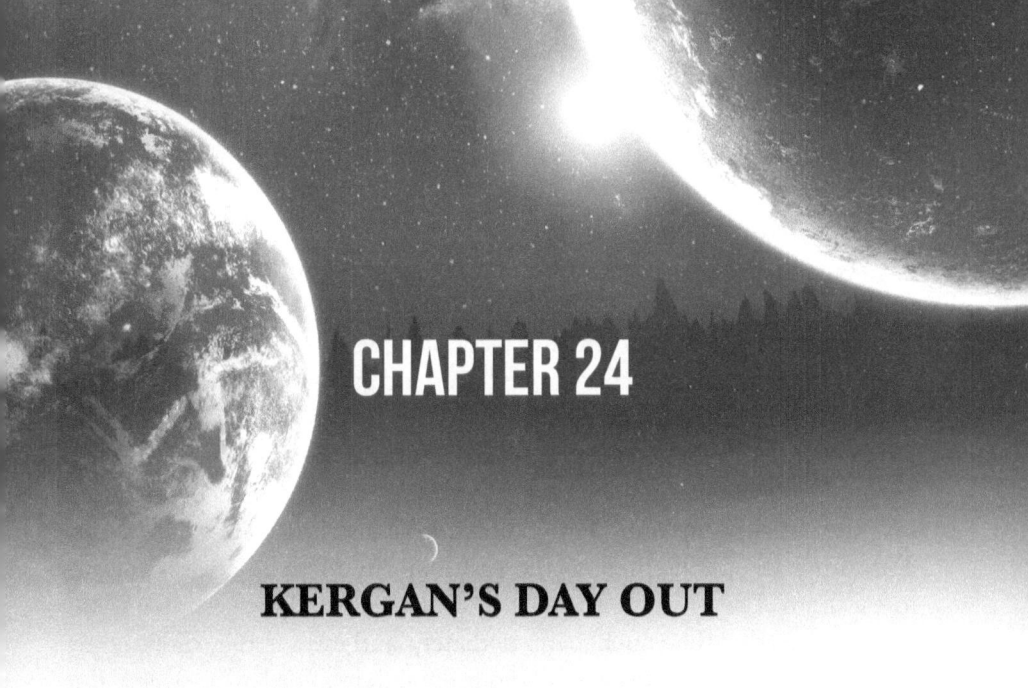

CHAPTER 24

KERGAN'S DAY OUT

"Gods, the feeling of the star on my face. It's so warm."

Kergan is walking down the business district in Chicago. In front of her is Cadyn. Beside her is Micel. Cadyn is moving her eyes constantly. Micel is calm.

"Cadyn, you're drawin' more attention to us, acting paranoid," Micel says.

"I'm doing my job. This isn't a holiday."

Kergan speeds up to saddle up next to Cadyn. "I'm going to *make* you have fun today."

Cadyn ups her pace to get back to a protective position. "We should be at home training you."

Kergan rushes to catch up. "Why? What is my training going to do to stop a bullet?"

Cadyn curls her lip. "Oh gods, you're right. We should start having *capulusno* parties instead."

Kergan puts her arm around Cadyn's neck. "Thank you for caring, Cadyn."

Cadyn elbows Kergan off with a grunt. Kergan smiles back at Micel. Micel points ahead, "There's the Barabara Autem Foretacen de CEO. We're starting there."

Cadyn shouts back at Micel, "Who did the preview?"

"Um, Mirkovic, I think. He might still be there. But it's ready to download."

Kergan asks, "Download what?"

"Layout of the building, exits, staircases, how many people are there…" Cadyn answers.

The wind has died down after a couple days of roaring through Chicago. There are still *draest* cans tipped over and garbage strewn about. The city has a team of *esnes* who clear the trash for food vouchers. (It is felt that food vouchers are best, so they can't blow the *feoh* on *ceren* or *pulveris*. They also put expiration dates on them, as it was rumored some *esnes* would save the vouchers up until they could afford a lavish meal at an *andoleofen*. This drove the public mad, as the vast majority of them couldn't afford to eat there. There was never any proof of this hoarding; common sense said *esnes* needed the vouchers immediately, and even if they didn't, they were so small they would never compile enough to afford an *andoleofen*. But rumors persisted despite facts.)

The air this time of year is dry with a slight chill. The city blankets the downtown with an aromatic mist which is supposed to be a neutral odor, but has a hint of lemon to it. The mist is a purifying agent developed by CEO Lero Coolage to try and keep germs under control. Fewer germs mean fewer sick people, which means fewer days of work missed.

Kergan covers her nose. "Why does it smell like lemon?"

Micel finishes explaining just as they enter the AFC. The interior betrays the exterior. The outside of the building looks modern, with crisp lines and plenty of glass. The star reflects off the metal and tinted glass giving the exterior a *kuangaza kama*. The block is clean; even the sidewalk is free of stray trash. But the inside is a throwback to centuries before. Rooms painted in dark hues, fake rocks jutting out everywhere, a lighting scheme which switches from room to room on a dime, depending on the era being depicted.

All of this made quite an impression on Kergan Satre II, who has been silent for the first ten minutes of wandering. She reaches out to touch some of the rocks and boulders, but is disappointed to find some are only holograms and the rest are soft and obviously fake.

The merger room has a holograph of the first two CEOs to merge their companies. After you enter, the room goes dark, then a soft male voice rains down from the ceiling, "While common now, the first merger occurred before there was even a name for such an event." A bit of a scene would play out in the middle of the room. "Rock Inc. and String Co. combined to become Catapult industries. The move saved over two hundred jobs and was celebrated to the ends of the Earth and back."

The group enters the gift shop, one of four in the AFC. Micel breaks away and meets up with a short balding man in a light blue jacket. Kergan watches the exchange as she pretends to browse the Nafuu Rebus section. She manages to pick out some *scelerisque* with raspberries but keeps her eyes trained on Micel, who's showing visible frustration with Blue Jacket.

"Cadyn, what's that about?"

Cadyn spits her reply. "None ya business."

Kergan presses Cadyn, "Their job is to protect me, and instead they're distracted. Why?"

"Well, it's Micel, right? So, it's either about a *taeflian* debt. Or *pulveris*. But it ain't your concern."

Without a warning, Micel picks Blue Jacket up with one arm, but Blue Jacket seems unimpressed, shrugging. Micel puts him back down. As Kergan approaches, she's pulled back by Cadyn, but can hear the parting words from the man: "This is a thing, Micel. I'm a warning. Make something happen soon."

Micel turns around, wearing a sullen face, the color drained from his usually red cheeks. He sees Kergan watching and flashes a smile. But Micel can't hold it.

"What was that?"

Micel bites his lower lip, "Nothing."

Cadyn says to Micel, "Rafe sent the preview for the surprise."

"What surprise?"

Micel frowns at Cadyn, "Subtle, Cadyn."

"What is the surprise?"

Micel replies to Kergan, "We're heading there now, so you'll find out soon enough."

They trio leave AFC. Kergan, again, tilts her face up to feel the star on her face. Across the street, two *magistratus* are hassling an *esne*. The *esne*—a woman—is discombobulated and confused. The *magistratus* are yelling at her, but she shakes her head and shrugs her shoulders.

"You need a fucking permit, do you understand?" one says in a mocking, drawn out way.

The other one pokes her with a metal wand and repeats the sentiment.

The *esne* falls back and shakes her head. At this point, the trio are mere feet away. Kergan starts to walk towards the scene, but is pulled back by Cadyn.

"You're s'posed to be *yoonkana,* right?"

Kergan curls her upper lip, "Well, what the *hell* is that?"

Cadyn pulls Kergan away. "My priority ain't to protect 'er, it's to protect *you*. Keep moving."

Kergan looks at Micel, who adds, "She's right, we can't draw attention."

They walk away as the yelling and pushing escalates. Kergan keeps looking back, and Micel keeps pushing her chin back around to face the front.

"Come on, then. We got a surprise for you." Micel brags.

Kergan isn't thinking about that. And she's visibly upset. "This is what my mom told me about Chicago."

"Yeah well, that's why you live on a ship. We all *gesen* there." Cadyn replies.

Kergan thinks for a second. "But Rafe is in charge."

"Huh?"

"Rafe is in charge, so you're not all the same."

Cadyn shakes her head. "He ain't in charge."

"Come on, Cadyn," Kergan begins. "There's an obvious hierarchy there."

Cadyn sucks on her teeth, then spits, "Ain't nobody my CEO. Not again."

"What do you mean, *not again?*"

Cadyn freezes for a second, then spits out, "Mind ya'self, kid. My past is none of your concern."

Micel points ahead to a *bryce* shop, just ahead of them. "There we go." He elbows Kergan. "Best *cripito barafu* you've ever had."

In front of them is a rainbow-colored storefront with pictures of smiling children in the window, their mouths plastered with melted *cripito barafu*. There's a red awning with the name of the shop stenciled on it: "Furaha Ni Glacias Cripito."

Kergan thinks for a second, then replies. "That's not hard; I'm not sure I've ever had any. My mom said food like *cripito barafu* is an infection that makes workers stupid and disorganized."

Cadyn groans., "Gods, kid, it's just *cripito*. You're not funding a CEO's murder squad."

Kergan looks at Cadyn, "I know, but the money filters up, does it not?"

Micel is covering his eyes from the star. "I believe it trickles down."

Kergan draws an imaginary chart with her fingers. "No, if you look at patterns of wealth—"

As they enter the store, the smell of hot *scelerisque* overwhelms. Cadyn, in a rare moment, closes her eyes and takes a deep breath. Kergan notices Cadyn starting to smile, but fighting it. Before Kergan can say anything, though:

"There she is."

Kergan Satre II recognizes the voice and whips around to find Gilead with his arms open. She runs up to him and they hug with her head buried in his chest. When they break their hold, Kergan's eyes start to well up. Gilead smiles at her and grabs her by the shoulders. "I'm told you are really coming along."

Kergan goes in for another hug. This time, they hold on for longer.

Micel is at the counter, perusing the flavors. "Hey, can I try the pistachio? Right there in the back?"

The worker uses a tiny spoon to scoop up the *cripito barafu* and holds it up to Micel. In Micel's hands, the spoon practically disappears. Before Micel can enjoy it, Rafe saddles up to him and gets right in his face.

Rafe nods toward the opposite side of the store. "We need to talk."

Micel groans, but follows Rafe. When they get to a corner, Micel tries to cut the lecture off. "I dunno what Cadyn said, but that was nothing at the AFC."

Rafe squints his eyes. "What?"

Micel crooks his head back. "Know what? Nothing. I got it handled."

Rafe shrugs. "Okay. Can I get to what I wanted to say now?"

Micel sighs out of relief and nods.

Rafe cracks his knuckles and explains. "Things may be more complicated than we thought. Sasha has apparently taken two trainees under her wings. Said to be real *cwyldrofs*."

"I'm shocked she's training anyone."

"Yes, well, here we are," Rafe begins. "I'm seeing an open contract on the girl circulating on the boards. Looks official from a *burgealdor* or a *meneja*."

Micel rubs his forehead. "So, we got no idea how many *bongers* are looking for 'er. That's great."

"It's a government contact, so only a few can take it on legally. The problem is—"

A melodic tone rings, signaling a customer's entrance. A man with white hair and a bit of a hunch enters the store. Or at least he tries—Cadyn cuts him off, sticking her neosiri out to block him.

Cadyn's sword is as still as a stone. "Closed now. Come back in a bit, eh?"

The man pets his pepper-colored mustache and thinks. He's wearing a yellow button-down shirt with a matching vest and an oversized black coat. His face is mostly covered by glasses and a brown fedora tilted over his face. His right hand shakes on the alabaster cane he's bracing. "The signal on the front of the store was green."

Everyone stops talking as they turn to watch the exchange. The worker behind the counter escapes to the back room.

Cadyn puts the sword down. "Well, this is sort of a *private party* thing."

The man scans the room. "Eh, there's too many of you to fight."

Cadyn furrows her brows. "You nuts, old man? Make yourself scarce, *now*."

He tips his hat in the direction of Kergan, winks, then limps out.

Gilead asks, "Do you know him?"

Kergan shrugs, thinks, and then says, "I don't think so."

Cadyn stalks over to them. "I'm not comfortable with you being here anymore. Time to go." Cadyn pulls her up by the arm.

Kergan pulls away from Cadyn's grip, "I barely ate any."

Rafe coming over, "Cadyn's right. It's best to keep on the move. You can take it with."

CHAPTER 25

BELLE'S SERENDIPITY

Belle slides open the giant metal door to her storage box. It's musty and has the smell of mold. She covers her mouth and coughs into a fist. The light from the star above is enough to illuminate the box, but Belle turns on the lighting mode from her phone anyway. She makes her way to the back and pulls down a blue sheet, exposing a rack of clothing.

These were her old disguises. Uniforms and badges she could use to gain access to office buildings or government facilities.

At her age, the easiest disguise for Belle to pull off was essentially camouflage—trying to blend in as a decrepit geriatric, of little concern to the producers and creators that filled Chicago. As soon as she has the disguise on, she studies herself in the body-length mirror propped up in the corner. "Good," she thinks as she put her index finger just underneath her nose. "But I'm missing something."

She took on a simple job, the killing of a dog. There wasn't a reason listed—but most likely the dog barks a lot or had bitten a kid. Belle always took these, but not because she enjoys killing dogs. Quite the opposite. Rather, she knew other *bongers* were heartless enough to dispel a dog if it meant getting paid. She would take the contract, kidnap the dog, take it to an *esne*. They always appreciated a good boy or girl.

Belle emerges from the storage box with a pepper-colored moustache adorning her upper lip and a brand new hat tilted over her face. The dog only lives two blocks over, so Belle heads over to scout the area and see if the dog lives in a doghouse in the back or if it lives inside. She will watch the house for three or four days to observe the dog's routine. Protected by her disguise, she'll be able to sit on the bench across the street and pretend to feed the *sprearwa* without drawing attention to herself.

When Belle turns the corner, she can't believe her eyes. Sure as the Andetenes Star in the sky, its that square-shaped *weaorud*. Ah, shit, what was his name? *MICEL!* Belle hadn't seen Micel in years, but had a casual acquaintance with him when Sasha and Rafe were…whatever they were.

She starts to raise her hand but notices Micel looking around, casing the area. There is another *weaorud*, but Belle doesn't recognize her. She is more intense, her gaze shifting all over the place and her hand casually draped over the handle of a weapon. *Bit over the top, if you ask me,* Belle thinks to herself as she notices a girl standing between them. *Weird.*

Belle commands her phone, "Display on. Search the CPR boards for the words Micel or Rafe." Nothing. Then, she checks the government listings. Micel brings no hits, but sure enough, Rafe's name pops up under a contract.

A mechanical male voice reads out the following: *"KERGAN SATRE II is requested brought in alive. Everyone one else involved in harboring her should be disposed of. Contract to be honored by Burgealdor Spencer."*

For Belle, this job is a hell of a lot more lucrative. But with it being posted on the board, there's also going to be more competition. She decides to pursue it, but stays far back, out of sight. Belle can't overpower the likes of Micel and Rafe anymore.

"Thank gods, I'm smarter than them," she mutters to herself.

While Kergan visits the AFC, Belle parks herself on a bench and tosses seed to the *sprearwa*. The tiny brown birds push and peck at each other to get their share. She concentrates on forcing air deep into her lungs, trying to dissipate the effects of her disease. Her left side feels like a thousand needles are poking at it.

"Stupid birds, you don't know how lucky you have it," Belle mutters as she tosses another handful of seed. A gold and black *sprearwa* flutters its wings, almost as if in response.

When Kergan leaves, Belle trails behind and spies her entering a *cripito barafu* shop with Micel and the other one in tow. Belle, again, finds a bench to sit on and tosses out seeds. Thankfully, this bench has an adjustable tensile strength, and it cradles her body. It's a relief to her aching lower back. She pulls out a flask filled with *pombe tenebris* and takes a few swigs. It mixes well with the pain pills she choked down an hour ago.

"The *magna eorl* of Rafe," Belle grunts to her bird companions. Then she has a spark of an idea—maybe something to test herself. She bracers herself on her alabaster cane and limps towards the shop. Rafe and Micel are off in a corner talking while the project and some old guy are at a booth eating and chatting. And standing at attention, right in front of the door, is the *weaorud* girl.

As Belle approaches, she gets a clearer view of the *weaorud* girl. She's not too tall, but her forearms are the size of Belle's neck. Belle can feel her gaze as she approaches the shop. The door has one of those sing-song bells, bringing more attention than was wanted.

The *weaorud* girl snaps, "Closed now. Come back in a bit, eh?"

Belle pets her pepper-colored mustache and thinks. Her face is mostly covered by glasses and a brown fedora tilted down. Her right hand shakes on the alabaster cane. This was not an affectation, but a side effect of the medication.

Belle coughs up some phlegm and uses it to disguise her voice. It rattles in her throat with each word. "The signal on the front of the store was green."

Belle can feel the room tense up. Her surgery keeps her nice and loose though, unaffected by the eyeballs looking her over. The left side of her lips pulls into a grin as the worker scampers to the back. It's been a while since she has seen that kind of fear.

The *weaorud* girl stands there, arms folded. "Well this is sort of a *private party* thing."

Belle knows she is no position, nor physical shape, to put up a fight—especially against this brick-house of a woman. But a part of her wants them to know who she is, that she's not an *ibora*. She raises her head slightly and looks over the room. "Eh, there's too many of you to fight."

The *weaorud* girl's laugh grates at Belle. She might not feel anxiety, but she sure does feel rage.

"You nuts, old man? Make yourself scarce now."

Belle runs her tongue along her top row of teeth. She briefly imagines jamming her *brazo*-plated *oeorfsear* into that girl's eye. But showing the better part of valor, she tips her hat in the direction of Kergan, winks, then limps out.

CHAPTER 27

JORGE, THE COMPANY MAN

"**T**his is *grornhof*," Gerwid whispers to Jorge. "It's just lacking the Ki-pangas tearing our guts out over and over."

Jorge is a bit uncomfortable. Not just because of the plastic stools they're sitting on, but because any conversation deemed threatening to the company's morale could be subject to sanctions and salary reduction. Even if it was outside of work.

Gerwid recently changed her hair to a bright blue. She's wearing a black hooded shirt and black pants with brown boots. Her eyes are bugged out, but not because she's excited—that's just how they have always been. She pulls out a jazz bag and inhales a thimbleful of *pulveris*. Her expression relaxes and she has that familiar glow around her.

Jorge's left leg is bouncing up and down nervously. "That's not smart—they can sanction your salary if you get caught."

Gerwid's voice has a hum to it now. "I mean, they make the powder used in *pulveris* at the factory right outside Chicago."

"Right, but that's not what the company means it to be used for."

Gerwid laughs and it sounds like four or five of her laughing. "Why do you think the company fought so hard against licensing the suppliers?"

Jorge shrugs and takes a guess, "Because regulation cages the soul of a company, the workers."

Gerwid shakes her head. "Do you really believe that *plable*?"

"I mean, we have to, right?"

"No, we really don't."

Jorge looks over at the booths, which are mostly empty, except for a group of interns chugging *ceren*. They are all fresh out of school and just dumb enough to enjoy drinking at a company bar. Gerwid's glowing begins fading, and she puts an arm around Jorge.

"Jorge, how long have we worked together now? A good few years." Jorge nods. "I think by now you can see this place for what it is, right?"

Jorge shifts in his seat, trying to use body language to hint that she should back off. "I guess, Gerwid. I just want to mind my own—"

He's interrupted by the door opening. Moose appears. Moose earned the nickname thanks to his protruding ears. He's startled by Jorge. "Oh, hey, Jorge." He says this in a drawn-out fashion, indicating it was time for Jorge to leave.

"Nah, he's *schway*," Gerwid vouches. "Get on with it."

Moose scrunches his face and points at Jorge. "This isn't some *ndege de phantasiam*. And Jorge is a company man if I've ever seen one."

Gerwid stands up and crosses her arms. "Well, I've drunk with this man for longer than you've been working, so I say he's fine."

"You hafta do better'n that, Gerwid."

"He was friends with Nalah—stood up with her in the face of Wildorlic."

Moose to Jorge, "You stood up to Wildorlic?"

"I—I mean I…was just supporting a friend."

"Point is, he's a man of honor. The last *kamuni dominus*. At the very least, he won't say anything." Gerwid snaps into a serious mode. "You'll keep your mouth shut—right, Jorge?"

Jorge puts his hand over his mouth and nods.

Moose saddles up to the bar. "So, it's a go with the Burgealdor. He's looking to make the push this term. And get this, he's heading the committee."

Jorge wonders what they're talking about, but doesn't think it's his place to say anything. He just turns his head and pays attention to whomever is talking.

Gerwid clasps her hands together. "That's like a dream. We may really get this to happen."

"I know. Since the Burgealdor is heading the committee, he promises he can force a bill through."

Gerwid is sporting a giant grin. "Wow, this time next year, we *gaderigen* might be a reality."

Jorge shakes his head. "Wait, wait, wait—what is a *gaderigen*?"

Moose doesn't look at Jorge and spits the words out of the side of his mouth. "Gods, you really are a company man, huh? Try readin' something not approved by a CEO for once, bud."

"A'ight, lay off. How many people remember *gaderigens* anymore?" Gerwid turns to Jorge. "You ever hear of the Scorching Biggencere War?"

"Yeah, I remember it from fifth year. Something about workers trying to ruin the economy by setting fire to the Happy Colman Factory. They were all caught and put to death."

Moose has a cutting tone in his voice. "I'm sure that's what a *weaorud* like you believes."

"Moose!" Gerwid scolds. "Anyway. So, if you read some of the *sui iuris* (indie) history texts, it's when the *biggencere* at the factory tried to band together and ask for safety measures after a little girl died in the *hund* pulverizing machine."

ADDENDUM

WHAT WAS THE WAR ABOUT? QUESTIONING THE MOTIVES FOR THE SCORCHING BIGGENCERE WAR

BY PROFESSOR OLIVAND REKI
Summarized by Olivand Reki II

Tumaini Ra, aged fourteen, died in the clutches of an industrial strength *hund* pulverizing machine. Designed by Joint Enterprises of Chicago, the machine was used to turn the tougher parts of the *hund*—the skull and bones—into a fine powder by crushing and churning. While at the time, these machines had safety mechanisms, which caused them to automatically stop if someone released the control, the machine at the Happy Colman Factory was an antique and lacked this update. No good reason was given by the company for never upgrading, and the machine was switched out with a new one the day after Ra fell in. The old machine, which was over thirteen feet tall and weighed as much as a ship, seemed to disappear overnight, severely hindering any investigation.

The narrative following is a tightly wound yarn of half-truths and fabrications on the part of both our government and our CEOs. For instance, early reporting by major news companies painted the child, Ra, as incompetent at her job. This is contradicted by her previous recognition in safety training and a spotless record in the previous eight months. She had even been put in charge of training the night crew on proper use.

This story wouldn't stick, so using the company-owned newspaper, they tried to smear the girl as a habitual user of *pulveris*. This was contradicted by accounts of her parents and friends denying ever seeing her partake in any sort of criminal infraction. On top of that, the public relations manager who wrote the story was sanctioned and fired.

I am laying out the following sequence of events, as I believe it lends itself to only one conclusion.

- The family of Tumaini Ra claimed it was offered stock in Happy Colman Factory
- The Ras rejected the offer two days later and retained a lawyer
- Pictures of Ra's remains circulated in the *sui iuris* press, fomenting anger by *biggencere*
  - These pictures were later proven to be false, as her body turned into dust after the machine crushed her
- The beginning of next year, Judge Kipaj Praeclum was randomly assigned to the case
  - Judge Praeclum was one of the two remaining judges who were not directly appointed by the Burgealdors and therefore had no connection to any corporation
- For reasons unknown, Judge Praeclum went on vacation as the trial was about to start and a new Judge, Naomi Betts, replaced Kipaj
  - Betts was an appointee of Burgealdor Gabriel who, in turn, was backed by Happy Colman Factory
- The trial ended in a clear-cut win for Happy Colman
- The *biggencere* walked off the job and marched through downtown Chicago
- Happy Colman's mascot Squirly Squirrel gives an interview where he promises the "streets will be flooded with the blood" of anyone who tries to form or join a *gaderigen*
  - The actor inside the Squirly Squirrel suit was the nephew of a CEO
  - He had a glow about him indicating he recently used *pulveris*
- The actor who portrayed Squirly Squirrel is killed in a riot as he leaves the factory
- The day after the death of the nephew, every *magistratus* is called in to quell the strike

At some point in our history classes, every young child is taught the Scorching Biggencere War. And it is stressed that the blame fell on the shoulders of rabble rousers who wanted to form a *gaderigen*. We're given excuses for Tumaini's death, even though they have been long disproven.

When the official history books get to the strike, they don't spare any detail of the war between *magistratus* (who were given carte blanche to end it) and *biggencere*. They even point out that despite the death of twenty-five protesters, the only person punished in any fashion was Chris Mogwai, who punched a *magistratus* when they were wailing on his husband with a club. Chris was sentenced to a lifetime of servitude. He was paroled at the age of eighty years, kicked out with no money or housing. Chris would die of Advanced Pulmonary Fibrosis a week later. All of this is meticulously detailed in our books.

The story is a Mace Rung, like the child's stories of rabbits who steal from *wenan (cats)*. And then some terrible fate befalls the rabbit. It's an attempt to intimidate anyone who would fancy the idea of a *gaderigen*.

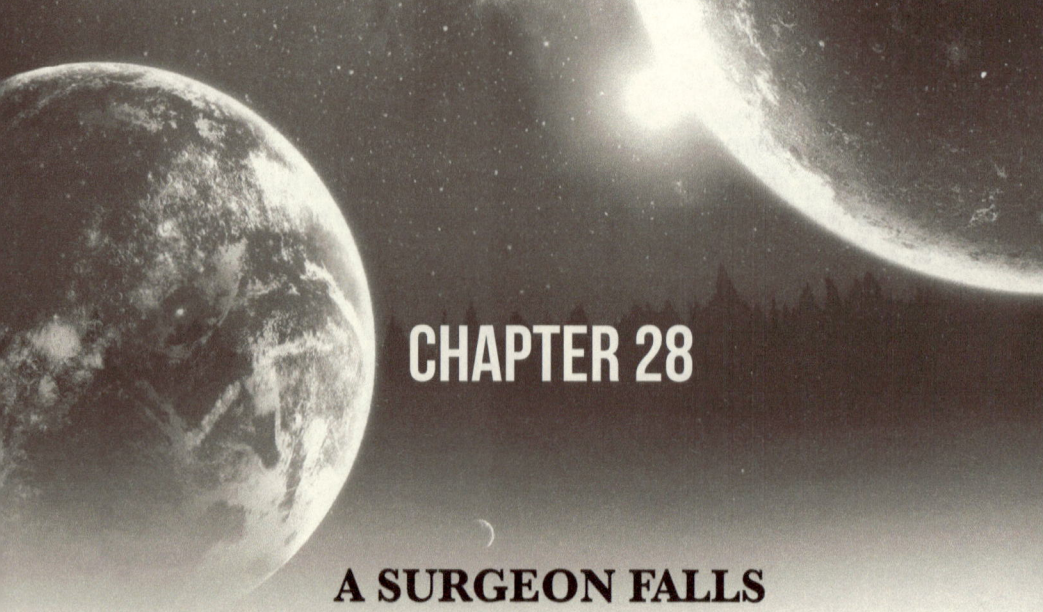

CHAPTER 28

A SURGEON FALLS

The *lareow*, Burg Merid, was a young genius, or *praeter asili* (wonderkind), who was on her way to becoming a full-fledged surgeon. She was the youngest person ever accepted into the surgical program and would have studied on Abakalic. The issue Burg was coming up against was her promise of servitude to the company that provided her schooling. She owed them four years, probably hacking away at a computer, living in the *huduma quartrum*. The *quartrum* was acceptable—companies tended to keep them stocked with plenty of entertainment and drinks. You were still stuck there, though, for almost the entirety of your debt.

Burg knew the lifestyle which awaited her. Surgeons had palaces on each planet and dined on hand-fed *hunds* and *fearh*. With their feasts, they drank *ceren*, which cost as much as most *biggencere's* paychecks. She planned to sit front row at every play, every *morgen pleghus* projection, even every *huntung* (though she was not a fan).

Living trapped by a corporation, like a *fearh* in its pen—well, that was too much for her. She earned the privileges coming to her. She was smarter than any teacher she encountered. She worked harder than any CEO. She sacrificed more than anyone her age. Why was this debt forced on her? Wouldn't she be more valuable as a surgeon?

One night, while drinking plenty of *ceren* at a teacher's annual party, she met Surgeon Rip. Rip regaled her and several students with stories from his time as a student. Specifically, he bragged about making *feoh* on the side, performing "off the books" surgeries, and graduating without any debt. That was all Burg needed to hear.

What Rip didn't brag about was how his father was a surgeon on LaRocca and had the necessary connections to keep any *magistratus* from investigating or arresting Rip.

Burg set about finding a spy spot in the residential part of Chicago. Somewhere out of view of casual passers by, our of the view of the *magistatus*. She settled on a windowless cellar below a house owned by the Markmen family. The Markmen, Saad and Liam, were an elderly retired couple who had lost their pensions. Saad's skin was loose and wrinkled, and her loose jowls vibrated when she talked. Her hair, a light yellow color, was thinning in the back. She had a bit of a hunch, which forced her to use a cane.

Liam was taller and thinner than the stout Saad. Liam wore circular glasses, which perched on the edge of his nose. His left hand was crippled, thanks to palindromic arthritis he developed in his forties. Even at his age, Liam was self-conscious and embarrassed about it. He would often stuff the hand into a glove when entertaining company or going out in public.

A year before Burg answered the couple's ad for a rental space, Blue Fish Market, the company they both worked for, declared a settler's bankruptcy. This allowed the people at the top of the company to use the pension fund to settle salary issues with current employees.

"Settler's Law," introduced by Clyde Settler, was sold to the public as a way to ensure workers were paid after bankruptcy proceedings. Previously, the workers had no such protections and had to hope for manna from the gods. Now, the pension funds would be opened up to make sure workers' pay was commensurate with their last day of employment. This proved to be a boom for CEOs, who received massive payouts in the form of a *quia debitum fikra which was a LaRoccan concept which mean a debt for genius.*)

The Markmen had also been denied permission to have kids four times. These factors, and seeing how friends of theirs were also treated, lead to the Markmen more than welcoming Burg. They were excited to assist her in circumventing the company she was indebted to.

Their house was—we'll say *cozy*. It was just outside Chicago in an *andred* called Forgrinden Park. Its main attraction was that it was adjacent to a childhood development park. They had even stored baby toys and a crib in the crawlspace. These items were bequeathed to the Markmen by Saad's older sister. She had won permission to have four children, though she was given special consideration, as her wife was a *magistratus*.

When the Markmen decided to rent out the cellar, which was more of a finished basement than anything, to make ends meet, they finally threw out the toys and the crib.

Word of mouth spread. A *praeter asili* was performing surgeries off the books. Look, you can find plenty of "dreamers"—a man who tried and failed his entrance exams, or, maybe if you were unlucky, a woman who "lost" on her way to graduation from a Surgeon School. (A percentage of people at the bottom were kicked out of school. This was labeled as *losing*.) But to find someone who was going to graduate, running a *buibui* was like stumbling upon *yttrium* in your back yard. Most people just didn't risk it.

To be clear, the offense was strictly about control. The government kept tight control over who could become a surgeon. It tracked any kind of slice and dice job done for assassins. Very few surgeons had the licensing to perform slice and dice jobs; rumor was, there were no more than a handful. The government was especially wary of someone getting a *planus wakati*, like the one Jessi has. This was strictly forbidden and one of the few crimes which would end in the government putting a worker to death. (The idea of someone being born with it, like Kergan, was thought to be a myth.)

Word of mouth was a double-edged neosiri; the more people knew, the higher the chances of being found out. Burg Merid was an artist, though. Not just fumbling her way through procedures like a beginner (with the help of Saad or Liam at her side), but gliding through them like a *spearwa* in the sky. It was as natural to her as breathing. Maybe that's why she took on Frank Fisher, an aspiring assassin.

The slice and dice job was a success; she removed his anger, as requested. However, Frank was the son of a CEO. A CEO who had groomed his child to take over as a CEO, not to chase some silly dream of being a Cysta Por Ruverno. But Frank was taken with the idea of harems and unlimited worldly pleasure at his disposal. A CEO had to study for years and work uncompromising hours. In Frank's teenage mind, by the time he became CEO, he'd be an old, dried-up prune like his father. He deserved to enjoy life *now*.

It was night when Burg arrived at the Markmen house to open shop. The door was unlocked, but that just meant Liam had already started preparing for tonight's procedure…though the light in the cellar was turned down low. When she took her first step inside, a repugnant smell filled her nostrils. It was like a school of *fyscynn* had swam up her nose and died. Burg could make out a shadow at the end of the room. It looked like Liam. She called out, but got no response.

Burg tried to slide her finger up the switch to turn up the lights but ended up cutting her finger. The switch was smashed, leaving jagged plastic exposed. She sucked on the finger and called to Liam again. Again, no response. Liam grabbed the wireless lamp and walked over to the shadow. As she got closer, she was distracted by a squishing sound under her feet. Looking down, it seemed like she was stepping on a pink rope. After a second, though, her *lareow* brain kicked in and she realized it used to be someone's body.

Seconds after realizing she was stepping on part of someone, she blacked out.

CHAPTER 29

SASHA AND ALVA

I can't feel my legs. Alva is holding me up by my armpit with her arm wrapped around my waist. Jorge is holding open the door to Bwana Freosan, my deep-freeze guy. Four times a year, I have my knees cleaned and vacuumed. Once a year, including this time, I have them do a total replace job on the ligaments and other…stuff. I don't know what all they do, but it costs a mint and leaves me in this state, unable to walk for twenty-four hours. Tomorrow, though, my knees will feel like I'm sixteen again. Mostly because the replacements parts came from a sixteen-year-old.

Workers look down on it, but I don't understand why. These kids have something in demand; they sell it for a nice sum. They can take that money and enroll in a training class or something to get out of their predicament. The average worker has no problem working for companies that'll hire me to eliminate competition, but they get queasy at the idea of some *unmagus* losing a few ligaments? It's *zushe*.

"Hey, you wanna get a stick of sleeved *hund,*" Jorge suggests more than asks. He's starting to sweat and, I'm guessing, is getting tired of hauling me around.

"Sure, Jorge. Just make sure the cart has up-to-date tags."

Across the street from us is the Holihan Magnus Inc. Park. Built five years ago, the park was where food vendors gathered for the lunch rush. Most had a keen setup with a barrel of food and a portable redeye. They couldn't compete in pricing (those were set by Mass Co.), so they fought over the best spots and tried to attract attention with gaudy signs.

To keep quality standards high, they were inspected by Mass Co. agents once a month. At which point, the agents would throw away any unused product. If you wanted a tag, you had to use Mass Co. as your food source. And when you used it as a food source, you had to agree to its pricing.

Alva requests a sleeve of favi vyombo which is a meat substitute made of beans pressed together and drenched in salt to provide flavor. And, once again, I'm left alone with her. I should try to relate.

"You know, I tried *favi vyombo* once," I start, "and it wasn't the worst thing I've ever had." Almost immediately I realize—good start, bad end.

"Yeah, it depends on where the beans come from. There are a few unlicensed places who get theirs from the people of the forest."

"That's illegal," I state as fact, not as judgement.

Alva shrugs. "I mean, you never had something off the market?"

"I did once. Caught Cyclospora…"

Alva slaps her knee and laughs. "Sounds like a VD."

"Cyclospora?" I ask.

"Yeah, sounds like something you catch off a sex worker."

"Oh, yeah. I get it. I thought it sounded like a weather report."

Alva squints at me; she changed her eye color to sky-blue last week. "I like that you don't laugh."

"Most people hate it."

Alva explains her reasoning to me. "Most people are worried about their corporate gods seein' 'em. It's disgusting. Fake. As if it's not enough that you have to perform at the office."

"People perform at their office? Like an act?"

"That's right—you never worked in an office. Yeah, sort of." Alva cracks her knuckles and stretches her arms. "How do your legs feel?"

"They don't."

"Right, but you feel nothing?"

"Not for at least a day. Which is fine. I don't have any jobs lined up for a few days."

She squints at me again and pokes at my leg with her index finger. I slap her hand away. "All right, that's enough."

"Weird." She is still staring at my legs. "It's like they're not even yours. Existing in some kind of limbo."

She's kinda right. "You're kinda right."

"When you get back on your feet, what's your next job?"

I don't know if it really makes a difference if I tell her. But I prefer not to. Where the fuck is Jorge?

"I really prefer not to talk about it."

"Oh." Alva pulls back and looks at her knees. "I didn't mean to intrude."

Ugh, I'm supposed to be getting close with her, right? "I'm doing a township foreclosure. Basically this *andred* is bankrupt. And a company wants to reclaim the land. And me and a bunch of *bongers* show up and clear the area."

"So you kill workers because the local government can't pay its bills?"

I shrug. "I don't know. It knew what it was signing up for when it moved into the *andred*. That's the risk you run. And we don't kill *all* of them."

Alva grimaces and shakes her head.

I mean, what is she not getting about this? "We just kill a few at first to scare the rest of the *andred* into compliance. Once they comply, you know, they're left alone to get their stuff and move out."

"You can't possibly think that's a good thing to do? I mean, I know about your surgery, but you don't feel anything for them?"

I get a brief flash of the girl with the blood-stained frog in my mind. Thankfully, Jorge interrupts before I must answer.

There's an *esne* limping along the sidewalk in front of us, bracing on a plastic cane. I hardly notice her until Jorge taps her on the shoulder. And then, for the love of the gods, gives her his sleeve of *hund*. Why?

"Why did you do that?" I ask as he hands me my sleeve.

"I dunno. Sometimes I see them and think *sped mchezo ludum*."

"Jorge, I have no idea what that means."

"It means *luck is a fickle game*."

Alva looks up at Jorge. "I thought it was *love*, not *luck*."

"Here." I use my phone to send him some *feoh*. "Get yourself another one, on me."

"*Schway*, Sash." He makes a fist and twists it back and forth. I return the gesture. I want to smile, but I fight it with a snort and mouthful of *hund*.

CHAPTER 30

CATCHING A GAME

"Hey, I'm glad you paid something this time, Micel. It makes it easier." Ashmir winks at Micel. Ashmir looks in a black bag and does some mental math. "It's not quite as much as my boss was expecting, ya know?"

Micel shrugs. "It's what I could get right now. We've been spending almost all our energy on this…" Micel things for a second, remembers how the Kergan job should be somewhat a secret, and says, "motor, this *motor revamp* for the ship."

They're sitting on metal slab in front of Big Sal's Tooth Emporium and Hair Cuttery. There's about a person's worth of space between them and neither is making direct eye contact. The sky is dark, a mix of violet and orange. It's pretty, but also portends bad weather.

"On you, Micel. The longer you take, the more *vig* we make." Ashmir takes a breath, closes the bag and stuffs it in her back pocket. "Speaking of which, hearing a nasty *uvumi* that you're taking chances with some other rustlers?"

Micel chuckles. "Rumors, huh?"

"That would not quite be in the spirit of our arrangement, right? Money ya gamblin' is money we ain't seein'."

Micel replies, with a stern face, "I'm smarter than that, Ashmir."

Ashmir looks to the left, then to the right. She leans in and whispers, "Between you and me, 'the one on top,' they ain't being too patient."

Ahsmir relaxes and leans back. "I mean, I love you Micel, you're real *schway*, but we live in a pyramid society, right? Each block leans on the one below it. And I'd hate to see someone I love crumble under the pressure—right, M?"

"You look out for me as much as anyone, Ashmir," Micel says through his teeth.

"How's the crew?"

Micel nods at Ashmir. "*Schway* as ever."

"They miss me?"

Micel, "You never come up."

"I heard I'm banned from the ship by Rafe?"

Micel scratches her nose. "It was politely suggested that I don't let you 'any-fuckin-where near the ship'."

"Yeah, well, it ain't my fault y'all such reckless gamblers."

"Some of it is finding Adrian hung from his stomach by his intestines."

"I don't do that part." Then she laughs. "I'm pretty sure that was Rafe's old flame, what's-her-face."

"That seems over the top for Sasha," Micel replies.

"Hey, man, these assassins are animals, M. You pay them enough, they'll hunt down their own children."

"I guess."

"No, seriously, the 'one on top' hired one and killed his own son."

There's an awkward beat of silence.

"So, I can't just sit around spitting with you, M—though it's lovely, I got other people to meet." Ashmir pulls out a bag of *pulveris*. She offers it to Micel. Micel accepts and does a pinch. Then she takes a hit herself. "The guy I have next—meeting 'em in the residential district—is a real rudder. One of those people so far in debt, he doesn't even keep track anymore."

Micel licks his top row of teeth. "I can't imagine."

She stands up. "It's fuckin' sad. The man on top is gonna end up farming this out to *bongers* soon. Guy has three kids and everything."

"That's sad."

Ashmir dusts her palms, then checks her nails. "Some people lose themselves in it, ya know. They don't even realize it. You get me, M?"

"Aye, that's not—"

"I gotta go. Take care."

Micel leans back and watches customers flow in and out of the barber shop. "You really shouldn't sneak out like that."

Kergan Satre II pokes her head out from behind an advert projection. (The ad was for faux wooden horses…a children's toy.) She's wearing a green dress which resembles an ill-fitting towel, and a matching wrap around her head. Micel doesn't make eye contact—not out of anger with Kergan for sneaking out, but because the *pulveris* hasn't worn off and Micel feels embarrassed being caught by Kergan.

"Who was that? The same person from the museum?"

Micel considers for a moment. Then says, "That was my bookie."

There's a beat.

"I like to gamble—that's who I do it through."

"Do you win?"

Micel chuckles. "Not nearly often enough."

"What do you bet on?"

"*Huntungs*, mostly. I'm goin' to one right now."

"You bet on it?"

Micel replies without shame, "Yup. It's what I do."

"Can I come with?"

"I can't send you home alone." Micel's phone flashes a green light and Cadyn's name pops up. "Ignore."

"Who was calling?"

"Cadyn. She'd go *woda de faereld* if she knew what we were up to."

"She cares, but she's nuts."

Micel replies with a belly laugh that ends in a fit of coughing.

A while later, the two of them are sitting inside Fudoh Private Club and Field. Kergan is on her tiptoes, her eyes frozen wide. She's picking at her cuticles to the point that they bleed.

"Let's go, put it on the ball!" Micel's voice booms.

Kergan puts her hand on Micel's shoulder and cranes her neck to get a better view. "You couldn't get better seats?"

Micel waves his back and forth, "Ain't no better seats than gambler's row."

"Gambler's row?"

Micel nods, "Yeah, it's where gamblers sit since they spent all their money gambling.

Kergan is bouncing up and down, "What's the name of the guy with the ball?"

"Rafael."

"He's really good, huh?"

"Yeah." Micel is not expressing any excitement—more of a tense anxiety, clenching and unclenching his fists with every throw. His phone starts flashing again, this time with a message from Rafe. "Open."

"You need to get Kergan back now. There's been a change in status."

"What was that, Micel?"

"Nothing." Micel then yells, "Fuckin finish it, a'ight?"

The stadium goes silent. The throw comes with a loud *thwack* and the opposing player immediately starts jumping up and down, followed by a mix of groaning and jeering from the crowd. The opposing player is joined by his teammates in celebration.

"Ow, that's a rough one." Kergan snorts, with her arms crossed.

Micel is just staring. Then, he puts his hand over his stomach and sits down, "I fucked up. Real bad."

Kergan puts her hand on his shoulder. "Hang on."

The crowd is rumbling again and Rafael is getting ready to throw. Micel looks around. "What happened?" Behind his eyes, Micel feels a slight headache coming on.

The crowd falls silent and the throw comes. Again, the sequence plays out, this time with a dull *thwack*, but with the players still celebrating and the crowd still groaning.

"Shoot, I can do it again," Kergan says to Micel. "It's all about odds, really. Eventually, he'll miss the ball."

Micel closes his eyes as a sharp headache attacks. It's so painful, Micel can only groan and slowly blurt out, "Yeah…do…it."

This time, the ball zooms past the opposing player. The crowd applauds and cheers. Rafael is hugging his teammates. Micel's head is hanging between his knees, a smothered whimpering sounds escaping his lips. Kergan massages the back of his neck and helps him to his feet.

As they leave the stadium, Micel asks, "So, no one noticed anything?"

Kergan wiggles her fingers as if performing with a marionette. "It'll seem like dreams to them, or maybe memories. But their minds will rationalize and file away the other results."

Micel, "Why do I remember?"

"We were physically connected. I'm not sure of the logistics of it, but it has something to do with you seeing time the same way I do for a brief moment."

Micel points at his temple. "That why I got a 'edache?"

Kergan taps her nose.

Micel looks away and sucks on his teeth. "Hey, let's go grab a treat before we head back."

Micel leads Kergan away from the crowd as she asks, "Did that help you win a lot of *feoh*?"

"More like it got me even with one of my bookies. Turn left here." They turn left down an empty street. The wind kicks up and pushes wrappers and leaves across their path.

"How many do you have?"

"Can you not ask me about this anymore?"

Kergan whisperers a response. "I'm sorry, but if I can help—"

Micel stops walking. "You can't fucking help me, a'ight? This is *my* hole. I dug it. Mind yer gods damn business."

Kergan curls the left corner of her lips. "Hey, fuck you!"

Micel releases a heavy exhale and glares at Kergan. Kergan shifts her weight and looks at the ground.

"What you did is very dangerous."

Kergan pleads. "No one noticed."

"If someone figured it out—figured out you were *cheating*—weight could come down on me."

Micel and Kergan stand there silently. The wind gives out a whistle. Another call comes through from Cadyn. This time, Micel answers it. "Yeah, Cadyn, we're coming back."

Micel pauses. Kergan leans in to listen but can't make anything out except some mumbling. She raises her eyebrows at Micel, asking him for information, but he just shakes his head. Kergan wears a bit of a pout and rolls her eyes.

"Looks like we're heading back."

"Bah, back to the *niti-dusque*."

"That was, what? Encasement?"

Kergan replies. "It's a forest slang for *prison*."

"Ah, damn, it has been a bit, ain't it?"

CHAPTER 31

RAFE AND SASHA

I didn't sleep at all. Spent the night trying to fight off memories. Distracted myself with a couple of projections. Tried masturbating (you'd think the one good thing about this surgery wearing off is my ability to complete, and yet nothing—like my body forgot how to). I even, for the love of gods, tried reading an old Riestovikian book of poems. I don't even *like* poems. Thought about an old man I blasted for some company because he had reached the *hatua kuvunja* point (basically the point where he was taking out more than he put in) of his pension fund.

I tried sorting my wardrobe, but everything I own is either black or dark blue, so I had to sort by sleeve length. Polished my sidearms by hand—damn, it has been a while. Thought about a mother of three I shot in the throat when I first started. Her kids shouldn't have been there, but they were. Nothing I could do. Cooked up some *hund*—or, more accurately, burned some *hund*. I'm going to need Jorge to show me how to cook properly before he and Alva move out. Dusted the worker's space, polished the floor. Dwelled on Kergan with the frog holding her dead mother, screaming. I used a tiny brush on the projector to clear out the dust and particles. They said it makes the picture clearer, but I dunno, I don't see a difference.

I sat in my window when the Andetenes Star was coming up. Watched it while sipping on some fresh-squeezed *wuddupple* juice. My mind flashed on the stomach of a project I had sliced open when a company thought he was selling leads to a competitor. Weird thing was, I'm pretty sure both companies were owned by the same corporation. Tried to masturbate again, this time in the bath. No go.

I'm leaving before anyone gets up, or the kids show up to train. I reached out to Rafe and set up a meeting. (Rafe…Now *he* could get me to complete.) It's early enough for him that most of his crew will be recovering from drinking and pinching *pulveris* the night before. Probably a bad look on him to meet with, well…I guess I'm the enemy.

In the morning, the hovering lamps on the sidewalks emit a seasonal fragrance. Right now, it's slow-baked *wudduPple* tarts with a hint of sage. There's a conspiracy theory that suggests this is used by Auntie Makers Corp to boost up *cecel* sales. They do sponsor many of the lamps. I dunno, I try not to fill my head with theories from the edges of society. The rain from last night left the air damp and cool. It's the first day of the work week and the streets are spotless. Those in servitude spend most of the night cleaning up alongside sweeping bots. The moving sidewalks aren't up and running yet; those don't begin until closer to the workday. Right now, the only people up and running around are service workers and criminals. Rafe and I fall on opposite sides of that line.

When I turn the corner down LaSalle Parkway, he's standing against a wall poking at a projection. It's some game from the phone where you pick out items at a store and try to match the amount of the budget the game gives you. The closer you get, without going over, the better your score.

I walk up and gently kick him in the shin. He signals for me to wait. So I kick him harder.

"Come on, I'm moving onto the car lot next."

I shrug. "I have no idea about those games. I thought you didn't play them because they were 'soaked in pro corporate messages' or some shit?"

Rafe shuts the game down. "Yeah, but I'm real good at this one."

There's a flash in my brain, a memory from when I left Rafe. Him calling me cruel. Me saying he knew what I was. I cough and close my eyes.

Rafe tilts his head to the side and asks. "You all right?"

"Headache."

"You look like the business end of a *hund*."

"Sleep's an issue." I reply with a sigh.

"You need someone to help wear you out?"

"Possibly—as long as you don't cry when I leave this time."

Rafe furrows his brow. "I didn't cry."

"Micel said you did."

"That big rudder."

I shrug. "It's not like I could. Maybe you did it for both of us."

Rafe looks confused. I recognize that look all too well.

"So, how's the girl I was hired to kill?"

Rafe answers. "She's still alive."

Chicago at this time in the morning is still—no wind, no rain. There's a slight humming sound from climate controls firing off in the surrounding buildings. It's quiet enough I can hear a *spearwa* hopping along the sidewalk. It's all white with a yellow beak. Barely bigger than the palm of my hand. The *spearwa* crooks its head to look at me, then hops behind a garbage can. There's a hiss. I can see the *spearwa* start to fly up from behind the can but a hairy paw slaps it down. A few seconds later, a tabby cat emerges with the *spearwa*, still twitching, clamped in its mouth.

Under my breath I say, "Poor thing."

Rafe studies me for a second, raises his eyebrows, then continues. "Anyway, she's alive and well taken care of."

"I'm hired to kill anyone who is helping Kergan Satre II."

"You set up this meeting to...*kill* me? Make me tell you where the ship is cloaked?"

"Listen, the contract was open to all government contractors, so it's not just me coming for her now. And there's a lot of money at stake."

Rafe shrugs. "I don't know why I'm here yet."

"Your crew, while...spirited, are *idiots*. Addicts, too."

"They have their *daemones*."

"Addicts do desperate things."

Rafe nibbles his lower lip. "What is this?"

"My surgery. It's worn off."

I massage my temple, trying to relieve a rhythmic thumping in my skull. Rafe raises his eyebrows.

"I went to a foreclosure and spent the time saving people." I chuckle. "I almost killed Drake."

"You should have." Rafe tugs at his brown pants, which are barely held together by patches of mismatched fabric. They're tight on him, forming a nice picture of his...body.

"That's it—I couldn't. Though, I was able to tell my *leornes* (trainees) to execute—"

"You have *leornes*?"

"Don't interrupt me, you know . . . "

"You *must* be off your surgery," Rafe says with emphasis on the word *must*.

"I can't stand that. Look, I'm in a place where I don't want to kill Kergan. For some reason, I want to help her."

"Well—and I may be mistaken—but I *believe* you off'd her ma."

"I did finish that project, yes. As I was hired to." We stare at each other for a few wordless seconds before I continue. "This isn't guilt. I keep flashing back to the child, with her mother's blood…I just need to help."

"The only way to help is to end the contract. Can you kill the *burgealdor* who put out the contract?"

"If I want a contract on me, sure."

"Maybe that's the sacrifice you need to make things right?" Rafe suggests.

I'm suddenly aware of how much space there is between us.

"Look, I'm not a *takifu sanctus*, I just want to get rid of the distractions in my head." My headache is as intense as ever.

"You think that's all it takes, huh? People like you and me?"

"We're different—you're an actual criminal."

"And what are you? Not a *takifu sanctus*, right?"

"I'm a freelancer who does his job better than anyone else in the field," I grunt the reply through my teeth, trying to fake conviction. Rafe is the wrong person for me to try that on. "What I do is a job. It's sanctioned. I have corporate authority in carrying out contracts."

Rafe simply replies, "All right…"

"Most of these projects deserve it. They're not following the rules that we all agreed too."

"Kergan deserve it?"

It's like there's a nail being driven into the back of my eyes. "I don't… This is how things work, that's all. Why—" I vomit. It just explodes from my mouth, so forceful some of it reroutes through my nose. Next, I feel Rafe's hand on my back. He holds back my hair as more vomit pours out.

"Sasha, you know you can't stay like this?"

As soon as I'm done dry-heaving, I slap his hand away. "I can do whatever I put my *breostloca* to."

"Right, I don't doubt that, Sasha—but why?"

CHAPTER 32

GRANDMA BELLE

"Hi, I'm Mickey."

"I can't afford to buy anything, kid. Try the idiot two doors down—he'll do anything for some company."

"Um, you're Grandma Belle, right?"

Belle squints her eyes at the phone, trying to get a clear look at the young man's face. He's familiar, but not somebody Belle can place. "Who are you?"

"I just called you grandma. I think it's pretty obvious."

"Can't be…My ungrateful son won't let his kids even talk to me."

"He doesn't know I'm here."

Belle walks over and opens the door. Standing at attention is a blue-haired kid, slightly shorter than Belle. He's dressed in a green and brown suit with a black fedora on top of his head. Mickey is pudgy, but not fat, with rosy cheeks and bright green eyes. He appears to be a teenager, maybe slightly younger.

"Told Father I had a job interview."

"And here I thought you dress like this to impress me." Belle looks him over. She tugs at the lapel on his jacket to straighten it. "You do look very handsome. You have eyes like your grandfather."

"Can I come in?"

Belle looks back at her place and realizes it looks like the home of an old, lonely spinster. A single drink-stained recliner. A single chair at the kitchen table. Underwear hung up everywhere to dry. It's sort of embarrassing. So she suggests, "How about we go out and get some food?"

They're sitting at a *bryce* shop, enjoying some late morning breakfast. The conversation is sparse, at best. Both pretend to be taken in by the food, keeping their mouths stuffed to avoid talking. After finishing his meal, it's Mickey who breaks the silence and gets things rolling.

"Is it true you were an assassin?"

Belle puts her arms on the table and squints, giving Mickey the once-over, trying to decide how he'll react. She decides to pull the ripcord.

"Yes. That's true. I was a killer. But I always operated under the law. Well usually. When it was convenient."

Belle can tell Mickey is a bit awed. He's trying to force out his next question, but can't get anything to come out. So she helps.

"I was trained when I was slightly older than you. By one of the most brutal *bongers* to ever unsheath a neosiri."

"A *bonger*?"

"Slang for assassin. It's a slight insult we use among each other. I executed my first contract…Um, the new in-home projections had just been released, so maybe…fifty years ago? Killed a couple while they were leaving the old Wuddupple Brand Morgen Pleghus. I followed them there, watched the whole thing, sitting two rows behind them. When they stopped to kiss in an alley, I shoved my blade through her back and into his gut. It was very efficient. I had these serrated blades attached to my armband, used 'em to cut their throats real coarse-like. The amount of blood shocked me, but thanks to my surgery, I was able to keep me wits about me. Oh, I had—well, not by choice, but I had anxiety removed. Useful in my field of work. You see these hands? Steady cutting a *hund* or a project."

Belle takes a sip of *capulusno*. Gives out a cough. He's leaning in, rapt with attention. Belle continues, "I took a lot of jobs other people didn't want. I had no problem killing anyone, any age and, I'll confess, I did 'em all. At least in the beginning. In my thirties, when I was the best on Earth, I was hired by a CEO to kill a judge. Thought it would make me a leading candidate for Cysta Por Ruverno. Did the job perfect. Got away clean. No trace back to the CEO."

Mickey, "And?"

"And nothing. Realized CPR was about who you knew more than how good you were. I got jaded after that. Lost the zest for the job. Retired about a decade later."

"Do you know how many—"

"No idea. Lots. I executed a lot of contracts. Maybe two hundred in my biggest year. That was towards the end when I was rushing to retirement."

Mikey frowns. "So none of your killings bothered you?"

Belle shrugs. "Nah, nothing I can think of. Look, can you—This is awkward but, um…I can't access my accounts right now, something with the bank system. Can you cover this?"

Mikey tilts his head, purses his lips, then says, "Yeah…Um, sure."

They're standing outside the *bryce* shop, facing each other. Belle is smiling as she reaches out to hug Mikey. He resists a little, but she pulls him in tight.

"I'm so happy to get to meet you. Thank you so much for this."

Mikey doesn't respond.

Belle pushes a piece of his hair out of his eyes. She puts her hand on his cheek and taps it gently. "And don't worry, I won't mention this to your father."

Mikey is looking down. "I know you won't."

Belle chuckles. "So please, I'd like to…When is your birthday? Maybe we can go somewhere for…"

The motion from Mikey is smooth and practiced. The blade he had hidden up his forearm sleeve does the job and opens up Belle's throat.

"You won't tell my dad—cause you killed him."

Belle falls to her knees, one hand over her throat, another searching her coat pocket.

"I'm not your fucking grandkid. Gods, how pathetic, you don't even know what your own grandchildren look like?" Mikey spits on Belle, who is thrashing around on the sidewalk.

He gets down on one knee. "I guess I'll leave you the same way you left my dad: gasping for breath, crying with a mix of pain and fear." Mikey looks around. The only person in the area is a passed-out *esne*. He starts to run before anyone comes along.

Belle finally finds her *formeltan* iron, a mini one stashed in the inside pocket of her coat. Her hand is still, but she can't really see where she's aiming it. Belle keeps her breath paced and consistent. She's about halfway through closing the wound when everything goes black.

CHAPTER 33

OAKWOOD

The *andred* is called Oakwood. There's me and the kids. We're standing just outside of town, the other side of a large concrete bridge.

"We're here first," I announce. Without saying it, I'm proud.

Jonas is dressed in tight-fitting clothing—all black, as I instructed. Jessi, well…Terror Girl is less concerned with function as much as showing off her biceps and shoulders. I guess I would be, too, if I had those. You can trace the strands of muscle on her arms, they're so fit. She's wearing an orange, sleeveless top and green shorts. Can't fathom why she picked that color combination.

Jonas asks. "So, we can scout the area?"

Jessi replies, in a mocking voice, *"So, we can scout the area?"*

I pull the hood back on my sweater. "You two creep around the perimeter. Get a sense of the ways in and out of Oakwood."

They leave and I take out a sweet roll I wrapped in foil, and take a bite. I'm perched under a tree, watching for movement. It's late—most workers have gone to bed to meet their sleep requirements for work.

There's a shove to my shoulder. I turn around and see Drake Siri in his tacky, gold-cuffed shirt and his blindingly shiny silver pants. His hair is wavy and blond, running down his back.

"Sa! What is going on, Sa?"

"It's *Sasha*."

He chuckles at me.

"I tell you over and over, Sasha."

He turns around and yells, "Hey everyone, it's Sa!" Then he turns back and shoots me a grin, letting me know he's doing it intentionally.

He goes to hit me on the shoulder again and I shove his hand away.

"Still no sense of humor, huh?"

"Still no sense of self-awareness?" I mean this literally. That's what he had removed. Why? I can't fathom.

"Let's see." He scratches his cleft chin, giving the appearance that he's actually thinking. "Last time we met, I believe you stabbed me."

"You were going to kill a baby."

"I was going to complete a job. And what does it matter if it's a baby?"

"I'm not going to explain it to you."

He leans in close and whispers, "You ever redeye the meat of a baby and cover it in *sylfling*?"

I roll my eyes. "You've never fucking done that."

He pulls back. "Yeah, but you know I ate me some people, right? I 'ave."

I don't know why he thinks that's something to brag about.

"Hey, hey. See those two over there?" He points at a couple, boy and girl, slightly older than my trainees. They're wearing nothing but some rags covering their genitals. Both have a dying glow around their heads. This was a thing Drake did. Even with no empathy, I found it tacky. Now, with my surgery wearing off, he makes my stomach hurt.

"They love watching me work. Seeing big daddy Drake in action. Blades through flesh. Gets them going, ya know?" He pulls out his *beadomece* from the sheath on his back. It shines from the Fyllejnod rays. The Fyllejnod is full tonight, with the occasional cloud slicing it into pieces. Jorge says, on nights like this, it's hanging so low you can almost touch it.

"Whaddya think? I just had it sharpened and polished."

I can't tell if he's admiring his *beadomece* or his own reflection. "It's very good, Drake." I look away, hoping this conversation—

"You wanna make a bet?"

"On what?"

"On which of us runs more workers through?"

I just shake my head.

"Oh, come on, you have side arms, that gives you an edge." He leans in close to my ear. "And maybe you join us after I win?"

I curl my lip. "Gods fucking burn it all. *Go away.*"

"You fu—"

As he opens his mouth to say the word, I jam the barrel of my pistol in it. He freezes.

"You gonna go away?"

He nods furiously in response.

"And you'll keep your distance during the raid?"

He nods again, his eyes wide open.

"Great, let's start by keeping promise number one," I say and I pull the gun back.

He backs up as the kids return. As they approach and it becomes apparent they are with me, the idiot stops again. "Hey, would they—"

I shoot him in the chest. I know he had a steel plate implanted there and the bullet just bounces off. But the point is to freak him out. Drake lifts his head up and looks at the smoking hole in his shirt.

"You damn rudder, you have any idea what this shirt costs?!" He rolls on his side and stumbles when he tries to get up. "Get over here, damn it!" The two kids who came with him float over in a *pulverian* haze, and gently help Drake up by his arms. He snorts through his nose, spits at the *gor* in front of my feet, and stomps off.

"Who the fuck's that?" Jessi asks.

"Someone who deserved my aim to be higher."

"Should we kill him? I mean, it's not a problem." Jonas helpfully offers.

"Not just yet. But when we start, don't spare him either."

Jessi asks, "Why's he dressed like a light show?"

"What did you find?"

They give me a layout of the escape routes. They're surprisingly thorough. Down to the details of how wide the path through the forest is, and which part of the north bridge has cracks. It is solid work.

"Well, that was a great job," I say. I start to reach out to touch Jessi's shoulder. She recoils, as though my hand is white-hot, so I try Jonas. My hand lands safely on his shoulder. He looks at it. I notice I'm holding my breath. I start to exhale with a high-pitched squeal.

Jessi asks me, "What on Earth are you doing?"

"Trying to...show affection?"

"Why?"

I pull my arm back. "I don't know."

Jessi shudders and looks away. "Yuck, let's get back to planning."

And so we do. But for a split second, when I took my hand away from Jonas, I saw him bite his lower lip, sniffle, and look at the shoulder I was holding. He liked it. And for some reason, that realization makes me feel…content.

A little while later, the three of us and about thirty other *bongers* are sitting at the edge of the town. Our group is on top of a grassy *beorg* (hill). The houses are lined up two-by-two down the main street, the artery of the town. That's where the action will concentrate. We'll try to force people to the center so the reps from the company can detain as many as possible. After that, they determine if the worker has enough value left to pay off his or her debts. I don't know what happens if the worker is deemed not valuable, and I've never thought to ask.

Pigo Autem, an assassin who specializes in *kulpuka*, launches a couple of his *cargast* bombs. When they explode, they cover everything in the area with a chemical. He told me the name once—it's long. The chemical burns extremely hot but also slow. If it gets on your skin, it melts your flesh more than burns it. He claims he's seen it burn straight down to the bone in seconds.

There's screaming, wailing. Men and women. Things are kicking off and the various other *bongers* charge in. I stay still. Jessi and Jonas have their blades out and are in a sprinting position. They're waiting for me to give a signal.

I can already hear the bargaining of the workers. "Please, let me live!" or "You can have anything you want if I can just go!" Some are begging for the lives of others. Some *bongers* are taking flaming pieces of the first houses and using them to ignite the next row. It's all so much for my senses now. I think back to that girl I stabbed who was begging for her father's life. Fuck.

"Um…Are we going to go in?" Jonas asks.

"Yeah," I say without conviction, then grab Jonas by the shoulder. "Don't kill anyone until I say so, all right?"

They both look at each other.

Jessi curls her upper lip and spits out a question. "Um, why?"

I snap at her. "You're my *leorne*. Stop questioning me!"

Jessi shrugs and looks down.

"And *Terror Girl*," I say, using her nickname because it bugs her, "don't use your *temporis wakati*. If these animals find out about it, it would be dangerous for you."

"Whatever."

We march down the beorg and enter the chaos. The kids are tense; there's a lot of action surrounding them. I can see their heads snapping left and right. A worker, female, bumps into Jessi. Jessi goes to stab her but I grab her hand. "I said we *wait until I say*."

Jessi shoves the worker to the ground and she scampers away, whimpering something about her wife. I'm gonna guess the wife is dead.

We've moved closer to the heart of the town. The area has cleared out already. Workers running for their lives, mostly to be met by the blades of assassins.

"So , what are we doing here?" Jessi, of course.

"Go then, find someone to kill. I'm not interested."

The both look at each other. Jonas puts his blade down at his side. He tilts his head. "Do you think, like, what we're doing is bad?"

I sigh through my nose.

"This is the job," Jonas starts. "This is how the cycle of business concludes."

I should smack him with the back of my hand, hard enough to crack his lip. That's what Belle did to me. Often. Instead I just say, "I don't need a *leorna* lecturing me on the merits of society. I understand the balance far better than you two."

I grab at my chest; it's tightening. I don't know what this is. Maybe anxiety? No wonder Belle had hers sliced and diced. It's terrible.

"Come on. Let's leave. We don't need this *feoh*."

Jessi shoots me a look that I can only interpret as her thinking I'm crazy. "Um, you definitely do…"

I ignore her and start to lead them out of Oakwood. As we're walking back, I can hear a little girl screaming. I shouldn't look. Just leave. But now I can't. I stop and look at a brown house with a *pembe navale* in front. Drake is there, with a young girl pinned to the ground under him. His blade is pressed against her cheek. The two kids he brought with him have a strong glow to them and splatters of blood on their skin. The girl has her eyes closed. He's petting her hair. He's pressing the knife into her. He's growling through his teeth as he does it. Spit is dripping from his bottom lip onto her. He stops. He jumps up. He's screaming and holding his thigh.

I throw the flaming piece of furniture, which was dripping with the remnants of *cargast* bomb, to the side. I help the girl up. Jessi and Jonas kill the kids, as I instructed. I put the girl on my shoulders and start to leave with her. At first, I feel a bite, or what feels like a giant needle tearing through my back. I look down and see the sharpened and polished *beadomece* sticking out of the left side of my stomach. There's a loud humming in my ear. Colors all fade out…then everything goes black. Like a computer monitor being shut off.

Then, like the snap of a finger, I'm standing with the girl on my shoulders again. No blade through me. The last few moments are swirling in my head like a dream. I turn around. Jonas is attacking Drake. Terror Girl is swaying back and forth, frothing at the mouth. Gods, I hope no one sees her.

Drake is too powerful for Jonas and quickly overwhelms him. I pull my sidepiece out to wound him, but his cell phone has the new *baec* view. He twirls around, holding Jonas in front as a shield, and puts the blade to his throat.

(I can't kill another assassin if he isn't attacking me. And I can't claim it's because he killed me a couple of minutes ago.)

"What the fuck just happened?" he yells.

"Nothing, Drake, let my charge go. You have no contract on him or me."

"What the fuck just happened? Why is she a fucking *cargast*!"

"Drake you need—"

He shakes his head. "Wait, *wait*." He points his sword at me. "You're dead; I just killed you."

"What sense does that make?"

"You're dead and then, I'm back here." He's thinking hard. It's not pretty. And honestly, he's so distracted…Why hasn't Jonas es—

Jonas heel-kicks Drake in the groin. I pick the kid back up. Jonas is dragging his sister. And we all head for the exit. Out of the ether, Pigo pops in front of me. His face is smudged with ash and dirt, his hair, a bright yellow, is singed at the ends. Unfortunately for him, he startles me.

"Hey, Sas—"

I nail him with the butt of my gun, right on his nose. Bit over the top. To be fair…I did just die. Probably could have just said *move*. Too late for that now.

Holding his nose, I can hear the word "Why!?" trailing us as we leave Oakwood. It's probably the first time I've heard that question from a *bonger* at one of these.

CHAPTER 34

1ST ATTEMPT

There's about twenty-five crew members in the Banquet Hall. It's Sifa Njema Pug night. In the squared circle, two men and Micel are standing about, shoulder width apart. Rafe approaches them with three pieces of rope. The crew watching stands around the circle, anticipating their turns. They crack knuckles and roll necks. They tug at gloves and tighten shoes. They shout encouragement at the three combatants in the ring. By encouragement, they yell suggestions for levels of violence the three should escalate to.

"I wanna see you knock 'is teeth out, M!"

"Don't stop till the floor is painted in blood, boy!"

Rafe holds up all three pieces of rope for the audience to inspect. Then he yanks on them, sparking a line of fire to run their lengths. There's just enough space at the end to grab ahold. He hands one piece to each combatant. The first one wraps it around his wrist (the wrist has a fire-resistant tape wrap; however, the heat can still singe). The second starts cracking it like a whip. Micel, body relaxed, rests his hand by his side, limp. Rafe furrows his brow at Micel, but Micel just cracks a slight smile.

"All right, this is the first match of the night. I want to remind everyone the fight ends when the other person quits or when I say so. There's no attacking the eyes, no hooking the mouth—"

"Shut the fuck up and let's get on wit it!" Cadyn yells. The crowd roars in agreement. Standing next to Cadyn is Kergan Satre II. She's dressed with a bit more flair…green pants and a light blue shirt. Her hair is tied in a braid, then looped into a bun, thanks to Cadyn. Cadyn suggested the bun (and by suggested, she threatened Kergan bodily harm) so Kergan could hide a *cnif* in the wrap. At this point, Kergan knows better than to question Cadyn; her threats were not idle.

As the combatants stand off in the ring, Kergan asks, "Are *you* going to fight?"

Cadyn is too busy watching the action.

Kergan asks again, louder, "Hey! Are you going to fight?"

Cadyn, eyes trained on the fight, "Yeah, maybe. If I meet the right *slag*, I might."

Micel already has one opponent trapped—his legs wrapped tightly around his throat. The other fighter is whipping Micel, but eliciting no reaction. The first fighter gives up. Micel stands back up to face the one who's been whipping him.

The fighter hesitates, then yells, "For the gods!" He charges at Micel, punching him in the gut a couple of times. Next he hits Micel in the chin with uppercuts. The fighter gives kicking a chance. Micel chuckles, takes his fist, and hammers it down on the head of the fighter—who then crumples to the ground like a house of cards.

There's a cheer, then a rush of murmuring. Rafe jogs over to the man on the ground. He's as limp as a blanket. While Rafe checks on the fighter, Micel winks at Kergan—but Kergan is worried about the man on the ground. Rafe raises his fist and twists it back and forth, to the relief of the crowd. He helps the fighter back up and walks him to a chair over against the wall.

A tall woman, Pascal, with fuchsia-colored hair, enters the circle. She has red string tied around her arms to highlight her biceps and her stomach is painted with the Riestovikian symbols for pain and love. Despite her musculature, she looks lithe, sort of serpentine. Pascal tosses in a box of bronze stars. Even sharpened to a point, they make mediocre weapons. But being made of *brasu* bronze, they can fetch a good amount from a smelter.

There's a buzz in the crowd as everyone waits for—

"I'll take ya on, rudder!" shouts Cadyn.

Everyone looks over at her. She snorts through her nose and grinds her tan leather boot into the floor. She takes off a brown coat and hands it to Kergan. Then Cadyn kneels down, facing Kergan, and redoes her shoelaces.

"I trained 'is one, aye." Cadyn whispers to Kergan. "Just like you. I want you to watch her defense. Watch how she uses 'er feet 'specially. Pascal was a natty at balance, a bit a *wenan* in 'er.""

In contrast with the last fight, this one is about technique. Both test each other out, but keep their defenses tight. Cadyn takes a few shots at Pascal's legs, but to no avail. Each time Cadyn leaves her defense down slightly, trying to trap Pascal, Pascal will not fall for it.

Kergan follows Pascal's moves, trying to anticipate what's coming next.

Pascal lands the first clean blow—a knee to the chest—knocking Cadyn to the ground. Pascal jumps on top of the prone Cadyn. Despite having a smaller frame, Pascal almost engulfs Cadyn, using her limbs to wrap her up.

It looks like Pascal has complete control, but Kergan notices something. Pascal is gasping for air while Cadyn's breath is calm and measured. Cadyn's arm breaks free and she begins to chop at Pascals liver like an ax. Pascal has to release to protect herself, but Cadyn follows with a hold of her own, locking her arm under Pascal's chin and tying her right arm behind her back. Pascal kicks and spits, but she's losing strength. The combination of the hold and her uneven breathing has worn her down.

"Linnan! Linnan!" Pascal yells.

Cadyn releases her hold and stands up. Pascal is gasping, on her hands and knees. Cadyn tries to offer her a hand but is slapped away. Cadyn responds by kicking Pascal in the ribs.

"Ingratus!" Cadyn says as she picks up the *brasu* stars. She walks past Kergan. "Let's go. I'm hungry."

Kergan doesn't move.

"Hey, let's go!" Cadyn demands.

"I wanna fight."

Cadyn pauses. Then shrugs. "All right." She walks over to Kergan and hands her the box.

Kergan, shocked that Cadyn is allowing this, edges towards the squared circle. Once she's in the boundary, she places the box gently on the ground. She eyes the crowd, and in her head, prays the bigger opponents stay away. She's so involved in the moment, she doesn't notice the room is silent.

The eyes of the crowd dart about each other. No one wants to be responsible for hurting the project. Cadyn steps up.

"Anyone who can beat my charge"—she looks at Kergan before continuing—"can have my room and all the *innierfe* permanently."

This releases a wave of chatter in the crowd. Everyone knows Cadyn has the biggest room. She beat Rafe for it a while ago. They also know she has the most comfortable accommodations, as she is meticulous about care and cleanliness. That's a real rarity on this ship of malcontents.

Alois steps forward, cracking his knuckles. He looks down and pushes on the corner of his left eye. The eyeball plops out into his hand. He turns and hands it off. He replaces it with a dark red eye, the pupil a pulsating red light.

Alois snorts through his nose like a *hund* getting ready to charge. "What are the rules here? We can't risk killing 'er."

The crowd murmurs in agreement.

Cadyn replies. "No weapons, just hand-to-hand combat."

"I could still kill 'er"

Cadyd scoffs, "You may be a hell of a thief Alois, but you ain't no fighter."

Alois runs his hand through his hair, then shakes his head a couple of times. "Aye, I could, a'ight? I've killed before."

Cadyn catches her breath. "This isn't some old *slag* you took a jewel off, Alois. This is a machine of my build. *Machine De Cadyn*."

"What do you want on the line? I got some—"

"The eye. The red one." Cadyn stated.

Alois looks Kergan up and down. "Yeah, all right."

Cadyn pulls Kergan over to the side and pretends to give her advice.

Kergan whispers, "What's with the eye?"

"It's a high-end model; we can sell it for a bunch. 'ere, don't move." Cadyn slips a *cnife* into Kergan's bun.

Kergan's eyes widen. "I thought we weren't allowed—"

Cadyn hushes her. "An emergency. *Kushinda tu*. Just win."

Kergan steps forward into the ring. Alois is bouncing back and forth on the balls of his feet. Kergan puts her feet shoulder width apart and puts her fists in front of her cheeks. They move in a circle, too far apart to even touch. Alois throws out a taunt with his hand. But Kergan doesn't react.

A random voice from the crowd yells out, "Aye, this ain't a dance—you gonna fight or what?"

The rest of the crowd cheers, agreeing.

Cadyn cups her hands over her mouth and yells, "*Attack*, don't retreat!"

Kergan pushes forward and tries a couple of punches but is easily blocked by Alois. She takes another swing, and before Kergan knows what happened, she's flipped over on her back. She blinks her eyes rapidly and sighs through her nose.

Alois leans over her and tries to pick her up by the hair. Kergan responds by punching Alois right in the chest. It's hard enough to stun him, buying Kergan time to nip up. She attacks with a series of jabs and kicks. One or two land, but mostly they wear her out. Alois sweeps Kergan to the ground and starts trying to stomp her, forcing Kergan to roll almost out of the ring.

Kergan pops up and gets her bearings. Then Alois charges at Kergan, who shifts her body to the right. As she shifts, she catches him with her leg.

Micel raises a fist in the air. "There it is, girl!"

Cadyn stands with her arms crossed and shouts a simple instruction. "Pounce!"

Kergan jumps on Alois's back and wraps her arms around his neck. It was like a hold Cadyn used whenever she spared with Kergan. Alois collapses to the ground, frothing at the mouth, gasping for air. Kergan can't even hear him yell, "*Linnan!*" She holds tight until Kergan and Micel pry her off.

Kergan is shaking, her eyes wide. Cadyn holds her by the cheeks and looks into those same eyes. "Relax your breathing."

"Relax."

"Relax."

Finally, Kergan begins breathing normally.

Cadyn gently slaps Kergan's right cheek. "I think we opened up something you ain't know ya had, huh?"

Kergan looks down at the ground.

"S'alright," Cadyn starts. "It's what you're here for. It means I'm doing my job. Now come on, let's sell that eye and have some *baerodast* and *carnis. Carnis* slow-cooked over a real flame. Been a while since I've had that."

Kergan shrugs. "I wasn't stopping. I was going to—"

"You were going to do what I trained you to do. Nothing less."

"I'm going to my room."

Micel grabs her shoulder, but Kergan shakes it off and leaves.

"Fuck 'er." Cadyn elbows Micel. "Let's go eat some real food. Safer for 'er to be in 'er room anyway."

Micel licks his lips, snorts, then nods.

CHAPTER 35

WE ARE PREGNANT

"**W**e're pregnant!" Jorge yells as soon as I open the door. His cheeks are red. He has a bit of sway to his stance. His breath reeks of *ceren*. He's *druncnian*. And smiling.

He hugs me, and I hug back. Alva runs over and joins in on the hug fest. All three of us are just kinda saying words, but not making sense. Jonas then wedges himself into our group hug. Jessi walks past and heads to the kitchen.

When we all release, my stomach gets heavy. I think about the baby I saved from the foreclosure. Then I think about the ones I didn't. A pain shoots up my neck and my stomach cramps. It's enough to double me over.

Alva is the first one to notice. "Sasha?"

I'm concentrating on my breathing. A nice, even pace. Something's wrong with my eyes; the edges of everything are fuzzy. There's a hand on my back. I stumble over to the kitanda and sit down so fast, the kitanda slides back.

Alva repeats, "Sasha?"

Jorge asks me, "Hey, do you need water or anything?" He looks at Jonas. "Get her some water."

Jorge and Alva sit on each side of me.

I can't bear to look at him when I say this. Which is odd. For years I've shared my exploits with Jorge. But now, I can't when I say, "I've *killed* babies."

My hands are shaking. The pain in my neck is throbbing and expanding to my head.

I'm staring at my feet, hunched over. "Like yours—or the one coming. I've killed them."

There's no sound around me. People are talking, but it's like I'm under water. I blink a few times, but everything is still blurry. I feel like I have to belch, but that's not it.

It's amazing how much energy you get when you're about to vomit. For a minute, I couldn't move, like there was a *hund* on my chest. Now, I'm sprinting to the bathroom. It burns my throat coming up. And the more I look at it, the more I vomit until I start dry heaving.

"Fuck's wrong wit 'er?" I can tell it's Jessi asking.

Jonas replies, "I dunno. I think she's freaked out over babies."

Jessi then yells at me. "Hey, Sasha, fuck's wrong with you?"

I grab a towel and wipe my mouth. I use the sink to brace myself and stand. "I'm all right. Just the results of the surgery wearing off. I'm remembering things more often." I wash my mouth out. At least the stomach pain is gone, if not the head.

Walking out, I look at Alva. "I ruined the moment; I apologize."

Alva laughs, but I can tell it's because she doesn't know how to respond. "It's—it's all right, Sasha."

I nod at her, then retire to my room. I fall asleep quickly, like I haven't slept well for days. When I wake up, the headache is gone. My mouth feels disgusting. My throat is sore. I'm not sure how long I've been down. It's dark now, but is it *early* dark or *late* dark? I get up and walk out to the worker's room. The kids are watching something on the projector. Some show they're practically addicted to where a guy reviews old weapons. I don't know why; I train them in weapons weekly.

Jorge comes up to me, taps me on the shoulder, and motions for me to follow him into the kitchen. Alva is waiting for us, sipping *capulusno*. She's wearing a black and red *cynereaf* Jorge usually wears.

Jorge folds his fingers together and sits down. "Hey, that back there, has that happened before?"

I shake my head. "Not to that extent. I've had issues sleeping and get flashes of projects I worked, but nothing like that."

Alva has her hand on her belly. "What do you mean, *flashes*?" I shrug. "Like seeing things?"

I nod.

They look at each other.

"How sure are you that you don't want to get the surgery again?" Jorge tentatively asks.

"More now."

Alva tilts her head to the side and asks, "More now that you've had a breakdown?"

"More now that Jorge is having a baby. The intensity of the feeling I had when you told me…I wouldn't feel that with another surgery. I'd be able to recognize it, but I couldn't…*fenlyss de dael*."

Alva lets out a sigh.

"I'm sorry, Alva. I'm saying Jorge because I've known him longer than you."

"No, I was sighing because what you said was sweet."

Jorge looks at Alva. "I don't…What is *feiniss dole*?"

"*Fenlyss de dael* means *share the feeling*," Alva explains before asking me, "Have you seen an assassin go through this before?"

"No one I've known. I've heard that sometimes an assassin becomes so poor, he or she can't afford it. Again, no one I know."

"How long does it last? When will you know it's completely worn off?"

I shrug. "Probably when I stop vomiting at the idea of babies."

Jorge coughs up a laugh.

Alva reaches out for my hand. "Well, we'll be here with you every day."

Jorge is taken aback. "I thought you wanted to move out?"

Alva snaps, "We can't *leave* her like this."

"Great," Jorge says.

Alva nods to the worker's space where Jessi and Jonas are still absorbed by that weapons show. "What about the kids? Are you going to stop training them?"

"No. They need guidance. Just cause I want out doesn't mean I can cheat them. The *leorne* and *lareow* contract is binding. And if they were to screw up enough jobs, some *burgealdor* or company president might put a contract out on them. And now, with how I am, I'd feel responsible if they weren't trained correctly. I'll just make sure the proj—*people* we assassinate aren't…you know…"

Alva finishes my thought. "Babies?"

CHAPTER 36

DRAKE BEU NYOKA

Drake is smashing in a skull with the wide side of an axe. The skull formerly belonged to a Riestovikain diplomat. Drake had been hired to "not just kill, but send the message that they're not needed here." And so, Drake left with the woman's head, brought it back home, and put it in a display case with some of his other favorites.

There are quite a few these days, but no one keeps count.

Drake Beu Nyoka was born at home with the help of doctors hired by his parents. Home is the top suite in the Yttrium Tele Towers. He operates entirely out of this building, though his parents left him property all around Chicago.

The Nyokas were painfully successful. They were one of the original Earth families, and played a part in the structure of Earth's society. The Nyoka's were *de boc*, or *of the book*. Hugo Nyoka even developed the first engineering curriculum at the college formerly known as Lakeside, now known as The Alamedies Institute of New Technology. Alamedies was a dietary supplement company. Lakeside's science lab had produced a study connecting its dietary supplements with violent rectal bleeding. So Alamedies bought the college and buried the study. Lakeside was far from the only college on Earth this happened to; it's been an accepted practice for decades now.

The suite is painted *hwit*-shell white. There's crown molding that runs everywhere but the bedrooms. The floor is real wood, very expensive. Drake often yells at anyone who spills on it, "This floor is worth more than ya damn life!" Besides housing the finest of kitandas, there is also a projection system installed in the ceiling of every room that retracts when not in use. The kitchen is staffed by rotating *cocopannes*…a different one for each meal.

The second floor of the suite is dedicated to his craft. A weapon's room, a sparring room, an *uzito vitae* and, towards the back, a consecration room. This is where he worships the gods. When he gets around to it, at least. Not so much *worship* as much as him asking the gods to provide material goods.

The consecration room is home to the display case, and currently home to Drake's temper tantrum.

"Pincern! Pincern" Drake yells out, hammering away at a new skull.

"Yes, Rand Drake?" the pincern replies. Drake's *pincern* is left over from his parents' days. The *pincern* is short and round. He wears a blue and yellow suit with shoes he shined that morning.

"Get me *ceren*, pickled *fearh*, baked *sceota*, two *cecels* and *pombe tenebris* for after."

"Of course, sir. Will your…companions be joining you?"

Drake spits on his own floor. The *pincern* walks over and uses a napkin to wipe it up.

Drake is shouting, despite the *pincern* being just feet away. "No, I need you to send Clarence out to find me more. Wait, no—who *tollebonted* the last two? Whoever the fuck it was, send them."

"Rand Drake, while me and your staff are entirely loyal to you, it might be prudent for you to find partners who are…*willing* and don't need to be plied with *pulveris*?"

Drake's phone alerts him to a call. It's from current CPR Malcolm Ritchie, Jr.

Drake groans and lulls his head before telling the phone, "Answer."

Lakeside College reflected early Earth life. The admissions process was, as one student put it to a newspaper, "Do you have a pulse?" And the curriculum was collaborative, with students doing very few projects on their own. There was a tempered pace to the classes that matched the rhythm of Chicago.

Hugo was not on board. He correctly pointed out how Universities on Riestovik and LaRocca produced engineers at twice the rate Lakeside did. This was the ultimate goal of colleges and universities, in Hugo's mind—to "produce as many engineers as the society will tolerate." He was *abrugdon,* watching the brightest of his students become "pummeled into mediocrity by silly teachers more concerned with ideas than results."

After having his planned curriculum rejected by his department head, Hugo spent the next year maneuvering to take her place. Hugo and his small band of followers (a mix of students and intern teachers) protested against the administration. This included chaining the doors shut on admissions day, when new students were signing up. In class, Hugo's students bombarded teachers with question after question. Always arguing and attacking—putting the teacher, the administration, and the very *breostwylm* of the college on the defensive.

The tactic worked—and as a way to stop the chaos, Hugo was made head of his department. In a year, he would be head of the college and able to mold it into his vision of education.

"Hey," Malcolm says, greeting Drake. His voice is monotone, with little sighs at the end of each sentence. It's as if each word were a boulder he had to lift over his head.

"Yeah, Malcolm."

"Um, I need you to refer to me by my title."

"Why? I've known you since training," said Drake.

Malcolm smacks his lips before saying, "It just…matters."

"*Cysta Por Ruverno,* Malcolm. What can I do for you?"

Malcolm mumbles out a weak, "Thanks."

There's a bit of silence.

"Malcolm, why did you call me?"

"You know that girl you fucked?"

Drake plasters on a giant grin and pats his stomach. "Which one?"

"The other assassin—Sasha?" Malcolm's voice becomes nasally when he says her name.

Drake had lied years ago and said he slept with Sasha. "Um…yeah?"

"Contract breach. We need her fired."

"Wait—seriously? You're giving me a contract on Sasha?!" Drake is all smiles.

"That's what I said."

There's a bit of silence again.

"Oh, and this other girl. I don't know if you fucked her or not—Kergan Satre II."

"That is irrelevant, really. I thought they wanted her brought in alive?"

"He wants you to make it a priority," Malcolm practically mumbles, his attention stolen by something off screen.

"Hey! Hey! Malcolm!"

Malcom pushes a couple of strands of hair behind his ear. "Yeah?"

"Do they want Kergan dead or alive?"

Malcom looks off screen again and answers, "I…I don't remember, Drake. I'm just relaying a message."

"Yeah, but you're missing a giant…" Drake stops, as Malcolm isn't paying attention. "Hey! All right, let the *Burgleador* know I'll make it—"

"Not a government official. Higher."

"A CEO?"

Malcolm nods in agreement. "Said to tell you, besides the money, it would be good as far as favors go. And we both know you tend to need a lot of favors."

Drake coughs and pulls at his earlobe.

"So…we're done." And just like that, Malcolm hangs up.

It took a decade, but Hugo's influence on the college started to bleed into the world. Hugo made Lakeside College into the most exclusive engineering program on Earth. In fact, there were rumbles on the other planets that it might be the best anywhere. But Hugo had one more issue: the open admissions policy. It was tradition and reflected values which pervaded Earth's sense of fairness and justice. He couldn't just cut it. So in his tenth year, as the head of administration, Lakeside College began to charge a fee for attending. The fees acted as a deterrent to "questionable pupils," as Hugo referred to them. It was the first time a college on Earth was funded by anything other than taxes.

Hugo stood in front of the school one year and took in what he'd accomplished. He had built a school which solely functioned to produce engineers. He told his wife, "*Imeundwa de deorum siwezi forlor,*" which roughly translated to, "*What I make, no god can destroy.*" When the first all-engineering class graduated, Hugo swelled with pride to the point of tears.

What Hugo didn't count on was the profit Lakeside College began to make. And with profit, came CEOs. Hugo refused to give up control. But inside and outside pressures bore down on him, broke him down. Hugo was found with his throat cut while engaged in the bathroom. It was ruled suicide by a judge. The silver lining was Hugo's family kept claim to the college as an investment. This enriched them for generations and established the Nyokas as the first family on Earth who "came from money."

It's a less well-known fact that Hugo was the first victim of a legal assassination.

CHAPTER 37

THE GADERIGEN FOREVER

Jorge is bundled up in a puffy black coat. "It's *schway* you're coming with."

Alva is wearing a similar style coat, but blue and with her hood up. "I live for this. Down the CEO rule!"

Jorge looks around but the only person to hear is an *esne* who is apparently sponsored by Menglin Wash Pads and Chemicals. It says as much on her shirt. And she's busy fiddling with her projection device.

"Jorge, relax, all right?" Alva insists.

Both turn down an alley. Their jackets are not enough to keep the wind from cutting through the fabric. Alva shivers, and Jorge pulls her in tight with his arm. He shields his eyes and looks at the wall. Jorge starts pressing with his left hand, but is only hitting concrete.

Alva puts a sleeve in front of her face to block the wind. "Check the map again?"

Before Jorge can pull it up on his screen, he sees Moose turn the corner. "Hey, Moose! Good to see you."

"Jorge! Glad you could come." They both twist their fists at each other.

"And this is Alva," Jorge says, beaming.

"I remember—from the dinner a few weeks ago. You wanted to push for childbearing to be a personal choice. That's an old-world idea, Alva. I like it."

Jorge points at the wall. "Yeah, so we thought the place was here, but—"

"It's *above* the spot," Moose says as he raises his hand and pushes through the wall. "We moved them around on the wall so it's harder to find." He nods at Alva and Jorge. "You first, aye?"

The inside is a hall jammed tight with forty people. There's so little room, one can barely turn around. Jorge and Alva can feel the heat and humidity; beads of sweat immediately form on Jorge's brow.

"Is there anywhere to put the coats?" Jorge asks.

Alva points to a corner where coats are piled up on top of each other on the floor. "I'll keep mine on."

Gerwid approaches. She's wearing a friendly grin, but the bags under her eyes betray her mood.

Moose leans in and whispers, "She's been getting no sleep; thinks the company is watching her."

Jorge greets her. "Hey Gerwi—"

"No phones. You have to shut your phones off completely," snaps Gerwid.

Jorge and Alva look at each other, then to Moose—but he's already walking past to find a chair.

"Jorge, *off*. Just off the whole time you're here."

"Yeah, of course, Gerwid."

Gerwid turns her attention to Alva. "Who are you?"

Jorge leans in. "It's all right, she's with me."

Alva purses her lips. "Hey, I don't need you talking for me, Jorge. I'm Alva. I was at the dinner a while back."

"So?"

Alva glances at Jorge, then makes eye contact with Gerwid, "So I support the cause and wanted—"

"I need to get this thing started." Gerwid spins on her heels and marches to the front of the room.

Jorge looks to Alva, shocked. "*Wow*, that is different. Gerwid's usually the calm one."

Gerwid stands in front of everyone, tapping on a wireless mic, trying to get the room's attention. Slowly, the murmuring of the crowd dissipates. Gerwid holds her hands flat against one another in a praying position, then she folds her fingers over. With a deep breath, she sits in the prayer position again. Then exhales and folds her fingers together.

"Our *Burgealdor* has informed us of a judge who supports our cause. They obviously can't come out and say it yet. But when the *Burg* makes his move and recognizes *gaderigen*, there will be a judge backing them."

"So what?" yells a voice from the crowd. There's hissing from random people in response.

"This is the *amaerecian* times. The backing of a judge means we can have our *gaderigen* recognized legally," Gerwid explains.

"And then what? They kill us!?"

More hissing from the crowd.

Gerwid cranes her neck to see who is yelling. A man stands up in the second row of the crowd. "We are fighting companies who won't hesitate to hire assassins to kill us. We need to meet violence with violence!"

Now there's a mix of hisses and clapping from the crowd.

Gerwid tightens her grip on the microphone. "Plochman, you'll get your turn—"

"You have your turn every damn week, Gerwid!" He starts talking to the crowd. The man is short and stout with a long beard that reaches down to his stomach. He pulls at it when he talks, his words spilling out all at once. "If we get the body of a CEO, that'll scare 'em. It'll let 'em know we have the power."

The crowd is talking in a jumble, no one listening to each other, just a wall of words. Moose stands, picks up his chair, and slams it on the ground.

Everyone stops talking and turns to him.

"If you want to continue the system of violence, perpetuate it, make us no better than them—you are free to leave. The point of establishing a *gaderigan* is to fight for better treatment, sure. Change how companies control our culture, sure. But more than that, it's to come together, unite as siblings. Your wounds are my mine. Your hunger is mine. And Plochman, your anger and fear are mine."

Plochman looks at the ground.

Moose relaxes his pose and lifts both hands palm up to the sky. "*Kama croda levavi*—"

"—*ego levavi*," the crowd finishes.

Gerwid says, "Remember, Plochman—once we are legally recognized as an organization, we will have the same rights as any company."

A crowd member asks, "Like it was back then?"

Another member adds on to the first question. "Any word from the forest people?"

Gerwid bites her top lip. "Thank you for asking that." She starts nervously tapping her foot. "Up next...um..." Gerwid shakes her head and squeezes her eyes tight. The crowd is humming again. "Up next is a Mr.

Gilead Lakes. He is the de facto leader of the forest people until Kergan Satre's replacement is of age."

Gilead steps to the front of the room. "We want you to know you have our full support. The lifeblood of a new Chicago will be the *gaderigen*. And once you're established, my people can work with you to start pushing for similar rights and restitutions. The time of the CEO is coming to an end, and this is where it starts." There's a slight cheer. "I said, *this* is where it *starts!*" More cheers. "Our children will grow up in a Chicago born anew!" The crowd is standing. Gilead points at a man. "Will you join me, my bother?!"

"Yes!" he responds.

Gilead points at a woman. "Should my pot be empty, will you help me fill it, sister!?"

"Yes!" she replies with a jump and a hand clap.

The crowd closes in on Gilead.

"My child," he starts. "If your brother in the *gaderigen* has no shelter?!"

The young man doesn't seem to respond, but the crowd is so loud, it's impossible to tell. Gilead moves on, but the young man keeps focusing on him. When Gilead's back is turned, the young man pulls out a sidearm and shoots him in the back of the head.

Gilead collapses face-first, his body contorted unnaturally on the floor. Like a marionette tossed into a corner.

The group is shocked, at first. And before any of them make a move, the young man announces, "This killing was legal, dispatched, and charged by *Burgleador* Spencer. I apologize for the mess, but if you wait, someone will be along to clean up the body."

The kid is bald with dark brown eyes. He's tall, with hardly an ounce of fat on him. The kid puts his pistol back in its holster and turns to leave. As he approaches the holo-door, his path is blocked by Moose. The kid's eyes are at half-mast and his tone is disinterested. "Can you *move*, sir?"

Moose demands, "Why would you do that?"

"As I said, I was hired by Burgealdo—"

"You didn't have to do this for a living, though, right? You *choose* it. Just like you choose to sneak in here. And chose to shoot Gilead Lakes."

"I mean, that's the job. If you're going to talk about family or the kids he has, don't bother—I had my guilt sliced and diced."

"Another choice you made."

"Look, I really need to—"

Before he finishes the sentence, Moose's hands are around his neck. The kid goes for his gun, but Moose slaps it away and gets back to draining the life from him. They fall to the floor, locked together. Jorge runs over and puts his hand on Moose's right arm.

"Let go, Moose. Let go."

A tear rolls down Moose's right cheek, and his eyes are bloodshot. "Plochman's right. We have to answer violence with violence."

"Let go, Moose. If you do this, you'll kill the movement and end up dead yourself."

"So what!? Look at what they just did—they'll never let us be recognized!"

"Let go, Moose. Please."

The kid's face is purple and his mouth is open. You can hear him trying to force air through.

Moose, let's go.

The kid catches his breath and runs out of the hall.

When Moose collects himself, he looks over at the body of Gilead. Gerwid is sitting next to him, crying into her hands. Plochman pipes up and says, "I'd of finished him off."

Moose punches the wall, leaving an indentation as he exits the hall, back into the cold wind of Chicago.

CHAPTER 37

I TELL SPENCER TO GO AWAY

"**B**urgealdor Spencer, it's me, Sasha," I say into the camera at the front gates. The gate is ornamental, a cheap aluminum, the kind they used on disposable lawn chairs at auditoriums. The guard glaring at me is not ornamental. Might know what happened to her friends. Probably does.

She searches my person and takes the sidearm. The gates retract into the ground. I nod at the guard, a tall blonde woman with her hair in a ponytail. She spits at the ground in front of me. So, yeah, she's aware of what happened to the guards who visited me. As I walk up the cobblestone driveway, my mind wanders to flashes of projects I worked on that spit up blood. A tanned, orange-haired man in his fifties I shot in the gut, slumped against a brick wall outside his office. Normally, I would have shot him in the head but his wife requested it as part of brief experiment I had in marketing. This was my "Ndefu Hearm" package. The other two were "Perdita Kiung" and "Dominus Abredwian."

Basically, it was a way for consumers to choose how they wanted the project to die. But it quickly spun out of control. One guy wanted me to train *fearhs* to like the taste of flesh and then lock the projects in a pen with the flesh-hungry *fearhs*. I don't even know where to begin with that. Actually, I think Pigo Autem took the job. But he just blew the project up and fed the pieces to the animals, mixed in with their food.

"Sasha! Is that Sasha?"

Before I knock on the door, it's opened by a servant. The floors are wood, or made to look like wood. I can't tell, even when walking on them. There is a rug running from the doorway to the worker's space. It's white with this red and blue double helix running down the middle.

Burgealdor Spencer is waiting for me, standing by a gigantic *fyrhus*. The electric flames are dancing about with the occasional pop, simulating wood burning. In his left hand is a drink, and in his right, a *reafian*, similar to the one I keep in my safe.

Spencer wipes his chin with his sleeve before he greets me. "Sasha! I'm so happy you're here. I have such burning questions for you—"

"Yeah, I'm sorry but—"

Spencer's assistant is sitting behind a desk and looks to be reading. "Don't interrupt the *Burgealdor*, Sasha."

"So, tell me, yes—where are you in the hunt for our little miscreant?" Spencer asks.

I pause to make sure he's done talking. "I have not yet ascertained where the ship—"

Spencer clicks his tongue. "Have you found or killed anyone who is harboring Kergan Satre II?"

"No, sir."

"So, you didn't meet with Rafe Fortune a few days ago?"

I remain silent.

"Maybe my *jasusi* was wrong, yes? Maybe she saw you with another rudder?"

I have no clue what to say.

Spencer motions at a *fehrwerd*, who is standing as still as a plant in the corner. He leaves the room. It's silent.

Spencer takes a big gulp before asking, "Would you be a fan of the *huntung*?"

I shrug.

It's quiet again. Spencer takes another gulp. You can hear the assistant turning a page. When I scratch the back of my head, it's as loud as a maraca.

The *fehrwerd* returns with three large compatriots and a slight woman wearing an unfamiliar type of eyeglass. They seem to be almost attached to her head. Her hair is unkempt and drags down by the heels of her feet. When I do make contact with her forest-green eyes, they betray nothing. As if she had the same surgery I did.

"I've heard you have lost what made you the most calculated assassin in Chicago, yes? You've become more humane?" Spencer snaps his fingers and looks at the assistant. "What was that fellow's name?"

"Drake, sir."

That rudder.

"And while you may think getting back that part of you is a good thing, it seems to be hindering our little project, here." Spencer walks over to me, close enough that his gut is pressing against my folded arms. He finishes off his drink and drops the metal cup on the ground. The assistant scurries to pick it up. Spencer whispers at me, "Did you not want to kill because you felt bad, with your new…disease? Or was it because you have no respect for me?"

Now I'm getting a bad feeling. The guards are closing in around me, and Spencer steps back. They all have tasers and clubs in their hands.

"Well, come on then. Let's give it a go," I taunt.

The first *fehrwerd* is an idiot and charges with his taser down and his club above his head. I easily catch him when he swings down, disarm him, and—

At first, it just feels like a vibration—your organs start shaking violently enough, you collapse to the ground. As the feeling wears off, another wave hits, but this one is stronger. It's so painful you throw up on the nice white carpet. When you finish dry heaving, you get a hit to the back of your head from a club. You black out, but just for a second, and find yourself being held up by two *fehrwerds*. They're tying your hands together, but you don't notice until it's too late, still dizzy from the hit to the head. The sounds of people talking sound like you're listening from under water—muffled and dissonant. You're still dizzy, but not like a kid who just rolled down a hill, more like a ship in tumultuous waters.

The humming in my ear starts to clear up and I find myself tied to a table. Looking down at me is Spencer, the woman with the dirty hair, and the assistant.

"Sasha. I want to help you, yes? Help you take care of your debt to me. Help you escape this sickness you must be going through. All those people you killed, flooding your memories."

All I can think to say is, "Really, I'm fine."

"This person, here. This is *Burg* Merid."

"Hey," she weakly says.

"*Burg* here, is a former *praeter asili*, yes? Do you know what that is?"

"She's smart or some shit."

"Well put, Sasha. What you need to know is that, at one point, she was on her way to being a top flight surgeon. *Was* until she got caught in some nastiness. Now she works in servitude to a CEO. Bad news for her. Great news for you, because you'll have sure hands working on you tonight to repair you."

"I don't want to go back—or be *repaired*."

"Hm, Sasha…How can I explain this so you'll understand, yes? When a chair's leg comes off, you don't just ignore it and keep using it. You don't try to sit at an angle. You put a new leg on it, yes? Or you throw it out. Would you prefer I throw you out? You…broken chair?" Spencer has a smile on his face from ear to ear.

I wait a beat, then say, "Don't kill the girl!"

The *Burgealdor* Spencer loses his smile and scrunches his face. He is so confused, he doesn't even notice his assistant is missing his head. When he does, Spencer falls onto his back like a wall tumbling down.

Jonas unties me and helps me up. Jessi has Spencer pinned down with the point of a neosiri. I walk over and take the neosiri from Jessi, pressing it into the cheek of the Burgealdor. He turns on his stomach and crawls with the agility of an intoxicated turtle. I kick him in the side, and he rolls onto his back with his palms up.

"Now, now, now, Sasha…Don't be rash, my dear. You don't want another murder on your *dhamira*, do you?" He's forcing laughter. I've seen this in a lot of projects—they laugh when scared as a coping mechanism. This teenager, she laughed the whole time she was bleeding out from her neck. Died with that smile. Even then, I found it creepy. "You'll have me haunting your nightmares forever."

Wow, he really thinks he can talk his way out of this. Maybe he could have, but this is not the route. His pride is keeping him from just flat out begging.

"I'll be able to live with it," I press the edge into his throat just enough so blood dribbles down onto his chest. "I want you to cancel the contract."

"Of course, of course, Sasha. I'll cancel the contract on you."

"Not me. The one on the girl."

Spencer's voice is shaking. "Right, hold on. Phone, open contract files. Terminate contract for Kergan Satre II. Yes, yes, *confirm*." He looks up at me expectantly. "All right, it's gone."

I glance at Jonas, who's viewing the assassin boards on his phone.

"It's still there," Jonas.

Spencer starts spitting out words. "I don't—I can't—I don't *have* the authority to cancel it! It's above me!"

"Like a judge?" I ask.

"No, a…CEO. They want the girl. They want her alive. You are… incidental. The CEO is the one who wants everyone who helped her killed. They don't want anyone to know about her."

I yell back, "You have to know *why*. Why does she matter?"

"She's a *puer temporis*."

Jessi asks me. "The fuck is that?"

"A child of time." This can't be real. "Is it true? Do you know for a fact?"

"The CEO sure is spending countless resources getting to her."

I start to think about what to do next. First things first, I guess. I plunge the neosiri into Burgealdor Spencers's throat. There's a bit of a blood spray, which hits my pants. This is why everything I own is black or dark blue.

Jonas' mouth is agape. "You just killed—"

"—a Burgealdor, I know," I finish for him.

Jessi walks over to Jonas and I can hear her whisper, "That's the *schwayest* thing she's done so far."

CHAPTER 38

THE FUNERAL

Micel lightly shoves Kergan Satre II in the arm. "You been prepared for this? Speaking in front of your people?"

Kergan shrugs. "They're more Gilead's people than mine. More my mother's than mine. I've been away so long, babies are now walking."

Cadyn says, "I told ya to write a speech out."

Kergan just stares at the empty podium. She starts to sweat.

Micel speaks in a slow, measured manner. "Hey, it's gonna be all right. You say a few things and leave, right?"

Kergan's left hand starts shaking. Cadyn grabs it and snaps Kergan out of her trance. "Hey, don't be a fucking *ibora*."

"Thank you for the sage advice," Kergan says in a montone.

Cadyn barks back, "Good, now I hope ya forget everything up there. Make a *hund* of yourself."

"All right, I'm sorry, I'm…My stomach feels empty and full at the same time."

Micel starts to explain, "It's normal…"

"They're going to expect me to be *great*."

Cadyn grunts her frustration through her nose and begins to say, "I don't know why—"

"You two forget," Kergan interrupts. "Last time I was at a big speech, I ended up holding my mother as she died."

Micel puts his arm around Kergan. "I know Kergan, I'm sorry."

Cadyn looks off to the side and kicks some *gor*.

Later in the day, the big star in the sky is getting tired and starting to hide behind the horizon.

"And I'll close with these words from Gilead," the woman says as she fumbles with a piece of yellow paper. "If justice is our goal, oppressing the oppressor *can't* be our goal. Revenge will leave the forest stripped bare and salted." She clears her throat and waits for some scattered applause to dissipate. "And now—" Before she can finish, the crowd—which consists of the entire town—is humming with whispers. "The daughter of Kergan Satre would like to say a few words about Gilead."

Kergan, sitting between Micel and Cadyn, stands up and walks forward to the wood podium. Standing there, she is unsure what to do with her hands. Puts them to her side at first, but that's too formal. She starts to rest her forearm across, but…no good there. She settles for grabbing the sides of the podium with both hands, as though clinging to a sled.

"I don't know what to do with my hands," she says, quite serious. The crowd laughs anyway. "I guess I could honor Gilead and do the whole speech with my hands." She uses her arms and hands to exaggerate the statement. "Gilead wanted a lot for us: better treatment from Chicago, access to its medical care, so on and so forth. But—and this is something he and my mom argued about most often—he wanted to change Earth's *structure*."

There's agreement in the crowd. Kergan walks away from the safety of the podium. "He wanted to see an end to hierarchical structure that chokes opportunity for us." There's more cheering. With each subsequent sentence, her tone becomes more confident—and when called for, defiant. "He wanted to see an end to the use of the violent machines of intimidation called assassins. He wanted to see CEOs held accountable for turning humanity into nothing more than capital. He wanted a system where people could choose *Burgealdors*, so they'd work for the people and not for the corporations."

The crowd twists their fists in the air and stomp on the ground, expressing their agreement.

Kergan softens her voice and takes a deep breath. "He wanted a return to dignity and respect for people who don't worship at the altar of the corporation. Respect for our land that Chicago's suburbs continues to sprawl into, and dignity for people. People who beg in the street at the convenience of CEOs who value *ricea* over workers. People who are coerced into servitude by laws designed by the lawless!" The last syllable echoes.

Kergan takes a deep breath, allowing the audience to take one themselves and to build up the ending.

Kergan looks down and says, in a hushed tone, "They murdered Gilead for trying to start a *gaderigen* because they are terrified of our power." She looks up at the crowd with a smile on her face. "They should be."

Slowly, the crowd starts to cheer, then stand up, yelling and cheering… jumping and clapping. They even twist—every sign of approval they can think of. Kergan bows multiple times before bouncing back to her seat, her face aglow.

Cadyn's arms are crossed, but she still musters up a compliment. "You did well."

Micel eyes are lit up, "It really was *schway*."

Kergan plops down in her chair. "Yeah, the first couple of times weren't great—but I really got a feel for the crowd after that third attempt. Rafe is here, by the way. In the back."

"Yeah, I didn't have to go back too far, so I think the headaches will dissipate pretty quick."

To be sure, the rest of the *mawasilisho de corpus* was a somber event. After the speeches were finished, the *faru de kufa* began. People shuffle past the box holding Gilead's remains. Some put dirt in the box. Some leaves. Many put *cannes* of his favorite mead inside. Next the town moved onto the *baelblyse*.

Cadyn asks Micel, "This is a forest baelblyse? More festive than the ones in the city. Think you'd have little more respect."

Micel replies, "The idea is we're celebrating the dead's return to nature. The idea is human beings are separate from nature, it's the source of frustration and anger. In death, we leave all that behind and are absorbed back into the *gor*."

"Fuckin' supid."

Micel just shakes his head and walks away.

This was an event the likes of which city dwellers like Cadyn and Rafe had never seen before. A giant bonfire with real wood was started in the center of town. The horizon is a light pink color mixed with swirls of yellow as the star above falls and the *Fyllejnod* appears. Two tables, each about twenty feet long, stand next to each other at the very edge of the party. One holds drinks and is serviced by six forest people. The other is covered, *every inch*, with food. The *hunds* had been smoked for two days so that the meat melted in your mouth. The *fearhs*, roasted over the course of eight hours, fell apart before you could even cut them. Most people could be seen pulling strands of meat off with a fork. About twenty full *carcases* of *cicen* are on the table next to a gravy made from their fat and blood. Mixed together with various wild berries, it left a savory and tangy taste in your mouth.

Cadyn and Rafe are leaning against a signpost at the edge of the party. It reads, "*Ut non uno.*" Cadyn is keeping an eye on Kergan. Both eyes, actually. Staring would be a more appropriate description. And Kergan can feel the eyes on her. She occasionally makes a face at Cadyn, encouraging her to relax. It's about as effective as asking a *hund* to sing Chicago's anthem.

"You ever smell that before?" Rafe asks Cadyn.

"Huh?"

"The bonfire—you ever smelled one before?"

"Yeah, years ago on Riestovik. I was—*gods*, I don't know how young. It was huge, though." She closes her eyes and breathes in through her nose. "It reminds me of solstice celebrations. That smell. Makes me think of my parents." Cadyn opens her eyes and looks down at her feet. "My dad made a delicious grilled *fyscynn*. He'd catch 'em on Jezero Lake. Pickled 'em special for the last night of solstice."

Rafe laughs to himself.

"What?"

"I just never thought about you having parents."

"What does that—"

Two kids interrupt and are circling Cadyn with sparklers, singing a nursery rhyme. Round and round. Singing the same line over and over. Round and round. Cadyn calmly licks the tips of her fingers and smothers one of the kid's sparklers, putting out the fire. The little girl stops, looks at her sparkler, and then runs away crying. The other girl quickly retreats to avoid the same fate.

Rafe retrieves a couple of drinks from the table. He walks over and hands Cadyn a wooden *canne* filled with *ceren*. "You got a real touch there with the kids, Cadyn."

Cadyn is smiling. "Might surprise you, but I 'ate kids."

"Yeah, that follows. But you've done a great job with Kergan."

Cadyn presses on her left nostril and snorts through the right. A wad of snot shoots out. "A brat. And strong-willed."

"But…" Rafe says, trying to lead her.

"But what? She's impudent and slow to learn."

"Come off it, then, you rudder." Rafe elbows Cadyn.

"*Fine.* And I'm only saying this 'cause I'm on me ninth cup of *ceren*. She doesn't quit. Ever. She'll be all right."

Cadyn looks over at Micel, who's dancing with a few people. Micel has the *pulveris* glow and is dropping *voluptatem stilla*. His dance moves are, at best, jerky. Like a *hund* swatting at flies with its tail.

"They 'ave a problem," Cadyn says, nodding toward Micel.

Rafe looks at his cup and swirls the light brown liquid around. "Half the ship has a problem with *pulveris*. Even half of Chicago."

Cadyn looks at Rafe to let him know she's serious. "Eyes need to be kept on M. Liability."

The sky is lit up by the *Fyllejnod* and a few torches placed throughout the clearing. A group of seven play instruments off on the side: fast-paced, upbeat songs. The band ranges in ages from a small child shaking a bell, to an old woman playing a flute. The songs last a minute or so. Then there's a twenty second break, and then the band starts up again.

Cadyn nods to the beat. "The music ain't *weaorud*."

"Yeah, it's catchy. Songs kinda run together, though."

"You have to listen to the rattles in the back row." Cadyn explains.

Rafe closes his eyes and concentrates. "Hm."

Cadyn is still nodding. "Take in the texture of it. How the sound feels."

"I was talking to M, and we miss you playing." Rafe says, with his eyes still closed.

Cadyn stops nodding. "Nope."

"Nope what?"

"I ain't starting up again."

"Come on, why not?"

Cadyn's tone changes to a growl. "Cause I don't fucking want to!"

A few people interrupt their feast and look at Cadyn and Rafe. Rafe puts his hands up to reassure them. Cadyn is less concerned and keeps going.

"When I did, not *one* of ya rudders showed the least bit *anlec*. I take it serious. Not a joke."

Rafe is taken back. "Hey, I understand, Cadyn. People on the ship aren't like CEOs or *Burgealdors*. It was just pleasant. A break from the usual activities of…" Rafe starts sniffing the air, taking deep, measured breaths. "Hey, Sasha is meeting us here. So you know, and don't kill her."

"I still might kill her. She's a weapon for the CEOs."

"Maybe not anymore. She killed a *Burgealdor*."

"Sorry, but isn't she hired to kill the girl we protectin'?"

"True."

"Is this a trap for her? You want to lure her in and we all attack?"

"Nope."

"I don't—"

"You don't like her—assumed and noted, Cadyn."

Micel bounds over, wearing a big smile. "Gods, I forgot how much I missed—"

"Did you know Sasha was coming?" Cadyn interrupts.

"Um, yeah, she's coming to live with us."

Cadyn whips her head around to look at Rafe.

Rafe is looking into the forest surrounding the party. "I's gettin' to that. Do either of you hear anything coming from the forest?"

Without warning, an *arwe* shoots inches away from Cadyn's head and ends up sticking in Micel's arm. Micel reacts casually, reaching to pull it out, betraying no pain. There's a loud *pop*. The head of the arrow explodes, like the *cargast* bombs Pigo Autem uses. Micel's eyes widen as the burning sensation ripples through his arm, consuming him.

Micel falls to his knees, groaning loud enough to drown out the music and bring attention from the rest of the party. Another *arwe* lets loose and hits Cadyn in the calf. Rafe dives to pull it out before it pops, and manages to get it free. However, this just allows the burning chemical to explode over his hand, landing like needles on his skin. The initial pain is so intense, Rafe instinctively grabs for his neosiri to cut the hand off. He's panting and looking for water.

"Cadyn, grab Kergan," Rafe orders, but Cadyn has already taken off to get her. By now, the party has turned into panic mode.

Micel tips over a table, which they both hide behind. "Is this Pigo?"

Rafe is still tending to his hand. "No, he wouldn't use *arwes*."

"Any idea where it came from?"

Rafe waves his hand back and forth liberally. "Over there?!"

Rafe looks down at his hand. The burning is as intense as before, but it's not registering. He's too busy examining his now sieve-like hand. Micel's forearm is exposed, almost to the bone. He keeps shaking it, hoping the chemical will come off, but it won't. Then, from behind them, a voice comes.

"I got the cure." A voice yells. "I got the cure for those burns."

An giant man, over seven feet, strides over to the two with his left hand behind his back and his bow in his right. He's wearing green pants and a black sweater with a green hood pulled up. His mouth is contorted into a smug smile as he intermittently licks his top lip. He stops a few feet away from Rafe and Micel.

"I have the cure. But be assured, I have more *kulpukas* also." He takes a long circle around the table to get a better view of his victims. A couple of men, forest people, charge at the tall man from behind. He whips around and puts an *arwe* in each in their throats. "Not smart."

He turns his attention back to Micel and Rafe, whose faces are red and scrunched, trying to get through the burning.

"I'm Welsly. I'm going to capture your project, Kergan Satre II. It'd be much faster and easier if you would call her back on your phones. First one to do it gets *this*." He holds up a tiny bag. "This is the powder that will neutralize the burning."

Kergan starts laughing, "Yeah, sure, we'll call Cadyn and tell her to bring the kid right back."

Micel joins in, alternately chuckling and grunting. "Hey, I'll make the call. hang on. Phone, call Cadyn."

"Wow, this is going much smoother than I thought."

Micel shakes his head. "Hey, Cadyn! Yeah. Can you bring Kergan back here? What's that? Well, the assassin who attacked us is here and would like to capture her…Well, he has a powder to…What was it you said?"

"It will neutralize the burning. Tell her I will kill you two and everyone in this *draest* town."

Micel shrugs. "Sure. He says he will kill everyone here, including me and Rafe. Yeah, sounds good." Micel looks up at the tall man. "She said she looks forward to being the leader of the crew."

"That doesn't make sense. It's giving up one person versus me slaughtering a whole town."

Rafe explains, "Cadyn's guiding morality is that she completes her job no matter what."

Micel mumbles, "Yeah, she's…intense."

The pain had developed into a throbbing. It couldn't be ignored anymore.

Rafe groans out a request. "Can we just pay you for the powder?"

"I mean, there's a lot of *feoh* on that girl's head. You can't make up for it."

Micel is grunting in a simple pattern, matching the throbbing of the pain. A sliver of bone is exposed at this point. "You're going to get nothing as it stands now. Also, killing the town is a bit excessive."

The tall man appears to be thinking. "Huh? Oh, no." He waves his hand. "I wasn't going to do that." He pulls his hood back, revealing a tattooed head with some scarring on the forehead. Micel and Rafe look at each other. Though tattooed heads were somewhat common on Riestovik, the practice had died off on Earth.

The tall man works on his phone, mumbling into it.

The two injured parties look at each other and start to stand.

"I'll put an *arwe* in each eye before you got close enough with your neosiris."

Rafe groans and falls back down. "How about if we tell you where she's going?"

The tall man laughs. "You'd just give me a fake location."

Rafe puts two fingers over his heart. "I resent that, sir. I'm a *kamuni dominus*."

The tall man is still studying his phone. "Let's see, Rafe Fortune, the *weaorud* who promised to help the assassin Sasha kill a family. But instead told the family about the contract and smuggled them into the forest for a handsome sum. You used Sasha's intel to screw her over. And she was your girlfriend at the time."

Rafe smirks and replies, "That's bullshit. I didn't take the *feoh*."

"So *adumbian and* a liar. Great combination." The tall man hums to himself before saying, "Send me this amount and you can have the powder. That's from each of you."

After applying the powder, Micel punches the table they were hiding behind, snapping it like a toothpick.

"Hey, it's not all bad. We kept the girl safe and got the powder," Rafe says.

Micel stares off into the forest.

"What's wrong, M?"

"I needed that *feoh*." Micel whispers his reply so that Rafe can barely make it out.

"Huh? I couldn't hear you, M."

Micel turns around. "Let's get back to the ship."

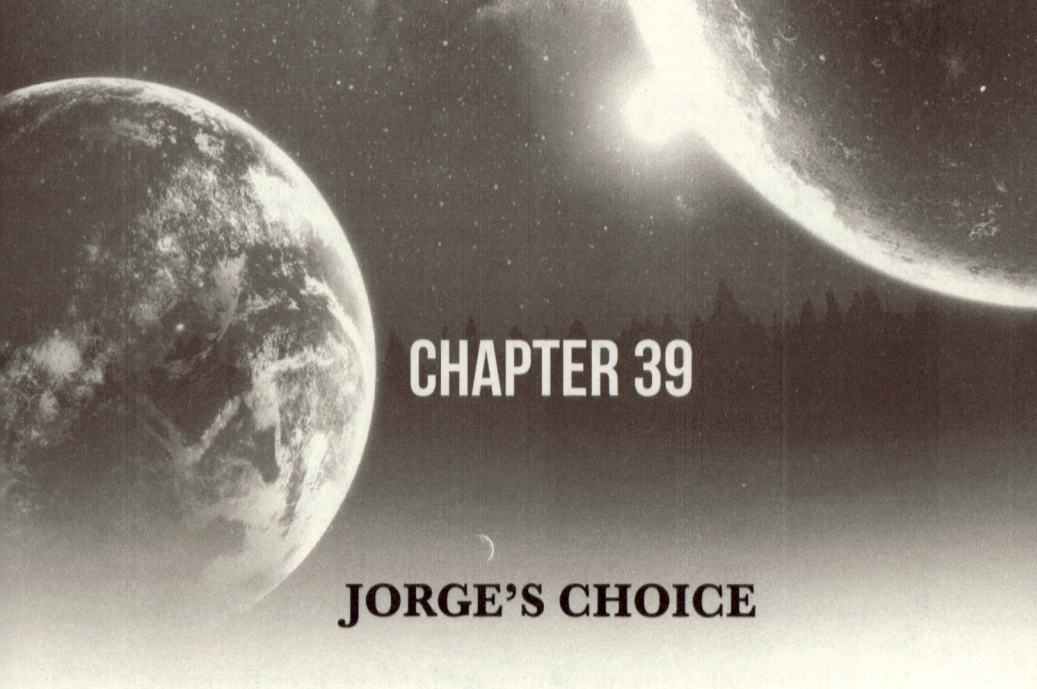

CHAPTER 39

JORGE'S CHOICE

"Jorge, you remember me? I'm Wildorlic, from Notitia."

It's early in the workday and Jorge has just got his computer up and running. The border around his cubicle is light pink, which means he has just arrived but has not yet logged onto the phones yet.

Jorge turns around in his chair. Wildorlic is wearing a blue, collared shirt with mustard yellow pants. His head is shaved on the sides, revealing a tattoo of the company logo. It's a unicorn in front of a blue shield.

"Yes, Mr. Wildorlic."

"Would you be so kind as to follow me, please?"

As they walk down the hall, Wildorlic attempts small talk. "So we had a good week for margin, last week, huh?"

"Sure, I guess."

"Are you looking forward to the late quarter push?"

"Um, yeah."

"I remember I would get here hours early to go over my goals and calibrate my strategies. Exciting times."

"Right," Jorge responds.

"But working in Notitia has its benefits," Wildorlic says as he opens the door to an office Jorge didn't even know existed.

From the outside, it looks like an *afeormian*. But instead, instead of mops and buckets, there's a thin staircase lit by a single hovering light bulb. The staircase goes so far down, Jorge can't see where it leads. Wildorlic presses his thumb against a panel and the door slides shut.

"Go ahead, Jorge." Wildorlic's words echoed.

Halfway down, Jorge looks back at Wildorlic, who says, "Go on, then."

The light runs alongside them, illuminating the next step, but nothing further. Jorge can make out a clanging sound, like a wrench knocking against sheet metal. It's mixed with a whirring buzz, like a redeye or an automatic blender. Jorge peers over the side of the stairs, looking down.

Jorge chuckles, "They doing construction down there?"

"Yeah. Construction. Sure."

"What's that sound—"

"It's just ahead here, a few more steps."

When they reach the bottom, a door frame lights up and the floating bulb that followed them heads back up the stairs. Jorge watches the bulb. When it disappears, he has a sudden anxiety attack. He rubs his stomach and slows his breathing.

Wildorlic engages a retinal scan and sweeps his left arm to open the door. Jorge enters first and notices the smell. While descending down the staircase, the air was musty and stale, but in this hallway it switches over to a fresh *wudduple* scent. Each square of floor laminate lights up a bright white when you step on it. Jorge smiles at this and starts hopping around.

"Stop—*stop* that! Hey!" Wildorlic starts. "This is still on company grounds. Please act professionally."

Jorge follows Wildorlic down the hall, noticing the numbers on all the doors they pass. "Mr. Wildorlic, where are we in the facility?"

"This is statistical company asset management."

Wildorlic stops suddenly and turns to face a door with the number thirty-five on it.

Jorge feels that anxiety come on again. "Is this the…the hurt room?"

Wildorlic snorts. "That's not the official name of it. The official name is Heuristic Inquiry for Asset Allocation. But yes, among the workers it is commonly known as the *hurt room*."

"I'd rather not go in there."

"I don't doubt that." He opens the door and nods at Jorge to go in.

Jorge slides his left foot across the threshold, then his right. The door closes behind him, and Wildorlic is gone. A soft yellow light comes on, revealing a worker's room setting.

A couple of sofas. A seven-foot fur *kitanda* with a triangle of three white fluffy pillows in the middle. A *capulusno* table, seafoam green, with a couple of empty glasses next to a jug of water. There's also a plate of *cecel*. Jorge picks one of the little *cecels* up with his fingers and pops it in his mouth. The dough is buttery, flaky, and the fruit on top is fresh.

Jorge plops down on the *kitanda* and looks around. The area he is in is lit up well, but surrounding him is darkness. He can't make out where the room ends in any direction except the one he entered. There's a shuffling sound simultaneously from his left and right. Jorge turns his head back and forth, squinting, but can't make out anyone. Until they hit the light.

"Jorge, I'm *Magistratus* Singleton."

"Jorge, I'm *Magistratus* Dominus Deebo."

Singleton is dressed in a drab grey uniform, complete with grey fedora. He's round, with a large potbelly testing the strength of his shirt buttons. His eyes are squinted, like he's studying you at all times.

Deebo's uniform is the same style, but with hints of blue. He's significantly taller than Singleton with a medium build. The one distinctive feature Jorge notices is Deebo's long fingernails. On some fingers, they're starting to curl over.

Singleton asks, "Jorge, I trust you're comfortable?"

"Yeah, these are delicious *cecels*."

Singleton nods at Deebo, "Deebo's husband makes them fresh every morning."

"Yeah, but they're premade, he just redeyes them."

Jorge twists his fist in appreciation, "Still very good."

Deebo pinches a *cecel* between his thumb and middle finger. He nibbles at it, then puts it back down.

Singleton sits down and crosses his legs. "The management tracker has a very positive view of your output, Jorge."

"I'm sorry, do you work for the company?"

Singleton ignores the question. "Looks like, as an employee, you're in the top five percent."

"Yeah? Didn't keep them from cutting my salary."

Deebo and Singleton look at each other. Then Singleton continues, "We didn't realize that. We'll take care of it immediately and restore your pay."

Jorge raises his eyebrows. "Wow, I appreciate that, thanks."

Singleton says, "On top of that, Jorge—speaking on behalf of the company, we would like to extend an offer for a promotion."

"Wait, so you *do* work for the company?"

The two look at each other. Singleton, again, ignores the question. "So this is a reward for your loyalty, Jorge. You're a part of a family here and an extremely valued asset."

Jorge looks back and forth between them and asks. "I…what is the new role?"

"Don't worry about it for now." Deebo talks to his phone. "Contract. Send to Jorge Burprofen."

Singleton uncrosses his legs. "If you just acknowledge it and agree, we can get you set up. There's a used office all set up for you."

"That's great, but what am I agreeing to? This contract just has the word 'promotion' on it a bunch of times. What's the pay bump?"

Singleton motions with his index finger. "Scroll down."

"Oh, shit. I'm sorry. Oh, *wow*." Jorge squints and studies the contract.

Singleton claps softly twice. "So, if you would kindly agree, we can go ahead and get that processed."

Jorge hesitates. He thinks about Alva. About having a kid with no company sponsor. The *feoh* is vital. "I mean, is it a supervisory position?"

Singleton asks, "Would you like that?"

"I've really wanted to work in the information department for a while now."

Singleton nods in affirmation. "We can do that."

"Wow, all right, that's—" A smile breaks out on Jorge's face. "That's *great*. Exciting."

"Good to hear."

There's silence for a minute. Jorge leans forward, grabbing another *cecel*.

Deebo interrupts the quiet. "We understand congratulations are in order."

Jorge sits up straight. "Huh?"

Deebo drums his fingers together. "Ah, yes—I get you'd want to keep this private. But things have a way of getting out."

Jorge tries to lie. "I'm not sure what—"

Deebo smacks his lips and shakes his head. "Jorge, we've been honest up to this point, let's not break that trust. Lying to us is lying to the company."

Jorge looks down, snatches a *cecel*, and nervously nibbles on it.

Singleton crosses his legs again and leans back. "The medical cost for the birth alone is going to bankrupt you, Jorge."

Jorge stops eating. He unconvincingly replies, "We've been saving up."

Deebo and Singleton chuckle and look at each other.

Deebo stands up and looks down on Jorge. "Jorge, the company wants to be reassured that you are part of our family. The company is reaching out with this promotion. *Are* you part of the family?"

"Yes. This has been my family for years now."

"Family members don't turn their backs when times are tough. More than that, we stand up for each other," Deebo concludes.

Singleton continues the thought. "And since you are going through a rough time, we want to reach out and offer to sponsor your future worker."

Jorge shrugs, "But we need permission from both companies."

Singleton grins, exposing his teeth. "Rest assured, we can get that for you, even with Alva's…um…past choices."

Deebo's hands are folded in front of him. "Yes, but just as we're helping you out, the company needs you to reciprocate."

"*Nihil liberum es christendom*," Jorge replies with a chuckle.

Deebo nods, "Of course, nothing is free—how would we ever maintain order otherwise?"

Singleton lays out the proposition, "We know you're a part of a group that is trying to establish a *gaderigen*. We need to know who the *burgealdor* and judge are that are backing you."

Deebo shrugs, "Just two names and your child's fortunes go from a gutter worker to limitless."

CHAPTER 40

DRAKE RECRUITS

Pigo Autem twirls a tiny red stick between his fingers as Drake and he walk down an alley. Behind Drake, his *pincern* is dragging a large brown bag—large enough to hold a person. Pigo tosses the red stick at a *draest* can. The stick explodes on contact and flips the *draest* can over.

Drake rolls his eyes. Pigo takes out another stick and starts twirling that one also.

Drake grunts out a question, "Aren't you afraid it'll blow off a finger?"

"Know what I'm doin'," Pigo says. "I know 'ese chemicals better than most people know their spouses."

There's no wind today, and the *Andetnes* star is beating down on Chicago's residents.

Drake is sweating profusely. "I feel like I'm gonna fucking melt. *Pincern,* did you bring my water?"

"Yes, I most certainly did."

Drake snatches the bottle, chugs some water, then tosses it on the ground for the *pincern* to collect.

"I think it's right over there. It's in between the 'No Parking' signs," Pigo points.

"Yeah, this the place they sliced and diced you? This place is for fucking *victoses*," Drake says with biting disdain.

Pigo shrugs in response. "Come on, Drake, you said you wouldn't call me that anymore, man."

Drake laughs. "Yeah, I did, didn't I?"

Pigo shakes his head and reaches out his hand. It disappears into the wall. "Here we go."

All three of them enter the hidden doorway with the *pincern* diligently dragging the bag.

"Hey, Mom!" Pigo exclaims when they open the door to a waiting room.

Drake shakes his head. "Of course."

"Pigo, my baby!" She rushes up and kisses him on the cheek. "So good to see my handsome boy." She turns to Drake. "And who is your friend here?"

"I'm not his friend," Drake snorts. "I'm Drake Beu Nyoka."

Pigo's mom is taken back. "Oh, wow, what an honor to have a member of the Nyoka *cynling* —"

"Yeah, it's a real treat for me too. Can we see 'er?" Drake rushes through his words thoughtlessly.

Pigo's mom shrinks down, "Oh...um, of course. Right this way."

She leads them down a bright pink hallway. The floor is white laminate and there are railings on both sides.

"What's in the bag?" she asks.

"A human being," Drake replies.

Pigo's mom looks at him. He grins and shrugs.

"Anyway, um, here we are, boys." She points at a brown door with a small round window at the top. "She just started talking again two days ago. Doing very well, considering."

Drake enters the room first. He looks over at the bed where the patient is turned on her side, presumably sleeping.

"Belle, you awake?" Drake asks.

Belle sighs, as if disturbed. "I am *now*, Drake Beu Nyoka."

"Hey, Belle, I'm here recruiting people for a contract."

"If it's about that kid, forget it. I'm not interested." She sits up. "I'm not interested in any of it."

Drake nods at his *pincern*, then says, " But,I brought an *offering* for you."

The *pincern* undoes the bag and drags out a body. A pudgy young boy with blue hair and bright green eyes. He's hogtied with his hands behind his back and his mouth has been sewn shut by a *formeltan* iron. His nostrils flare with each breath.

Belle tilts her head and studies the offering. "Mikey?"

Mikey realizes who he's in front of and tries to scream while wiggling around. It's no use.

Belle stands up and walks over to Mikey. "How'd you find him?"

"I just talked to an *esne* who witnessed it. Well, *I* didn't talk—I had one of my *pincerns* talk to it."

Belle gently pushes Mikey with her foot, then looks at Drake. "I don't have a neosiri on me. Not even a *cnif*."

Drake unsheathes his neosiri and hands it to her. She points the tip of the blade at his throat. "Mikey, I want you to know I'm sorry you lost your father. But you can't make business personal. That's the lesson you need to take from this, okay?"

Mikey nods furiously. Belle cuts his hands free and slices open his mouth so he can open it again.

Belle isn't looking at him, but says, "Please, don't try to kill me again."

Mikey appears to be in shock, his hands shaking.

"Well, boy? Run on now," Belle demands.

Drake puts his hands up in the air, "I don't know what that was, but I'm taking you freeing him as you accepting my offering."

Belle is still holding his sword. She studies the blade, then looks at Drake.

"Belle, now, don't get any ideas," Drake says.

"What do you want for the offering?"

Drake promptly replies, "Sasha."

"Then go find her."

"You might be the only person in our world she trusts. I want you to set a trap for me."

Belle snorts out a laugh.

"Hey, this isn't a fucking game, ya old rudder. I made an offer and you accepted—right, Pigo?"

Pigo shrugs.

Belle speaks in monotone. "It's fine, I'll help you. She's the one who can lead us to Kergan."

Belle hands the neosiri back.

Drake cracks his knuckles. "I thought you wanted nothing to do with the kid."

"If I'm going to help execute a contract on someone I raised like a child, I'm at least going to get paid well for it."

Drake looks at Pigo. Pigo nods. Drake grins, "Sounds like a deal."

CHAPTER 41

SASHA MOVES IN

I saw Jorge briefly this morning. And Alva. I gave them a small sweater I bought, along with tiny shoes. Also, some kind of *bridd* toy where when you push on the beak, it displays the alphabet and recites it to you. When I think about it, my stomach churns and I can feel my eyes start to water. There's a real possibility I'll never meet their baby.

But I'm happy for them. They're two people of integrity and they deserve all the happiness the Earth can afford. And I believe the gods are generous to people like them. People like me....

It's the first night I'm on Rafe's ship. This will probably be the last place I ever live. The kids, too. Right now, we're eating in the *triclinium*. Kergan was here, but left the hall the minute we entered. She's none too thrilled about us being here. Well, me, at least.

Cadyn walks over to me and leans down, her eyes locked on mine. "You know what you are?"

I shrug.

"Proof that Rafe is weak." She takes a finger and sticks it in my sparkling *ceren*, stirs it around, then walks away. I can't tell if that was Cadyn's attempt at flirting or not.

The kids look at me, waiting for me to react. I don't feel like it. I don't know—I think the reality of the situation is setting in. And the more I think about being stuck here, the more claustrophobic I feel. I wonder if Jorge's kid will like the toy.

I leave the table and head to our cabin. I say *our cabin* because I'm sharing it with Terror Girl. Kid Kill is sleeping on the floor of Micel's room. Our room is small. Too small for two people. But Rafe assured me something will open for Terror Girl. There's a couple of plant projections on the bedside table. No dresser to be found though.

When I look at my stuff piled in a corner, and Terror Girl's stuff piled in another, I realize how unfair this situation is for them. I sit on the bed and go over everything in my mind. If I just had enough *feoh* to pay off my debt. I could have saved more, maybe. I know many workers who are just starting out are cutting back to one meal a day. Maybe I should have done that.

I miss Jorge. Usually, I'd talk to him about these things.

A purple light flashes in the corner of my eye, indicating a video message has been sent. In order to keep the ship hidden, phones—which have tracking devices built in—have to be kept offline. You can send and receive messages, but you can't make a live call.

"Open."

"Sasha." It's Auntie Belle. She's coughing in between her words. "I need to see you. I'm sick and I need help. Can you meet me at my apartment, please?"

This is a *fealle*. And an obvious one. She's not even bothering to hide it.

"I'm practically bedridden. Come as soon as you can."

If she really wanted to see me, she'd insult me and call me stupid.

"Delete." I say out loud. I see a shadow cross the threshold of my doorway, then see Kergan standing there. I can't read her face; it's blank. I don't think she knows what she was going to say, or she did and forgot the second she saw me.

Kergan's still wearing that frog pin.

I'm not going to be the one to talk first. She looks much older than when I was hired to kill her and her mom. There's been a weathering of her face, and her skin looks unhealthy, ashy. Probably too much time on this ship. But I do notice, in her eyes, I can still get a glimpse of that young girl I almost shot.

Kergan was making eye contact, but now is looking off to the side. I stand up and walk over to her. She's still in the doorway.

I look at her directly in the eye and put a hand on her shoulder. She swipes it away with a scowl. I suck on my top lip for a couple of seconds, then motion for Kergan to follow me.

Kergan nods.

A half an hour later, we're knocking on Auntie Belle's apartment door. She opens the door, looking the worse for wear. Belle nods her head and opens the door wide. Kergan and I walk in.

Belle closes the door behind us. I walk up, give her a giant hug and whisper, "I don't know why you're doing this, but it's the wrong choice."

Belle responds, with a rasp in her voice, "I didn't have much of one. I'm sick. I need the *feoh*." She pushes me back, holding me by the shoulders. Her face hardens, her lips curl into a snarl. "You're a grave disappointment ta me."

There's a crackling sound coming at my head. I turn around and bat away a tiny read stick. It lands on the kitanda and blows up, kicking fabric and stuffing into the air.

Two more sticks are thrown. I swat them both away, but miss a third one, which explodes right by my ear. I collapse and all sound is drowned out by a hissing in my eardrum.

"Pigo, this is a bad idea, my guy," I yell out. He's probably in the kitchen.

"Good idea, Sasha. Lots of *feoh* to make."

I'm hiding behind the couch, with Kergan crouched next to me. I've lost eyes on Belle. Two more sticks land behind us and explode, causing the window to shatter.

"Pigo, let's be reasonable. You have no reason to hate me. Why attack me now?"

Pigo laughs a child-like giggle. "Wow, don't remember punching me for no reason?"

I don't, so I say, "No." I peek over the couch to try and get his position. "That's it? Because I hit you? You're a damn assassin."

Pigo has a desperate whine in his voice, "I like you—you were supposed to be my friend."

I have no idea where he got that impression. I even look at Kergan and shrug.

"We were—*are* friends, so don't you think killing me is pretty immoral, Pigo?"

"*Mji mkuu es morbus*," Pigo giggles again.

Kergan gives me a perplexed look, so I explain, "That's the Chicago motto. It means *money is morality*."

I have my sidearm out, check that it's loaded. Kergan is staring at it. I know what she's wondering, but I don't have time. I peek around the corner and can see spikes of blue hair sticking up from behind an overturned kitchen table. I shoot twice at the table, but the bullets just dent it and ricochet off.

Damn, Belle probably used braso bronze for the table as a safety precaution. It's smart, but really inconvenient for me right now. *Where is she?*

A glass ball rolls towards me on the ground. I turn behind the couch. I cover Kergan's eyes and close mine. Even still, the flash-bang is bright enough to temporarily white out my vision. I fire twice in the direction of the table (I think) and blink rapidly. Two more shots, hoping to hold him off. Nothing yet. I can hear footsteps running at us. I take a couple more shots, but they don't stop. Kergan is gripping the bottom of my sweater so hard, it's starting to rip at the stitching. And then, suddenly, the running stops.

I was expecting an explosion and am thrown off by the punch to the side of my head, right in my temple.

"We're even now," Pigo grumbles.

I'm starting to make out shadows of shapes, but not much else. I'm pointing the gun randomly, hoping to scare him off, but he slaps it away and gets on top of me, pinning me to the ground.

It's silent in the apartment until there's the sound of a lighter being struck. "You could'a been nice with me, Kergan. Could'a treated me well. You wouldn't be about to lose your head." Pigo follows this statement with another giggle.

I'm not fighting back yet—when I do strike, it'll work better as a surprise. I have my hand on his chest, not to push, but to get a map of where his body parts are.

I can make out the hiss from the fuse being lit. I jab him in the throat with my fingers. He reacts by opening his mouth and gasping. I roll us over, take the hand with the bomb in it and force it into his mouth. My sight is clearing up. Pigo is wriggling around, violently kicking and shaking, but I'm too strong. He reaches at my eyes with his free hand, and I have to pull my head back and turn my head to stop him. When the bomb explodes, his cheeks are shredded like curtains. His tongue—I *think* it's his tongue—is hanging out of the bottom of his chin.

Pigo is prone on his back with his arms curled up on his chest. I find my sidearm and hand it to Kergan so she can keep an eye on him as he, well—*dies*, I assume. I head off to Belle's bedroom and find her sitting in a *schlot* fchair, tilting back and forth slightly.

Belle stops rocking and says, "You know this chair is worth…worth…" She stumbles a bit with her words before looking me in the eye. "Worth more than *I* am at this point."

"I never thought it was real."

"My grandfather handed it down. Don't brag, cause I don't want it stolen. But yeah, it's real wood."

We look at each other. Not stare, but *look*. I can't kill her. "I can't kill you."

"Should'a fixed the slice and dice, then." Auntie Belle replies with raised eyebrows. She sucks on her teeth then says, "This contract is from the CPR himself."

"Shit really stirs up when you kill someone on the top of the pyramid, huh?"

"Yup." Belle shifts in her seat. I can see a flash of steel hidden under her leg. I hope she's not planning on doing anything. I would have to—

"Under your leg?" I ask, "That a neosiri? Silver one with the Abakalician carvings?"

Belle smiles. "Saw that, huh?" Belle pulls out the neosiri, admires it, then looks at me. "I gotta make the attempt, otherwise I'll be the one they contract out next. Which gun do you have?"

I point to my holster, exposing it as empty. "Kergan has it."

"Why'd you bring her?"

"Gave her the option. After what I did, she deserves it."

"Gods, Sasha, you really should have gotten fixed." She turns her head and lets out a wet, hacking cough. Belle takes out a blue mask and covers her mouth with it. When she inhales, it shoots into her mouth, like it was a spider scurrying to hide. Belle takes a deep breath with her eyes closed. When she opens them, they're glowing dark blue. "In the closet is a *beadomece*. Grab it so we can get on with this."

"I could just—"

"Gods almighty, Sasha! Go grab the fuckin' *beadomece* and let's get on wit it!"

I walk over to the closet, with my eyes on her the whole time. Never trust Belle.

"It's behind the *forlisgleng*, the red one."

I push the cotton dress out of the way, still looking at her. Maybe it's because my hearing is still shit, but I'm caught off guard by the hand reaching out and grabbing my wrist. I can't dwell on it as a fist slams into my chin. It's off-center, more of a graze, but enough to drop me to a knee. From the back of the closet, Drake's face slithers through the garments. His grin is sickening.

I look at Belle. "Gods, Belle, this *weorud?*"

Drake kicks me in the side, and I roll belly up. He grabs me by the hair and slams my head down. Everything vibrates when my head hits the floor. He does it again and punches me in the mouth. Drake wraps his hands around my throat with his thumbs pressing into my trachea. I can't get any breath in. I look at Belle, who's walking over to us. She stops. Puts both hands up and starts to back away.

I look up at Drake, who's baring a toothy grin at me as he puts pressure on my throat. "This…is the best feeling I've ever had. I'm glad Pigo didn't kill you."

I can still manage the strength to spit in his face. If it's my last act, so be it.

CHAPTER 42

WHERE IS SASHA?

"Where's your *lareow*?" Micel asks Kid Kill and Terror Girl. They're sitting in Micel's cabin, drinking *ceren*.

Kid Kill doesn't even bother to look at Micel, "I have no idea. She went back to her cabin, I thought."

Cadyn comes stomping down the hall towards Micel. "I can't find Kergan anywhere."

Terror Girl suggests, "Just use the tracking on her phone."

Cadyn curls the corner of her lip. "Tracking's disabled on this ship. For obvious fuckin' reasons."

Jessi just rolls her eyes and takes another gulp of *ceren*.

Micel, under his breath, says to Cadyn, "What if Kergan killed Sasha?"

Cadyn's eyes widen. "That'd be fuckin' great!"

Jonas glares at Cadyn, "Hey, that's our *lareow*, yeah? Leave it alone."

Cadyn looks at Jonas and pretends to wipe her hands clean.

Jonas stands up, sways a bit. He tries to pull out his weapon, but fumbles it to the ground. It's quickly followed by him falling facedown when he tries to pick it up.

"Probably turned Kergan in, that rudder," Cadyn worries.

Micel runs his left hand through his hair and pulls out a few strands. "That'd be a damn disaster."

Cadyn looks at him crossly. "Yes, it would." Cadyn spits out of the side of her mouth and snorts. "Well, let's go find 'em."

The foursome consists of Cadyn, Micel, Jonas, and Jessi. As they leave the ship, they're greeted by Rafe, who's hanging out on the dock. He looks worse for wear and has no shirt on, exposing numerous scars, including the one Micel gave him. He's pitching rocks into the lake and humming an old nursery rhyme.

"She went to see Auntie Belle," Rafe says in between throws. "Something about a trap. She told me not to follow, then knocked me out with the butt of her sidearm. Kinda like how we broke up."

Cadyn asks, "Is that the Auntie Belle that killed the Judge Moscato?"

"One and the same, Cadyn."

Jonas asks, "So, she would be in the palaces, then?"

Micel and Rafe both laugh.

Micel explains, "Gods no, she's in a *bolttimber* by Bucktown."

"You'd have to know her. She's not built for the residential section. Anyway, Micel remembers where she lives." Rafe says, tossing another rock.

Micel nods.

Rafe chucks the rest of the rocks all at once. "Off we go, then."

Micel takes the lead, with Rafe trailing well behind everyone else. "Quite the crew we make, huh? Three rudders and a couple a *leornes*."

Jessi looks to Micel. "The fuck's wit 'em?"

"He doesn't deal with heartbreak well. Or at all."

Jessi sticks out her tongue and shakes her head.

They arrive at Belle's *bolttimber* to find a man with his jaw missing and Kergan pointing a gun at him. The scent of gunpowder hangs in the air, along with a light haze of smoke.

Cadyn goes over to Kergan and lowers her arms, finally taking the gun away. Micel checks on Pigo, who is fighting to keep breathing. Rafe pushes through with his neosiri drawn and looks for Sasha. Down the hall, sounds spew from the bedroom. He turns the corner to find Drake perched on top of Sasha, with his hands around her throat.

Drake notices Rafe a moment too late.

Rafe's sword goes right through Drake's neck, slightly to the left of center. Rafe starts sawing back and forth. Drake grips the blade of the sword, the rest of his body in spasms. Rafe finally saws through the rest of Drake's neck, and Drake crumples to the ground. Decapitated.

Auntie Belle is still sitting in the *schlot* chair. "You're too late. He killed her."

Rafe turns and runs into the worker's room. He grabs Kergan by the arm and drags her over to Sasha's body.

"Fix it!" Rafe demands.

Jessi and Jonas appear behind Kergan.

Rafe points his neosiri at her nose. *"Fuckin' do it!"*

Kergan glares at Rafe. "She killed my mom. She was going to kill me."

Jonas asks, "Jessi, can you bring her back?" His breathings is short and fast. He runs both hands through his hair.

Jessi staggers back, then responds, "Fuck it, might be too long. I'll try."

In a few seconds, Jessi and Kergan are the only two people in their universe. Jessi looks Kergan up and down. "Who gave *you* this power?"

Kergan nibbles her top lip and replies, "I was born with it."

Both are suspended in a black space, delinquent of anything resembling life.

Kergan tilts her head and locks eyes with Jessi, "What is this place? Do you know?"

Jessi breaks the gaze and looks around, "Fuck, this is the first time I've been conscious in it."

"Maybe it's cause I'm here—makes it stronger."

"That makes no sense," Jessi says. She starts to bleed from her nose.

"What's that? You all right?"

"Yeah. Well, no. Some shit about people's minds aren't built to see time like this—flat or whatever."

"So, you get nose bleeds?" Kergan asks.

Jessi sighs and answers, "Worse. They say one day, I'll completely lose my mind."

"I'm sorry to hear that."

Jessi looks down and says, "My brother thinks if one of us becomes Cysta Por Ruverno, we'll be able to cure me. That they have access to treatments the workers don't."

"You understand why I don't want Sasha brought back, right?"

Jessi nods, "I don't understand why you didn't kill her yourself."

Kergan looks at her hands. "I've never killed anyone before. It's not that easy."

Jessi laughs a giant belly laugh. "Man, I don't even know where to start. I mean, it's just workers. They're replaceable assets."

"You know you're talking about yourself, right? Do you value your life that little?"

Jessi frowns, "I—I don't know—it's—"

"It's how you're trained to think. You can't value other people's lives cause you don't value your own."

"Gods, Mom, thanks for the lecture."

"I can't kill her precisely *because* I value my life. Human beings shouldn't be looked at as disposable assets. The goal of life isn't to improve a company's margins."

Jessi challenges her, "But you would let her die—how's that different?"

Kergan thinks on it for a second. "Maybe it's not."

Jessi scratches the back of her head, "Come to think of it, you let your mom die, too, didn't you?"

Kergan shrugs. "She didn't want to be brought back."

"Why not?"

"Don't know—my mom wasn't exactly an open book." Kergan looks around at all the nothingness. "This is the first time I've been here with someone."

"Yeah. I'd ask you how long we've been here, but—"

Kergan chuckles.

There's an interruption of light piercing the black background. More light beams show up around them and the primary colors start to appear.

"Well, here we go," Jessi looks at Kergan. "It'd mean a lot to me—*my brother*—if you saved her. I think you're the only person who can."

Kergan looks away. "Yeah. We'll see."

"Later." And with that, Jessi disappears.

The scent of gunpowder hangs in the air along with a light haze of smoke.

Cadyn enters first, kicking broken glass out of the way. Micel checks on Pigo, who is fighting to keep breathing. Rafe pushes through the kids with his neosiri drawn and looks for Sasha. Down the hall, sounds spew from the bedroom. There's the pop of a gun.

Rafe peaks into the room and sees Kergan holding a still-smoking sidearm. Drake is rolling around, holding his leg. Sasha is gasping for breath. She stomps over to Drake, who's screaming and crying.

"*Weaorud!*" Drake spits and kicks at Sasha. "You piece of *draest*! I'm fuckin' Drake Beu Nyoka, you rudd—"

The heel of Sasha's boot slams down on his chin. She braces against the wall, and kicks down over and over. The first few times, there's a *cracking* sound, but eventually it's more of a *crunching* sound.

Kergan slides the gun away and walks out.

Sasha turns her attention to Auntie Belle.

"I don't know what to do with you, Belle."

"You should probably listen, 'cause I have a way for you to stop being targeted by CEOs." Belle replies with a knowing grin. Sasha shakes her head in frustration, glances over to Rafe, then nods for Belle to continue.

CHAPTER 43

PURIFICATION

The old ones called it a *safi officium*. Basically, a job that cleans your debts. I'm still not in an emotional position to do the killing myself, but the job is easy enough for the kids. I told them to avoid the flair, painting letters in blood and shit like that. Just be *professional*.

The best part is I'm back home. I can be there for Jorge and Alva. Get to meet the little rudder spitting out soon. I'm looking forward to…life. I can't say that was true when I had the surgery.

"The crackling of that bacon is music to my ears, Jorge," I say, taking a seat at the table.

Alva waddles over (sorry to be mean, but it's accurate at this point in her pregnancy) and replaces a yellow *waridira* with a blue one. I'm starting to remember to ask people about their feelings again.

"How's the feet, Alva?"

"Getting fatter every day," she says, then waddles back to Jorge and steals some bacon from the pan. "It's a miracle Jorge's work decided to sponsor the kid. The meds I'm on are helping my back pain, at least."

"Yeah, Jorge, how'd you swing that?"

Jorge shrugs and doesn't respond.

A green light flashes in my eye. It's Kid Kill. "Hey."

"It's done. It worked out perfectly—they were both trapped in that warehouse."

"Good to hear." I think but don't say, *I'm free again.*

Terror Girl is wiping off her sword. "But I don't think they can fake these as suicides. We kinda sliced them up."

"Not our problem, we just needed to execute the project. So everything went smoothly?"

The kids look at each other and nod approvingly. "Yeah. I mean, how hard is it to kill a *burgealdor* and a judge?"

Byron Bartlett is a Chicago area author of vague renown. He graduated from a college that's no longer accredited. He was an editor and staff writer for a boating magazine that no longer exists. He works for a company that was swallowed by another company who was then swallowed by a larger company. He loves stories like Battle Royale and Ichi the Killer, and hopes to bring the same level of dark humor and viscerally titillating violence to his own writing. His debut novel, Violent Souls, is the first book in the Blood City Chronicles

GLOSSARY

*Because the language of Earth is a blend of the 3 planets (Riestovik, LaRocca, Abakalic) some of these definitions are rough approximations.

Rudder - bastard born of a Fearh (pig)
Hwicci - chest, hope chest
kuokua locus - safe space
ARMORY/GUN STORE- WAPENUS
Beomador - Queen Bee
Esne - poor person/panhandler
geboeric - Dog
rudder - Slang/insult bastard or bitch
magistratus - police
Feoh - money
Kipanga - giant falcon/eagle
Dryre - depository/trade shop
Wudduple - apple
Geneat - annoyance, like a gnat or mosquito
Woda de Faereld - A crazy action, the action of a madman
Ceren - wine/beer
Leona - Lion
Victos - loser
Apulder - village
Canne - cup
Ibora - coward
Guistarn - dress shop
Hund - cow/steer
Hnutu- piglet
Fleoge - grape
Iboras -archers
Ufalme - castle/palace
Mordu - A bear, particularlry referring to a large black bear
formeltan iron - used to heal cuts, close wounds
pura migale - pure gecko
Byrignes - cemetary

Rakishi - a jerk, denotes a partically mean jerk
Vrfebin - cubicle
Baelblys - funeral
frofro - Chit Chat
Ukoma-ritis - leporacy
Buibui - spit/chop shop
Bolttimber- building
Fearh - pig
voluptatem stilla - pleasure drops. Eye drops that give you a
rush
Cnif - small knife
Brasu cnif - small bronze knife
Oeorfsear - larger knife.
Fiigol - turkey
Foor - hog
conflandum in ore tuo - melt in your mouth
Egeswin - fish
Neosiri - longsword
Ingenii - natural ability
Genip - cloud, vapor
Planus wakati - time travel surgery
Fylleseóc - crazy,nuts
kuchimba madini - Mining drill
donum magnam - grand gift
Bearn - child
Dihtere - manager
Andred - City
Notitia - data department
kuzaliwa kwa mtoto - child birth
Hama - snake
Futa - eraser
Byre - hut
hordei ventilat - barley
Lodrung - rubbish, delusiona
Abrugdon - frustrated
Ligaturas - Raisins
scelerisque - Chocolate
amittunt marmorum - lose their marbles

Puer temporis - child of time
Morgen pleghus - movie
Imekataliwa - disenfranchised
Gagel - sweetie
Andoleofen - upscale restaurant
Draest - refuse/trash
deliciae temporis - taking ones time
Fyllejnod - moon
Reafian- Rifle
Jasusi - spy
studium liber - text books
Ceaster-wyrt- black market trader
Aethelbald - eldest child
deorcynn- animals
Alorr- bedroom
Clrfran - screw/forget
Greot room - utility closet
Hama - snake
Unanielewa - understand me?
Bitel - beetle
Pintreowl - pine tree
Winhus - tavern
Buc - jug
Beadomece - sword
Aurum ya dhahabu - gold for tag
CSD cum sicario disputabo - department for assassin tracking
Volant - fly
Elpend - Elephant
Fullfremens (perfect ones)
Baerodast - champagne/expensive wine
Spiritualibus - spiritual pain
Cicen - chicken
Pombe tenebris - Dark Booze
quae fortuna - what bad luck
Sanu - healthy
hoja ya minua - move to excite
Mi tibi kwako - I love you.
Cwild - plague

Kushanga Crustula - creepy people/anyone who makes you uncomfortable

Cantwaraburg - fortress

Koroga impotente - stir crazy

Cwyne - common wife/harlot vaguely insulting

Rali navali - rail yard in Chicago

Aldhem Castle - famous tower in chicago

Biggencere - worker

Huntung - sports event

Cecel- cake often covered in berries

cum capti kuwa mzuri - when trapped be pliable

Bur - cottage

Fehrwerd - guard

capulusno - coffee

beost - milk

Andeleof - fridge

Kitanda - couch

Barabara autem foretacen de CEO - The Great Hall of CEO's

kuangaza kama alwealda tabernus - shines like god's boots

Nafuu Rebus - cheap goods

Taeflian - gamble

magistratus - Police

Yoonkana - discrete/invisible

Gesen - intestines

Acendele iumenta - violent person, uncontrollable

Cripito barafu - Cream Ice

Ndege de phantasiam - flight of fancy

Tunweg - beasts

Meneja - manager

electi principes seges - elite of the crop

Weaorud - hund waste

melior quam yeyote - better than anyone

Yttrium - an element on earth that self charges, invaluable as a power resource

ornatu tabernam - costume shop

Gor - dirt

Spearwa - sparrow

Yrfebin - cattle box/cubicle

Baelbys - funeral
Kazi opera Kazi - work for work's sake
Amani - peace
Magna eorl - bravado/arrogance
Grornhof - hell's home
Pulveris - drug light effeects but very addictive
Wanuzi - intern
kamuni dominus - man of honor
Reggio - district
Gaderigen - collective of workers
sui iuris - indie
Wenan - cat
Bwana Freosan - Mister Freeze
Lareow -/teacher/doctor
Praeter Asili - wonderkind
Zushe - insane
Huduma quartrum - service quarters
byden botym - bottom of the barrel, a race to
quia debitum fikra - debt for genius
Forgrinden - to grind
Bryce shoppe - a cheap diner/greasy spoon diner
Canne - cup
Fyscynn - fishes
Favi vyombo - a meat substitute made of beans pressed together
and drowned in salt to provide flavor
Sped mchezo ludum - luck is a fickle game
Pipi lorica - sugar coat
Sylfling - soup
beorg - hill
Leorne - trainee
Baec - behind
Cargast - zombie/ghost
Nitidusque - prison
hatua kuvunja - breaking point/price point where you lose money
takifu sanctus - holy saint
Breostloca - mind
Innierfe - furniture+
Kushinda Tu - just win

Arwe - arrow
Druncnian - drunk
Cavas kifua - empty chest/especially as relates to feeling guilt
or nerves
Fenlyss de dael - share an emotion or feeling
Cynereaf - robe
Cocopanne -chef
Uzito vitae - weight room
Sceota - trout
Rand- boss
Pincern - butler
Breostwylm - vibe, tone
Imeundwa de deorum siwezi forlor - what I have created, even the
gods can't destroy
Gaderigen - union
Amaerecian - define
Croda - crowd
Ego Levavi - I am lifted
Kama - as the
Berans - to bear/wear
Ndefe - long
Hearm - to harm
Kiung - limb
Perdita - lost
Dominus - master
Abredwian - to kill
Dhamira - conscience
Baelblyse - funerals
Fyrhus- fireplace
Ut non uno - one we be
Anlec - Respect
Buc - jug
Afeormian - cleaning room
Andetnes star - Sun
Cynling - clan
Triclinium - dining hall
arc - chest of drawers
mji mkuu es morbus - capital is morality

BYRON BARTLETT

Schlot - oak wood
Forlisgleng - dress
Safi officium - purity job/cleansing job